WILD WORLD

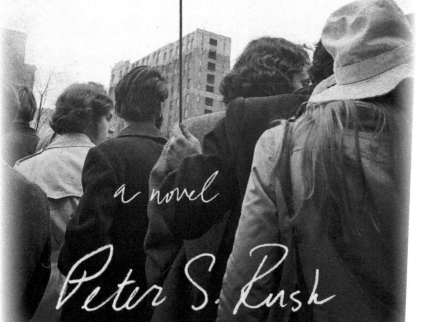

a novel

Peter S. Rush

To my family

Wild World

Copyright © 2017 by Peter S. Rush. All Rights Reserved.

For information about this title or to order other books and/or electronic media, contact the publisher:
Prior Manor Press
355 Lexington Avenue, New York, NY 10017
PriorManorPress.com

ISBN: 978-0-9990665-0-8 (hardcover)
        978-0-9990665-1-5 (paperback)
        978-0-9990665-2-2 (eBook)
        978-0-9990665-5-3 (ebook Student Edition)
        978-0-9990665-4-6 (paperback Student Edition)

Printed in the United States of America
Cover design: James Iacobelli

Library of Congress Cataloging-in-Publication Data is available from the publisher.

Praise for *Wild World*

"A deftly crafted and inherently engaging read from cover to cover, *Wild World* is an extraordinary and impressively entertaining read from beginning to end -- and showcases author Peter S. Rush as having a genuine flair for originality."
—*Midwest Book Review*

"[Set] in the early 1970s... Author Peter Rush vividly recreates those times and faithfully captures the mood on campuses around the country during those tumultuous years of protest against the Vietnam War, and demonstrations involving social causes... *Wild World* is a crime novel, a love story and a mystery all rolled into one... well written and keeps your attention."
—*Peace Corps Journal*

"(*Wild World*) is so very pertinent to our time that reading it brings into sharp focus those flaws in our present political condition: change is not only possible, but inevitable. Peter Rush is a sensitive and powerful writer whose future in American literature seems secure with the publication of this debut novel."
— *San Francisco Review of Books*

"A riveting exploration of one man trying to change a corrupt system from within... Rush's agile writing is impressive."
— *Clarion Review*

"*Wild World* takes us inside the Vietnam era on campus, and the author captures it perfectly. The devastating effects to the innocent are all here, especially upon those who try to set things to right."
—*Mary Ann Tirone-Smith author of Girls of a Tender Age*

"This is a well-written novel, one rich in period detail and dramatically dynamic."
—*Blue Ink Review*

"Set in the volatile days of the early 1970s, this superbly-written work is an absorbing story of youthful ambition tempered by real life."
—*The BookLife Prize*

"A complex and assured debut with a compelling storyline."
—*Auntie M Writes*

"Though *Wild World* is set in the '70s, it brings to light parallels between that era's cultural and political climate and today's tempestuous climate."
"Rush's greatest strength as a writer is his celerity. He is able to transition from scene to scene swiftly, propelling the plot forward at a rapid rate."
—*Wiki Lit*

CHAPTER I

FOUR DEAD IN OHIO

MAY 1970

When Steve Logan stepped into the sunlight that Monday, he began to make small decisions that would change his life. He felt a very different vibe on the Brown University campus. The mellow spring weekend had turned to an eerie chill. Students were pouring out of classrooms, not in their normal sleepy stroll but in panic and confusion. The action passed in slow-motion chaos as a knot grew in Steve's stomach. What didn't he know?

He grabbed a thin, intense kid with black glasses who looked like he was on the path to Faunce House, the student union. "What's going on?"

"They're killing kids on campus." The boy's acned face was a mixture of fear and incomprehension. He stood perfectly still, looking at the ground.

"What? Where? Here?"

"Kent someplace—shooting protesters. It's on the news."

Steve released the boy, who ran toward the student center without looking back. Killing kids on campus . . . anti-war demonstrations had been growing since Nixon had invaded Cambodia but. . . . It had to be a mistake. As Steve sprinted toward his apartment, his long brown hair trailing like a pennant, he thought how Nixon had increased the venom about college protesters. But shooting kids on campus? He stretched his legs, glad for the power he'd built through lacrosse, as the trees flew by—it was one more block. He had to get home to Roxy.

He dug deeper into his training for more speed. This was fucked up. It couldn't be true. It had to be something else—an assassination or madman with a gun.

Taking two steps at a time up, he flew to the third floor of the wooden New England floor-through. Roxy Fisher, wearing a white peasant blouse, was sitting in the maroon salvaged chair in the living room under a full-wall mural, whose screaming, clashing colors reflected the turmoil Steve felt. Her lips were drawn tightly, and small tears were running from her eyes. Steve bent and kissed her on the cheek, wiping her tears with his shirt.

His roommates, Cal Metcalf IV, a thin, over-achieving Boston prep-school kid, and Andy Powers, with his blond afro, were sitting on the sagging couch. They were watching Walter Cronkite on a small black-and-white TV on the table next to three empty Narragansett bottles. Steve inhaled deeply to catch his breath as he listened.

> *Today at Kent State University in Ohio, four students were killed and nine wounded when students attacked the National Guard troops as they were trying to prevent the students from taking over administration buildings. The National Guard said they were in fear of their lives by the mob.*

"Shit. Shit! Kids are attacking armed troops? We had a half a million at Woodstock last summer and no violence," Cal said, his face lined with sweat.

"A million march on Washington to end this fucking war. No violence. A bunch of kids at nowhere U, and the National Guard in full battle gear shoots them down. This is fucked up," Andy yelled at the television in his Long Island accent.

Roxy rose. "I can't believe I'm watching this. She buried herself in Steve's chest. "Is this the start of the revolution?"

Steve quietly stroked her head, trying to comprehend the scene on the television. He watched the Vietnam War—body counts—death on TV every night—it was destroying the country. His father's generation—the World War II veterans—didn't understand why his generation hated this war.

Steve tried to explain to his father that there wasn't a Pearl Harbor—the Vietnamese didn't attack. There were no front lines, no war objectives, just drafting kids as cannon fodder to fight little men in black pajamas. Nixon just expanded the endless war, dividing the country more than ever. And now body counts had come to the college campus. He felt the country had, without warning, begun devouring its young. College students like Steve and his roommates, students who should be making the world a better place.

He felt sick, like when the box on the schoolroom wall had announced President Kennedy was dead. These were just kids, like them, protesting just like them, not thinking of the consequences. Murdered by American troops?

Roxy turned and stared at the TV, small tears still seeping from her eyes. She was so vulnerable. Steve wanted to protect her because she had recently lost her father and sister, and her relationship with her mother was badly frayed. She leaned back against him and he surrounded her shoulders with his arms. He could smell the baby shampoo in her hair. Could he leave her for law school? He felt her quiver in his arms, and he pulled her tighter.

"Roxy, you're from Ohio. Is that some radical hotbed?" Cal looked over his glasses at her.

"Baloney with mustard on rye is radical. Why not Berkeley or Columbia?" She turned her head to Steve, and he could feel her rising sadness. He wanted to go back to yesterday, to Spring Weekend with Judy Collins singing on the green and Roxy's head in his lap. It was all so peaceful. How had the country come to this? The Vietnam War was wrong, and protesting was now punishable by death.

"Shut up," Cal snapped. "Let's hear the rest."

> *The students were unarmed, and observers said they posed no direct threat to the Guardsmen. It is reported that two of the dead were students on their way to class, who were not part of any demonstration. Two male and two female students were killed. Over sixty rounds of ammunition were fired at the unarmed students. Officials are questioning why the Guardsmen were issued live ammunition and who gave the order to fire.*
>
> *The students were protesting President Nixon's speech on April 30th, announcing the invasion of Cambodia by U.S. forces, further widening the war in Southeast Asia. Governor James Rhodes justified the shooting, calling the protesters, "un-American, bent on destroying higher education in Ohio."*

The television replayed tear gas and troops with fixed bayonets marching across the campus as students scattered in every direction. Steve imagined Cal fleeing in fear as the bullets cracked and Andy gasping for air as the tear gas cut off his oxygen. And he was pulling Roxy to safety while she wanted to confront the troops. It happened at Kent State to kids just like them. It could have been in Providence or any other college town. The country would not be the same—it couldn't go back. But where was forward?

Andy paced in a circle, his mustache flexing as he tightened his jaw and his blond afro seeming to grow. Finally, he pulled up and spat out, "They trained a generation of killers of women and children in Vietnam. Now it's come home. Maybe they will napalm this place and put us all out of our misery." The longest hairs of his handlebar mustache quivered as he spoke.

Students around the nation are calling for strikes on campus in solidarity with the students killed at Kent State.

Andy stood with his thick arm raised and shouted at the television, "That's right! We've got to shut it down!"

Cal jumped to his feet, fist raised.

"I'm so afraid. What's going to happen next?" Roxy's body tensed. Steve felt cold at the anger in the room. Was all he had been taught about America wrong? These were executions like in some Third World dictatorship. He always believed in the heroes, the good guys with white hats. Too many Westerns and war movies? No, he knew his history, and this was bullshit—just plain wrong. Was this the beginning of the revolution? Kids against kids—young against the old? But what would he do? He stroked Roxy's shoulder. Her moist eyes were set with determination, and he moved a strand of her dark hair from her face to behind her ear. Who were they? He had thought of politics in the abstract, like most people. But this time, it was very real to him and her. They weren't going to be spectators as the country went up in flames.

"We can't just watch this on TV," Roxy said. "Are you going to stay with me?"

Her green eyes danced under her raised eyebrows. He squeezed her hand. "Yes."

Cal and Andy were chanting at the tube, "Shut it down! Shut it down! Shut it down!"

Roxy pulled Steve's arms to her chest. These deaths had changed the stakes. He wasn't afraid but confused. Yesterday, life had been perfect. He wanted to take her away to live in a cabin in the woods or on some commune. But that wasn't going to happen. He wasn't going to run; he had to live up to his expectations. Life had seemed sorted out, with graduation only weeks away and law school. Now she wanted him to stay. So he was without a plan or a defined goal, questioning everything he thought he knew.

What was today about? Assassinations, riots, Black Panthers, peace marches, and Woodstock. Graduation at the end of the month had been the goal, but now he didn't know what would come next.

"Yes," he said trying to imagine some heroic gesture. "We can do anything."

Roxy smiled her liquid warmth, and he pulled her tightly to his chest, not wanting to ever let her go. What he was watching was wrong, he knew that, but what could he do to make it right? They turned and joined the chant. "Shut it down! Shut it down!"

What would he, could he do?

CHAPTER 2

WHAT ABOUT ME

I t was night, and the campus green, peaceful with dozing students one week before, was vibrating with excitement and emotions as Steve, Roxy, and their friends entered through the arch. Some students were standing with candles in more of a religious vigil. Professors huddled in a conclave by Manning Hall, an imitation Greek temple. Steve knew many had marched against the war in the fall. He guessed others felt violated now that the government had dared to introduce violence into their secure, sacred campus world. Signs read *Stop the war* and *Hell no. We won't go.* Many banners simply bore the word *Peace,* and the Peace symbol waved above the crowd. Steve and Roxy chanted with the other young men and women, "Stop the war! Shut it down! Stop the war! Shut it down!"

There was a raised podium overlooking the green. Professor Whitney, in his usual wrinkled khaki pants and plaid sport coat with leather elbow patches, jumped up on the stand and began tapping a bullhorn. Steve had met Whit in October, when he and Roxy had hitchhiked to Washington for an anti-war demonstration. It hadn't been an intimate first date.

Whitney shouted into the microphone, his voice raising an octave. "The faculty protests the undeclared war in Indochina and the shooting of students at Kent State University and has voted to suspend the remainder of the normal academic year." The crowd cheered. "Strike activities will include continuing workshops, discussion groups, peaceful demonstrations, mass meetings with important speakers, and educational efforts beyond the immediate university community. The strike is being directed by a twenty-one-member Steering Committee of students, graduate students, and faculty members.

"The administration has agreed to these demands, and finals and the remainder of the school year have been cancelled."

The crowd cheered and chanted, "Hell no! We won't go! On strike! Shut it down! Hell no! We won't go. On strike! Shut it down!"

He held up his hands.

"There will be a march Thursday morning at ten a.m. downtown to the state capitol building to exercise our rights as American citizens for peaceful assembly. We ask all of you to tell your friends to join us. Other schools in town—Rhode Island School of Design, Providence College, Roger Williams—as well as some schools from Massachusetts will be in town to demonstrate our revulsion with the Nixon administration, this immoral war, and the police-state mentality. We will be peaceful, but we will be heard."

The crowd cheered, but Roxy was coiled tightly as she moved forward in the crowd. Steve moved with her feeling her, anger in him yet reluctant to give it voice.

"Peaceful? Peaceful my ass," she shouted. "They shot those kids for nothing. Murdered them in cold blood! Four kids dead at Kent State. The troops are occupying twenty-one campuses across the country. Bayonets at the library—pigs on campus."

Whitney continued, "This is a mass movement. Already, over four hundred colleges and universities are on strike. And it's spreading to high schools. Our march will coincide with those around the country.

We'll need marshals, and we will have to follow a designated route. We'll gather on the green at nine a.m." He started making his way off the podium.

Roxy pushed forward and grabbed the bullhorn from him. Steve watched her transform; her eyes seemed to glow in the night as she looked out over the crowd. Her beautiful face was taut and determined. Her sweet voice was now hard, commanding attention.

"The march may be peaceful, but don't forget, they were peaceful at Kent State, and students like you and me were murdered in cold blood." The crowd cheered. "We are facing murderers who kill women and children every day in Vietnam and now Cambodia." The crowd cheered louder. "You can't trust them." Her face turned a shade darker. The crowd's cheers grew louder. Steve was filled with pride as a hint of fear crept across him. She had moved in with him in January; what else did he not know about her? But he felt her rage and chanted louder.

"We have to be brave and willing to die for our cause. They can't kill all of us." She raised her clenched fist in the Black Power salute. Steve saluted her back as their eyes met and the crowd cheered wildly.

"On strike! Shut it down! On strike! Shut it down! Hell no! We won't go! Hell no! We won't go!"

Coach Jackson stood in the locker room after practice in the converted poorhouse, the lacrosse team, in shorts and t-shirts, sitting on benches. He was a successful coach who had brought the program from nowhere to its current status as one of the best in the country. But he hadn't brought it all the way yet. He paced as he spoke, the little nervous twitch of his shoulder betraying his emotion. Steve had been flattered when he was first recruited; he was just a blue-collar kid from Long Island. Coach had always been tough on Steve, never really connecting with him on a personal level.

Steve looked around the solemn locker room at teammates who had struggled since February to get here. Andy seemed deep in thought. Bill Draper, a kid from Long Island who shared the same love of Jones Beach as Steve, sat pulling on his dark mutton chops as if counting the pros and cons.

"Men, you have worked hard to get here. I know the school has canceled the remainder of the year, but you owe it to yourselves to play this game. You are undefeated in the Ivy League." He looked around the room, knowing that a few voices would influence the rest. "This is for the Ivy League championship. This is what you have worked for since February. You seniors, you will never get another chance like this in your lives. You owe it to yourselves," Coach finished. Steve could tell that he wanted to continue like Vince Lombardi. Coach always complained that his athletes were more likely to discuss the existential nature of man or Nietzsche than listen to him.

"Coach, we'll have a team meeting," Steve said, fixing his long hair into a ponytail with a rubber band. A week ago, there was no decision to be made. Now Steve had to lead the discussion that wasn't about winning or losing.

Coach nodded. "This opportunity will not come around again." He pulled Steve to the side. "You and Andy are captains. Make sure they do the right thing," he ordered. "The war isn't going to end tomorrow, and canceling this game isn't going to change anything," he said in a conspiratorial tone. It was a voice he had never used with Steve, who knew the question wasn't about the strike or protests but about Coach's reputation—not showing up for a championship game.

Locking eyes, Coach put on his earnest recruiting face. "I have faith in you."

"We'll make the right decision." Steve knew no one at school cared if the team won or lost. This was a personal decision by the players and about the sacrifices they had already made.

"Good," he said and put on his plaid fedora. He was careful not to slam the door as he exited.

Steve nodded to Andy and looked around the room at his teammates. Bill was pulling on his droopy mustache. "Gentlemen, this is our decision. For some of you, the decision will be difficult. It is for me. What's happening in the world is now part of our world, whether we like it or not."

"What's the point of it? It's just a game." A sophomore from Baltimore was the first to speak. "We're talking about people dying. Being killed—on campuses, in Vietnam—and we think a silly game is important. We closed the campus for a reason. And all activities, including this game, should be canceled as well."

"Shit, playing or not playing isn't going to impact the war," Bill said. "For some of us, being here and playing is actually a big deal." He looked at the Baltimore kid and the button-down shirt he wore under his practice jersey.

"Yeah, but the symbolism is important as well. The government is lynching the Black Panthers in New Haven with trumped-up charges against Bobby Seale. I went to the protest. Are we just cogs in the machine, or do we have the right to think for ourselves?" Baltimore replied, his cheeks filling with color as he tossed his helmet into his locker with a clang like a recess bell.

"Think for yourself, not me," Bill shot back.

Steve was surprised that even a kid from the establishment of Baltimore was so vehement.

"They've got troops on over forty campuses. Students torched the ROTC buildings at Wisconsin and other schools. And there's going to be another protest in Washington," Andy reported, shaking his head in disgust.

More of the boys spoke, thick with emotion. The team was composed of kids from Baltimore and Long Island, with a couple of New England preppies. The arguments became heated, and Steve could feel the argument going on in his head. The game would be forgotten but

Kent State—never. Canceling the game would be symbolic, but would it be quitting? They had spent years to get here. Were they just going to throw it away with the finish line in sight? Steve stood and banged his wooden stick on the metal locker to get the room under control.

"Let's take a vote. Simple majority rules," Andy suggested.

There was grudging acceptance. "Let's make it a secret ballot."

Steve was unsure. He knew the war was wrong, and the killings at Kent State had brought it home to campus. The country was at the edge of open rebellion. But he felt he needed to finish what he had begun and not duck his responsibility. He had come a long way from the south shore of Long Island. He printed the word slowly—PLAY.

Andy collected the scraps of paper that contained the votes and counted them in front of the team. "Thirteen to play; eleven to cancel. I guess we're playing."

"We have to make a statement," Baltimore said.

"We could wear armbands with the peace symbol," Andy suggested. Others nodded in agreement, but the mood was pensive, not excited. The players left the locker room quietly in small groups, going back to campus. Steve sat alone in the quiet room. When he'd first entered this room, he was an excited freshman who couldn't wait to play. Now he was weighing the right or wrong about playing after Kent State. He slammed his stick against the locker. *Keep your feet moving,* he thought. The demonstration was a day away; the game was on Saturday.

Throngs of students and professors, many with their families, were milling about on the front green, looking down the hill. Roxy, Steve, Bill, Andy, and others with red peace symbol armbands were waiting for instructions as parade marshals.

On the podium, Professor Whitney adjusted his tortoise-rimmed glasses as he gripped the bullhorn.

"Stay in line. The Providence Police have promised that there will be no incidents. We have spoken to the governor and the mayor, and they understand that we intend to be peaceful, but we intend to exercise our right to assembly."

The march moved out of campus and down the hill on Angell Street, past the Unitarian Church used for graduation. Thousands of people were moving in a steady procession, with many students holding homemade banners on oak tag and bedsheets. The day was sunny and warm, and the atmosphere of the crowd was more of a party or an outing than a protest. Young men in shorts and women in tank tops were smiling, joking, and shaking hands. There was random chanting of "One, two, three, four, we don't want your fucking war. Hell no, we won't go" and singing, "All we are saying is give peace a chance. All we are saying is give peace a chance."

As they entered downtown at the park in front of the train station, rows of Providence police officers in riot gear—white helmets and batons—stretched the length of the park. Patrol cars and paddy wagons were stationed at each intersection. Many of the police were actively tapping their batons into their gloved hands and eyeing the crowd. The police line stretched across the road, blocking the protesters' path.

A thick-set captain with ruddy Irish features, his stomach overlapping his belt, stood on the back of a flatbed truck with a cigar stuck in his mouth.

"The mayor has issued a parade permit. You will keep to the exact parade route." The microphone shrieked as it touched his badge. He looked over the crowd, which was forced to look up at him. "Anyone who gets out of line will be arrested for disorderly conduct. Any violence, any disruptive behavior, anything un-American, we have orders to maintain the peace." He raised his arm like Moses, and the brown sea of officers parted for the marchers.

The mood of the crowd became less boisterous as scents of fear began to infiltrate the heads of the marchers. The show of force had intimidated even the most militant protesters. Roxy, Steve, and the group passed by the thick Irish captain, his badge reading *Lynch*.

"Hippie bastards. We should run you all in and ship you to Nam tomorrow," the captain sneered to the approval of his men.

A group of construction workers in hard hats assembled a make-shift counter-demonstration. They yelled at the protesters, "America! Love it or leave it, you hippie lowlifes."

Several of them took several aggressive steps toward the protest line with raised wrenches and hammers. Steve, Andy, and the other marshals moved the line forward toward the capitol, pushing the girls behind them to the center of the crowd. One man in brown overalls moved toward Roxy.

"You hippie cunt, you need a real man—" he grabbed his crotch with his right hand "—to show you what it's like, not these wimpy college fags."

Roxy recoiled at his intensity and the hatred in his eyes. Steve put himself between the man and Roxy. The man glowered at Steve, who moved into his athletic stance, ready to hit or be hit. Steve backed away slowly without breaking eye contact until he and Roxy turned the corner.

The line of marchers continued to move past the park, and the policemen in the line continued to pound their hands, looking to hit someone. The column proceeded from the square to the state capitol building, a smaller version of the one in Washington. Raised scaffolding had been set up so that speakers with bullhorns could address the crowd. The chanting and the singing of "All we are saying is give peace a chance" drowned out the words of Professor Whitney and the other speakers. The other marshals directed the crowd away from the capitol along the designated route.

The crowd began to grow tired as it snaked up the steep hill on Waterman Street, spent of their enthusiasm but still cohesive in purpose. Random scuffles broke out as kids dumped trash cans and spray-painted the peace sign on traffic signs. Several brown-shirted cops caught two boys and began beating them to the ground with their batons. Bill started to go to their assistance, but Steve held him back.

"You'll only get arrested. There is nothing you can do." Steve could see the anger in Bill, and he felt disgust with himself at not helping the bleeding kids. It wasn't right; the punishment didn't fit the crime. This wasn't a fucking dictatorship, or was it?

Back on campus, hand-lettered signs that said *Teach-in Cambodia invasion* and *Teach-in Making Washington hear* were nailed to trees or posted on the doors of various classroom buildings.

Roxy and Steve, arm in arm, were walking across campus toward their apartment. A hand-lettered sign in neat blue ink attached to the wall in the Faunce House arch caught their attention.

Sergeant David Durk, Amherst Graduate, New York Police Department. Reforming the New York Police Department. 7 pm. Alumni Hall.

"I've read about him in a big article in the *New York Times* last month. Really caused a firestorm in the city." Steve looked at the sign.

"Want to go?" Roxy eyed him.

The classroom was already populated by several dozen students who were sitting at desks arranged in a semi-circle around the desk in front. Sergeant Durk was sitting on the wooden desk in the front, and Steve paused before he and Roxy selected paint-chipped desks for themselves. Durk had a shag haircut that was too long for an active duty cop, dark eyes, a narrow chin, and a thin mustache that made him look like a young lawyer, not a cop at all.

The session was introduced by an adjunct professor, who started with some comments about the war but, he told the group that Durk was not specifically there to talk about the war. He said that Durk was touring a number of colleges to talk about making a difference.

"When the internal investigation unit started in New York, we didn't know what we were getting into," Durk began. "It didn't take long to realize that corruption was rampant at every level of the department, from the narcotics detectives taking money and drugs to the cops on patrol being paid off by bookies, after-hour clubs, pimps, and anyone you can think of," he said with a definite New York accent. "The systems in some of the precincts were elaborate, with designated officers assigned to make a weekly pickup and the money divided among the sergeants, lieutenants, captains, and precinct commanders. Everyone seemed to be on the take. We didn't think we would ever get through—and we almost didn't. We had to go outside the system to the *New York Times* in order to get the political cover we needed." He looked thoughtfully around the room.

"That didn't make you very popular in the department," an intensely acned freshman sneered. Steve stared at him, wondering why the boy had come.

"I'm still not very popular in the department, nor are the other honest cops. And there are a lot of them. It's just that scum often rises to the top. Taking bribes for not seeing something is very easy."

"Were you ever afraid for your life?" a student with a nasal accent asked.

"I have had many threats—anonymous because they're cowards. We aren't giving up. And I carry a gun, too." Durk smiled and tapped the pistol tucked into a shoulder holster under his blue windbreaker.

"Did they try to kill you?'

Durk paused and looked around the room as if he were sizing up a crime scene while he was formulating his response to the question. "There are threats. Not only personally but against any other cops cooperating, as well as against my family."

"Do you really think you can change anything? Or is this commission just a lot of whitewash by the politicians?" Steve asked, leaning in his chair while meeting the cop's eyes. He needed to know the truth.

"I think we did. That's why I became a cop after Amherst. Law is what separates the civilized man from savages. It's never perfect. We're just beginning, but we have made an impact in New York. You can't change a system unless you understand it and are part of it. That's why I'm touring campuses. You want to change how things are? You have to get involved. It's easy to talk about change, but to actually make the system change, you have to get your hands dirty, take risks. You have to have skin in the game."

The words had an immediacy. Protesting was exhilarating, intoxicating, and fun—and something he did with Roxy. But what next? He didn't believe in bombing buildings like the SDS did in Wisconsin. He was going to law school. Law was the civilizing force. He had never thought about policemen quite like Durk. But when he watched the cops at the demonstration, he knew he wasn't their enemy, but did they? Cops were referees. It was their job to keep the game in between the lines.

"Sometimes, you have to risk your life for what you know is right. And if you don't do it—if you let it pass—who will do it? Do me this one favor: think about it." Durk checked his watch. "I think our time is up . . ."

As the two-hour session finished, students filtered out, none coming up to shake hands with the cop. Steve and Roxy lingered. "Sergeant, you're the establishment," Roxy said. "Do you really think you're going to change the New York City Police Department?"

Durk looked carefully at Roxy and then at Steve, eyeing them as if they were suspects.

He spoke slowly and sincerely. "If I am not there, things go on as usual. When I'm there, they know that a conscience exists and that the law must be upheld. Before, I was a pain in the ass they could ignore. Now, I'm in their face. Sunlight is the best disinfectant. If it is out of sight, no one cares, but once we show it to people, things happen. What do you plan to do with your life?"

"I'm going to Georgetown law school in the fall," Steve said.

"Another lawyer. Just what the world needs." Durk looked down at his notes. "Your generation can change the country, but you can't just *turn on, tune in, and drop out*. You have got to be in it."

"Can you just beat people senseless like they did at the Chicago convention or shoot unarmed people down?" Steve asked. He was trying to understand it from Durk's vantage point. Could one person make a difference?

"It's not that simple. The system works, but it's not a one-shot deal. Life on the street can change in an instant. You can't wait to be shot—that's not the job. To be successful, you need commitment, and you will have to deal with the shit. And you will always be in danger of being set up and left out to dry." He let his words linger a bit, looking at the two kids.

"I could never shoot anyone, no matter how justified. There are other ways," Steve said. Roxy moved closer to him. Having said the words, Steve realized he had never really thought about shooting someone. It was an abstract idea from the movies. But Durk wasn't talking in the abstract.

"It is a dangerous world. Life is taking chances. Lawyer, that's safe—make a lot of money and move to the suburbs. But some people pay with their lives—look at the Kennedys and King. You know your history; go back to the Gracchus brothers. You put your life on the line for change." Durk's eyes were intense, almost drilling into Steve. He could feel the cop's passion.

Steve let the words sink in. Yeah, Classics 101: Roman tribunes assassinated for wanting to represent the Plebeians, the common man. This cop was the real deal.

"What does your family think after Amherst and everything?" Steve asked.

Durk laughed. "They think I'm crazy. 'Not why you went to college,' my dad says. But it's what I want to do." He stopped for a minute, looking at the now-empty classroom. "What else could they think?"

Steve had never thought about it as conscience. The *Times* article had forced the mayor in New York to appoint a commission—for the better. Durk was a realist who was making the system answer. How many more would it take?

They shook hands firmly while holding each other's eyes.

Returning to the apartment after the long day, the highs and lows were leveling out with the security of school. The sight of the armed phalanx of police hovering over the crowd at the march and the intensity of the emotions against the war still lingered.

In their room, the blue work shirt fell from Roxy's shoulders. She looked into Steve's eyes as he took off his shirt in front of her. He did not move, but rather watched her as she tossed her long hair over her shoulder and effortlessly unsnapped her bra, allowing it to slide to the floor. His breath quickened as she came closer to him, their breath meeting at the tip of their lips. They embraced gently, touching with their fingers, lightly, to feel, not grasp. Their tongues explored each other's mouth in slow movements, first hers, then his, allowing the taste buds time to savor the flavors of each other.

Before she pulled him to the bed, her panties and his shorts floated to the floor. On top of her, he supported his weight as he looked into her eyes, totally in her grasp. She pulled him down to her again, attacking him with kisses as their hands touched and explored. She guided him inside her and softly moaned, and he rhythmically stroked, gentle and slow, looking at Roxy, seeking approval before surrendering to her.

Roxy looked back at him with rapture and smothered him with kisses and sounds of pleasure. He could taste the saltiness of her as she began to sweat, little beads that sprang from her forehead to tease his lips. She tapped him gently, and he rolled to his back, holding her hips to not lose their connection. She swung her dark hair over his face, creating a tent of tresses that captured her sweet scents, which he inhaled.

She thrust her hips slowly and reached down to touch herself. She moved faster and he responded, meeting her every move, their bodies in total rhythm. He could feel her tense and begin to shudder, subtle at first as her excitement built within her. As she began to climax, her rapid breathing brought him to match her intensity. He matched her rhythm as he came inside her. She fell forward on him, her head on his right shoulder, her body still engaged with his now-softened member. They each took deep breaths.

"Now I understand what making love means," she said, wiping beads of sweat from his temple.

"I love you." He ran his fingers through her long, dark hair, now as damp as her skin. "I don't want this moment to ever end."

"What are we going to do with our lives? Anything anyone will remember?" she asked, looking at the ceiling from the comfort of his shoulder.

"Nothing. I just want this moment to last forever." His voice was just above a whisper as he ran his fingers down her back. "You know what I mean. Like Durk. He was upset how things were being done in the police department in fucking New York City. He is not afraid of the consequences," she said.

"Seems we college kids are scaring some people in Washington—that's a start. We won't settle for the suburbs like our parents." He turned to face her. "I don't know. What was Woodstock about? Why do we see things so differently? I don't want to be just a cog in the machine," he said.

"We're different. We don't blindly follow authority like the World War II generation. There's no great evil to fight. Maybe we've become the great evil. I think we can find a new way. Us. All of us." She was up on her elbow, one nipple pointed directly at his face.

He looked in her eyes. "I love you so much. I don't ever want to leave you, ever want to be apart from you."

"I am more me than I have ever been."

CHAPTER 3

TEACH YOUR CHILDREN

Andy sauntered into Manny Alameda's Ring Side Lounge in Fox Point with an Orioles cap perched on his blond afro. An all-American midfielder, he had been close to Steve since freshman year. He had a slow, deliberate way of speaking, almost squeezing the words from his lips. He liked to mock Steve's intensity on the field but admired how hard his roommate worked. Steve was sipping his Narragansett at a table by the side door under four posters of long-gone lightweight Latin boxers.

Manny's was the designated dive bar where the Brown students knew they could buy twenty-five-cent beers without fear of being carded. It was a popular hangout for the frat boys and athletes. The regulars from Fox Point, Portuguese immigrants, kept a quiet distance. Miguel, the bartender, knew many of the boys and appreciated them for their tips. The jukebox was playing "What's Going On" by Marvin Gaye.

"Any decisions on after graduation?" Steve asked. Andy had drawn number ten in the draft lottery in December. That night last December when the first draft numbers were drawn, all the seniors sat together, drinking to every number, high or low. Andy had gone very quiet, drinking harder: shots and beer. Steve watched the dull grey men in dull grey suits draw the ping pong balls on television that determined their future. When Country Joe and the Fish played, the room erupted in the chorus. "What are we fighting for . . ."

Andy stood, singing at the top of his lungs as he and Steve tried some harmony. "We're all gonna die." The draft had changed their lives and hung over graduation like a shroud: One more reason to hate the war.

"I already have the notice from the draft board to report for the physical," he said, flopping into a chair. "Good thing for this strike—everything is pass-fail."

Cal joined them at the small table, eating a hard-boiled egg from the bar. Cal was thin and bookish and had come from New England boarding schools. He affected a worldly weariness from his extensive international travel.

"I don't know what med school will think about it. I've asked some professors if they could give separate letter grades to me—at least in the courses I aced," Cal said. He liked being around two athletes as much as he liked putting them down as jocks. He paid for the beers.

"Any chance for the National Guard?" Steve asked.

"Not looking good. My father wants me to enlist. Says it's the right thing to do and that I should apply for Officers Candidate School. It would build my character. Right—a college lieutenant like me leading a bunch of grunts in the rice paddies. That would be a sure way to get a bullet in the back of the head. But I found out that Peace Corps is a two-year deferment. I just got the letter accepting me. I hope the war is over by then."

"Peace Corps sounds exotic," Steve said. "I've always wanted to travel, so I'm a little envious. Was it hard to get into? Did you have to take a test or pass an interview?"

"No. They have the application at the placement office. If you've got a foreign language and a college degree, they told me it's pretty easy. Travel for free where they aren't shooting guns. So I'll be serving my country making peace." He saluted with a mocking face.

"Where are you going?" Steve asked. He knew that Andy had made his decision—a decision forced on him by his draft number. He would get into it once he was there, but. . . . Why were they being forced to make these decisions?

"Latin America," Andy shrugged. "The reward for six years of Spanish: I can go anywhere from the jungle to the Pampas. I was hoping for Jamaica, sitting at Montego Bay with some grade-A ganja. Have you decided what you're doing yet?"

"I got into Georgetown Law. My dad desperately wants me to go. I don't want to disappoint him, and I don't have anything else to do. Lawyers get rich, don't they? My draft number's in the middle, so I should be safe. But who knows; maybe the Army will need more lawyers for the war crimes trials after the My Lai massacre."

"But?" Andy smiled, raising one eyebrow.

"I don't know. Still looking at my options. It would be nice to have a job here that pays money."

"You mean getting drafted into the Army isn't a good career choice?" Andy finished his beer and signaled for another. "I didn't know that."

"I start med school applications in the fall," Cal said. "The extra year will give me the double major that should me get into Harvard. And med school is a four-year deferment. And when I'm out, who knows?"

"Cal, you sure have changed since freshman year. Remember when I had to go out on the ledge of the dorm to convince you that LSD didn't convey the physical power to fly." Steve laughed.

"You both need to get serious about your lives." Cal's Boston accent increased an octave.

"Cal, you've gone from the acid freak to the career freak," Steve said. "You've really become a real grind. Doesn't all this shit that's going on in the country bother you?"

Money, career—if there wasn't the draft? Was the Ivy League about money and a career but not doing anything useful? Steve began thinking he was an idealist, but grinding away as a lawyer hoping to make partner and big bucks didn't have much appeal. Maybe being a great lawyer defending innocent and not-so-innocent people, like Clarence Darrow. But most lawyers just defend the system.

"The government may be fascist and the war an abomination, but I'm concerned about *my* future. You guys can change the world," Cal said as he left the table.

"That's a little fucked up. It's your country, too." Andy turned to Steve. "And you?"

"If you had a chance to change the world, do something really big even if you knew it would change your life, would you do it?" It was a rhetorical question. "I don't know anything about the real world. I grew up in a cookie-cutter Long Island tract house and went to school here. What do I know?" Steve was looking at his beer with a slight smile on his face. He was struggling wanting to do more, be more.

"What about law school?"

"Another lawyer or banker. Is that what the world needs?" He handed Andy a display ad for the Providence Police Department, torn from the *Providence Journal*. Andy read the ad and then read it again. The ad said that applications were open for the fall recruiting class, and there was a phone number at the bottom.

"Are you crazy?" Andy asked.

The challenge was right in front of Steve. "I'd know so much more when I go to law school. I don't mean for a career, but maybe a couple of years—until Roxy graduates. And see," he pointed to the ad, "Providence cop starts at ten thousand a year."

"What does Roxy think? Did you ask her?"

"No, not yet." Steve shook his head. He wanted Andy's approval first. "She wants me to be someone or do something. After meeting this Sergeant Durk, he's actually fucking doing it. The article in the *Times* says the mayor and the police brass appointed a commission. The media is all over the story. And Durk is the hero. He made an impression on me—something I never thought of—something real I can get my mind around. Law school is in the abstract. Durk is the law every day. Besides, leaving Roxy right now wouldn't be good for her. She's had too many people she loved disappear. She's having a hard time talking to her mother. I'm afraid she'd feel I was abandoning her. But we haven't actually talked yet."

Andy scowled. "Or good for you? I don't know; is this about her or you? Are you afraid of losing her?"

"Look at you—you're going to Latin America so you don't get drafted. And you might be doing something good: getting your hands dirty in the real world," Steve laughed. He was afraid of losing Roxy. A long-distance romance would kill him.

Andy laughed too loudly and sipped his beer. "Yeah, well, if Uncle Sam didn't want to ship me off to another jungle. But hey, this might change my life."

"Agreed. Peace Corps. New country, new culture . . . Thinking and living in another language . . ." Andy spun a quarter on the table, waiting for heads or tails. Steve felt he was nervous about his decision. "Two years . . . look what can happen in just one year," Andy said.

"You *will* be building something for other people. Maybe you'll help change their lives. It won't be this college-thing, ivory-tower shit. I don't think I could go to an office every day. I guess we're thinking the same way." Steve posed the answer almost as if he were asking a question.

"I guess you could be helping people—giving them tickets and hassling kids with long hair." Andy squeezed the words out with a stern face before he gave Steve a sideway smile. "Have you called yet? They might not accept a lowlife like you."

"No, just thinking about it. Just a crazy idea."

"Shit man, I leave in September. We can at least enjoy our last summer." Andy raised his glass and they smiled, satisfied. Steve trusted Andy's instincts as the idea continued to turn over in his mind.

"I have to go home to see my mother." Roxy's tone was concerned but not panicked as she put the black phone into its cradle. "Since they have canceled classes for the rest of the year, she wants me to come home."

"To visit or for the summer?"

"Probably for the summer. She's all upset about the protests. She says since Kent State, the National Guard has occupied Ohio State's campus, but the students are still protesting. She sees it on the news every night, and who knows where her head goes?"

"I can come. We can drive."

"Really? You would do that?"

"What would I do here without you?" He put his arms around her. "Plus, I always wanted to live in the Midwest." He figured he could find some kind of job.

She punched him, and then they kissed passionately.

They started out in the evening on 95 South for the 12-hour drive in the little VW Beetle. Roxy and Steve talked and laughed as he pointed out the wonders of the Jersey Turnpike like the Linden refinery, which gave New Jersey the noxious smell. She talked about her father and all the dreams he'd had for her. He was self-made, a union man who worked hard. She was his girl, and then he was gone—dead of a heart attack before he could see her graduate valedictorian of her class. Now it was her dreams of finding a cure for some disease. The Pennsylvania Turnpike was tight, built in another era, for less traffic. The pavement was rough; the potholes weren't yet filled from the winter.

The small A M radio struggled to find signals in the Pennsylvania Mountains, but when they found some, the news talked about the upcoming trial of the Manson Family for the murders of Sharon Tate and others in California. The police called them "dirty hippies."

In the little Beetle, he felt the world was shut out. It was he and Roxy against the world, and the summer would bring them closer together. She talked about growing up with her sister and putting a rope down the middle of their room to divide it. Stay on your side. She laughed at herself but turned her head to the window at the memory. Steve knew she was torn about going home.

Roxy dozed as Steve stole looks at her, wondering what meeting her mother was going to feel like. He knew Roxy didn't have much of a relationship with her, going back to the days after her father's death, when it had been up to Roxy to take care of her sister, Audrey. Roxy was, in fact, still angry about that.

But Roxy felt the obligation to spend the summer with her. Perhaps the time together would help heal the rift. Steve wasn't certain going to Ohio was a good idea for him, but he wasn't going to Long Island and didn't want to be in Providence without her. A few months in the Midwest would give him another point of view—if only about baloney. As he looked at her sleeping on the pillow against the door, he knew he had never really been in love before.

Steve thought about when she had moved in right after Christmas break. "I'm going to need more room. I need the top three drawers and most of that closet." She looked at the oak Salvation Army sideboard that Steve used as his dresser.

"Mom's fine. Praying and going to prayer meetings. My aunt and the cousins have her back into some saving religious moments." She rolled her eyes. "I may need this whole thing," she said, looking at the dresser, "if I'm going to move in."

"I'll go to the Salvation Army tomorrow to see if they have an old box for my stuff."

They laughed.

"I have to keep my dorm room for mail and stuff so Mom still thinks I'm living there. But it's on the way to class."

"Roomies covering for you?"

"Sure. They're delighted; more room for them." She finished emptying her last box of clothes and sat on the bed next to him. "I have a present for you." She reached into her black purse and handed him a round plastic container of pills sealed with a movable plastic top. He looked at it, confused. He turned it over to read the pharmaceutical name on it. She grabbed it away from him playfully.

"Men! I'm on the pill," she said as she twirled in a little circle.

"What? Isn't it illegal for unmarried women to have it . . .? You're on it . . . now?"

"Yes, silly. The law changed January first. We made an appointment at Planned Parenthood—Suzi, Liz, and me—before we left. We don't think you men are responsible enough. We went yesterday. Physical, prescription . . . all done."

"So we can do it . . ."

"Yes, big boy, any time *I* want." She was smiling at his confusion.

"I have something for you," he said, holding the moment while she looked quizzically at him.

He went to the closet to retrieve a shoe box with holes in it. He carried it over to Roxy, who sat on the Indian print blanket. He put it in her lap, and, as she opened it, a small black-and-white six-week-old kitten gingerly lifted its head to survey the surroundings. Roxy picked it up against her shoulder, and it began to purr.

"You said you were never allowed to have a pet and you always wanted one. So I thought it would be . . ."

"You remembered that. How? When did you get . . ."

"There was this lady on the Pembroke green with a box of kittens needing homes. And knowing what a softy you are, I couldn't resist."

"Oh, here, little one. That's a good kitty. What should we call him—her?"

"Him. I've been calling him Cyrano because he will always be in love with his fair Roxanne."

She looked at him a minute and then nodded at the reference.

"How sweet. Don't you think so, Cyrano?" She gave Steve a wet kiss and continued to pet the kitten.

Now he was going home with her to meet her mother. Roxy was an effortless beauty with a smart scientific brain that defied the stereotype of girls and math. She was as determined to succeed as he was, maybe more. They had the same fight in them, and he admired how far and how much she had already dealt with both her father and sister dying. He wanted to give her balance and help her—them. And the sex was great. Before her, it had been fleeting, illicit sex—and only a few times. Now they looked forward to exploring each other in a way he didn't know was even possible.

As the sun came up, he drove west on I-70, heading toward Columbus. He realized he had made a commitment to her without even discussing it with his father. That could wait; he didn't need any approval. Going with Roxy was the right decision, the only one he could make. Roxy began to stir with the light.

"You okay?" she asked, rubbing the sleep from her eyes. "You've been driving all night."

"Yeah, I'm okay. We need to stop for gas. I'll get some coffee." He smiled at her. "Can you get us home from here?"

Stopping at a Union 76 truck stop, Steve filled up the VW and paid the attendant $3.50 for the full tank. The thick coffee with some powdered Coffee-Mate tasted as if it was scraped from the all-night hot plate and placed into the cup. But it was black, hot, and caffeinated. He stretched his hamstrings, holding his toes from a standing position. Then he rotated his back in circular motions, followed by side-to-side twists. He wanted to do some sprints, but the parking lot didn't seem the most appropriate place. With the blood flowing again, he was ready for the final leg. Roxy had a black coffee and a copy of the *Columbus Dispatch*.

"How long to Westerville?" Steve asked.

"Half hour. We can take the ring road. This coffee is awful." She poured half of the hot black liquid onto the matching-colored asphalt parking lot.

"You don't know Westerville, do you?"

"Only that I'm going to be with you there." Steve was looking forward to a hot shower and cold beer.

"Welcome to the dry capital of America."

"What?"

"Westerville went dry in 1859. And the town was serious about it. The good citizens blew up the first saloons when they opened in the 1870s. In fact, the town was so staunchly dry that the Anti-Saloon League was headquartered here. It published more propaganda about the dangers of liquor than any other town in America and was firmly behind the 19th Amendment."

"And today?"

"Religious, not fanatical. You *can* buy booze in town. But self-righteousness is just below the surface of the politeness. I really can't stand being here—it's not home. I only went to senior year here and pretty much hated the entire year. But my mom is happy because she is near her sister and the cousins who, if you meet them, will make you understand why I don't come home much."

They pulled into an apartment complex comprised of four, three-story rectangular brick buildings. Entering through the green steel door to apartment 2G, Roxy was greeted by her mother's gasp of, "I can't believe you're here." She took Roxy's purse and ushered her into the small living room occupied by a yellow winged-foot sofa and Queen Anne chair that looked transplanted from a larger room.

"Mom, this is my boyfriend, Steve. I told you about him," Roxy said. Her mother stopped straightening a doily on the side table to look critically at him—long hair, mustache, jeans, a lean, muscular body, and a drawn complexion from having driven all night.

"Nice to meet you." Steve smiled and extended his hand to the small lady with her grey hair arranged in a tight bun.

Mrs. Fisher looked him over again and said politely, without taking his hand, "Nice to meet you."

She turned to help Roxy with one bag into the small second bedroom decorated in pink flowered wallpaper, with a single bed and a clown table lamp. "I redecorated the room for you in your favorite color." Roxy hesitated at the door of the room before entering, putting down her two other bags.

"Very nice, Mom, but pink is not my favorite color," she answered.

"Of course, it is, dear. I remember when you were little, you wanted your room painted pink, and Daddy did it one weekend."

"That wasn't my room. That was Audrey's room."

"I found a nice pink comforter which really brings it all together. And I found your old clown lamp—I know it's silly, but I thought you would . . ."

"Mother are you listening to *me?*" Roxy's mother stopped for a moment, looking at her. "Me, Roxanne, your other daughter. That was not my lamp, not the color . . ." She shook her head, giving up, not wanting to start an argument. She looked at Steve, shrugging to indicate she wasn't sure if her mother had grasped what she had said. He felt sorry for her. She had come out of duty, not because she wanted to. She looked at him and rolled her eyes.

"It's very cozy. This new apartment is smaller, but I know you will like it." Her mother followed her out into the hallway.

She was a compact woman with grey hair and heavy wrinkles on her forehead. She moved slowly, weighed down with life and a bad hip.

"Mom, I'm sure it will be fine. Thank you for decorating it. I will get used to the bedroom." Roxy looked at Steve, pleading for him to take her away, but he knew that was not an option.

"Steve needs to stay here until he finds a place at OSU," Roxy informed her mother, who looked unhappy with the announcement. "I told you about it on the phone. Don't you remember anything?"

"Maybe for a day." Mrs. Fisher looked around the room, moving protectively toward her furniture. "He can sleep in the living room, but he has to clean up." She looked at Steve, the side of her mouth turning down as if she had bitten a lemon. "I can't have his things . . . lying around."

"Yes, Mother. We'll take care of it." Roxy's voice was patient if strained, like she was explaining something to a child for the third time.

Mrs. Fisher looked at the two of them, and then abruptly averted her gaze as she entered her small kitchen.

After a dinner of canned tuna baked over egg noodles with a Campbell's cream of mushroom soup and canned string beans cooked grey, Steve picked up the plates and began to bring them to the kitchen, but Mrs. Fisher quickly intercepted him.

"Let me help you clean up," he offered.

"No, it's my kitchen. I will do it." And she quickly ushered him away.

"Aunt Irma and I will be away tomorrow, doing our volunteer work at the Crittenden Home for Unwed Mothers. Those poor fallen women need so much guidance. We'll be going to services on Sunday. I think it would benefit you to come." She looked directly at Roxy. "And you, too, young man. The way of Jesus is open to all. He is a loving Lord."

"Yes, ma'am." Steve nodded politely. He would go through it all for Roxy.

"Mother, Steve is Catholic."

Her mother shook her head. "Jesus has forgiveness for idolaters. You can learn the way of the righteous."

"He has to find a place to live, and we have to get jobs."

"God will provide." She sat down in the living room and turned the television to Lawrence Welk.

"Mother, we're going for a walk." Roxy took Steve's arm and walked him out the door.

From the apartment complex, they walked into a more residential area of small, tidy Cape Cods and Levitt-style houses, many with second-floor additions or dormers. Steve recognized the same house design, only a thousand miles away from Long Island. Were the people any different? He didn't think so. Roxy was silent in the warm summer air. The sound of children splashing and laughing in backyard pools echoed among the trees.

"I don't know if I can take it," she finally said, laughing and taking hold of his hand. "This isn't home. I feel like an animal in a zoo, on display. I don't think my own mother even knows who I am."

"Of course, she does. She has been through a lot. Give her time." Steve was doing his best to be positive, but he didn't see much chance that her mother was about to give him her blessing.

"You don't understand. I hate pink. I've always hated pink, but even more after Audrey got sick. It was her color, not mine—ever. Audrey was her favorite, but when Audrey got sick, Mom couldn't handle it. Not after my dad died. I was just in the way, but I was necessary."

"Don't say that. Parents don't feel like that." He was trying to help, to deflect the anger. They walked awhile in silence. "Was she always this religious?"

"She was brought up that way, but, around my dad, she dialed it down. We all went to services, but he was a union man—that was his religion. Dad died suddenly, and there wasn't any dam holding it back. And when Audrey died, the dam burst."

"It must be difficult for her."

"I don't know. She wouldn't even come with me to the hospital in Cleveland unless I begged. She wouldn't deal with it, with the doctors, with the decisions. I was only sixteen. I had to tell her what to ask, what to say. What did I know about . . ." Roxy began to cry. Steve embraced her, letting her tears run down his grey t-shirt.

"It may get better now that I'm here. Thank you for being my strength. I love you." They kissed. "Want to go to the high school? I can show you the place under the bleachers where the kids would go to fuck. Maybe I'll even show you how they did it." She smiled, taking his hand. They skipped to the high school field.

Steve and Roxy drove toward the sprawling Ohio State University. Traffic slowed as they neared the sandbagged National Guard checkpoint surrounded by rolls of barbed wire. It looked like the entrance to a prison camp.

The campus had been occupied by troops since the beginning of May. It was now June first, and the armored vehicles, troop trucks, command Jeeps, and fortified sandbagged sentry posts were still stationed in various configurations around the oval and designed to funnel traffic to the checkpoints. Storefronts whose windows had been shattered early in the demonstrations were covered with plywood. Peace signs and *Stop the War* and *Remember Kent State* were spray-painted in red and black on the wood. Several burnt-out cars, their tires gone, hugged the curbs behind the protective barbed wire, too late for their own salvation. The National Guard troops looked exhausted, tense, and young.

Steve slowed as the car in front of him stopped. He could feel himself tense, not from fear but because he knew this was wrong.

"This wasn't a good idea," Roxy said. "We should turn back."

Steve watched her eyes dart around at the armored personnel vehicles and fortified strongpoints.

"It's all right. I called the fraternity, and they said I could have the room. It's still a free country, and we haven't done anything wrong." He patted her hand gently.

He stopped his Volkswagen at the barricade, manned by two soldiers his age brandishing M-1 rifles with bayonets attached. The scent of tear gas emanated from the uniforms.

"What's your business?" the corporal demanded, putting his chin in Steve's face as he looked into the backseat of the green Bug. "Out of the car."

Steve was surprised by the order but exited the car. A soldier pushed him hard against a Jeep. Another soldier, who smelled of week-old dirt, roughly frisked him. He took Steve's wallet and handed it to the corporal. Two other soldiers circled the Volkswagen. Anger was boiling inside Steve—it *was* still a free country.

"New York plates on this foreign car," one soldier said.

"What's this about?" Steve asked, moving forward and squaring his shoulders. He felt violated but knew he had to keep his temper.

"Shut up." The solider raised his M-1 as he pushed Steve back to the Jeep, the bayonet in his face. Steve's anger was rising. He could feel the cold steel of the bayonet against his neck. He pushed down against his anger as he clenched and unclenched his fists. *Don't do anything stupid.* He felt he was caught behind the Iron Curtain. Who was in charge? Could they do whatever they wanted? Was there martial law in Ohio? Who the fuck were these storm troopers?

"You SDS? One of those East Coast radicals?" the corporal demanded.

Steve tensed and enunciated the words slowly. "I'm going to Lambda Chi Alpha fraternity on campus. I'll be living there for the summer."

A solider looked at Steve's collar-length hair. "But you're from New York?" He motioned to the driver's license. "You lost, or are you an outside agitator?"

"My girlfriend is from Columbus, so I'll be spending the summer working and being here with her." The guard peered into the car, and Roxy gave him her all-American smile. The boy soldier seemed to soften a bit and smiled back at her.

"Ma'am, where are you from?"

"Westerville. My whole family is up there." She batted her eyes flirtatiously at the tired soldiers, and two more came over to speak to her. Steve could see her animated gestures and her constant smiles. One of the soldiers smiled as she continued to work her charm.

"All right." The corporal looked Steve over with a weary disgust. "All public demonstrations are banned. Any group that assembles without a permit will be dispersed immediately or arrested. The campus proper is closed until further notice. Carry on." And he waved them through the barricade.

Steve gripped the wheel, his fingers blanching. He clenched his jaw as he put the car into gear. He looked at Roxy, who held on to her fearful smile. They were now face to face with the war. "Shit. This is straight out of a Costa-Gavras film; the generals have taken over," he said.

Steve walked through the gate to the employment office with the clipping from the newspaper advertising for temporary labor at $6 an hour. The application form was simple to fill out, and he sat in the sparse waiting room, needing to be cleared by the company doctor.

> *Buckeye Steel Casting Company is located on 90 acres off Parsons Ave in South Columbus.*

Steve read the company brochure on the table as he waited.

> *With more than 22 acres of factory under one roof, the massive foundry has produced railway couplers and other equipment for the railroad industry since it was founded by E.H. Harriman and Frank Rockefeller to supply the great railroad boom of*

the 19th Century. The company became an industrial giant under the guidance of its President, Samuel Prescott Bush, at the beginning of the 20th Century.

"Home from college?" The company doctor was middle-aged, with signs of alcohol wear on his face, which explained his current choice of careers.

"Yeah. Need to pay the bills."

When he reported to work, he was wearing the required steel-toe boots, a long-sleeve denim shirt, and jeans as instructed, despite the hot, humid day. The muggy air sat on his skin like a wet sheet, and Steve, who had never been in a factory before, immediately developed a new appreciation for the working class.

The foreman escorted the new temporary workers through a building that housed the blast furnace and the giant bucket that poured the molten steel into the various forms. The bucket was suspended on a series of railings that allowed it to be drawn down the row of forms—red hot batter poured into little cookie molds that made up the pieces of a railway undercarriage: couplings, wheels, frames, tie bars. Even from a hundred feet away, the heat from the liquid steel caused Steve to break out into a shirt-soaking sweat. Watching the glowing metal stream so smoothly from high overhead was like watching a ballet of industry, each movement endlessly rehearsed and executed, with every man filling his role perfectly.

The foreman, a man in his forties with thick arms and short hair, directed him to a metal stamping machine. He was instructed to cut metal bars into various lengths with a foot-operated stamp that made a loud chopping sound with each cut. Steve adjusted his plastic goggles and set to work, moving at an easy pace until he filled the two bins with the correct sizes.

When the lunch whistle blew, one of the other workers tapped him on the shoulder and gestured to him to go outside, where the noise and dirt were not as intense. Steve realized how loud the steady drum of machinery within the factory was when he sat on a packing crate in the yard. They could speak again in normal voices without the constant din of the factory.

There were a half dozen men sitting in the shade of the factory wall, where the temperature seemed cool after the relentless heat of the building. Each man had a metal lunch bucket, some with thermoses of cool liquids. Their faces were painted with perspiration streaks of dirt, each with a different texture or color from the swirls of grit in the air.

"Got to slow down, kid," a small, wiry man with jaundice-yellow teeth said, letting out a long stream of pale tobacco juice. Steve opened his peanut butter and jelly sandwich. "You ain't getting paid by piece work, so make the job last."

"Where you from, kid?" the bad-toothed man asked, taking a bite of some meat and then picking at his teeth with a piece of wire.

"Back east. New York."

"Ow-eye," a taller farmer said. "A big city boy."

"Not really. I'm from outside the city."

"I'm from Kentucky. *Up the hollers,* as people say. Been down here with kin. Once some of them found work, we followed. This is better work than the mines—at least there is daylight during lunch. What you doing here. Coming to work with us?"

"Summer job. Going back to school."

"Why here?"

"My girlfriend is from Columbus, so I came out for the summer."

"Pussy whipped already. I tell ya, once the old lady has her hooks into a man, there is no going back. Lead you around like a bull with a ring in his nose. Ain't seen no good come of it.

"Some time ago, young guy like you come work here. He wasn't getting any regular, like you. So we told him, you go over to the sand shed and you will see a big barrel with a hole in it about the same size as a pecker. Told him, you put your pecker in there and everything will be all right. So this boy goes over and comes back with a big smile on his face. Says, 'Boys, you were right. Went over to that barrel and put my pecker in and sure enough, I'm all satisfied.' So we tell him he can go over there every day except Thursday. Now, this boy is all happy about it, but then says, 'Why can't I go over on Thursday?'"

The Kentucky man paused and the other men smiled at Steve.

"'Cause that's your day in the barrel.'"

They all cackled with laughter, Steve with them. He admired how focused they were at their jobs, creating sand forms, assembling forged iron into working wheels and railroad undercarriages. He had never seen things made, and he was impressed at their skill. It was a workingman's world—honest work that they would do for the rest of their lives. What kind of life would that be for him, working in the mill for the rest of his life, hoping to make foreman one day? But he knew he wouldn't, and he appreciated that he had other opportunities. The whistle blew, signaling the end of the lunch hour.

"You're not going out looking like that?" Mrs. Fisher stared at Roxy, who was dressed in a yellow tube top and blue denim miniskirt. Her slim shoulders and legs were already tanned from the summer sun.

"You should dress like a young lady, not like some trailer trash," she continued.

"Mother, I know how to dress."

"Do you? What are you advertising? When will you be home?"

"I don't know. We're going into Columbus." Roxy rolled her eyes as she looked at Steve, who was standing helplessly, witnessing the exchange and knowing his opinion was not welcome. Roxy was looking very sexy, and he was hoping she would stay the night in his little frat house room.

"Well, be home by eleven."

"Mother, I'm in college; I don't need a curfew. I may stay in town with friends."

"Who?"

"Enough with the cross examination. We're going out. I'll see you tomorrow." Roxy gave her a kiss on the cheek. A scowl crossed Mrs. Fisher's face, and she turned her back to them, returning to her television.

As they got into the car, Roxy told Steve, "I don't know if I can take a full summer of this. I love her. She's my mother, but I can't stand her attitude."

"You're all she has left."

For several weeks, Roxy had met Steve at the door so he didn't have to come into the apartment. This time, she had invited him in before they went to the movies.

"I am going to a revival with Aunt Irma in Finley tomorrow night." Mrs. Fisher directed her remarks to Roxy, treating Steve like an unknown bystander or a piece of furniture that happened to be in the room. "We'll be back on Sunday morning after the services. Don't make a mess of things and create work for me." She smiled at Roxy. "You should come with us. Two days with the Lord will improve life for you."

"Yes, Mother. Have a good time. And give my love to Aunt Irma."

"I'll pray for you." Mrs. Fisher turned to Steve. "And you, too."

"We have a double bed," Roxy said when they returned from the movies and rolled her eyes to her mother's bedroom. It didn't take much encouragement, and they fell into each other's arms and passionately made love.

Roxy woke up in a panic, searching for a clock. "What time is it? Shit, shit. Steve, wake up," She shook him hard to wake him. "It's almost noon. I don't know what time she will be home."

He fell out of bed, heading for the bathroom.

"No, no! Not that one. Use the one in the hall." Roxy was hurriedly pulling the sheets onto the bed. She then carefully made hospital corners at the foot of each side and pulled the bedspread up over the pillows.

Steve walked to the bedroom door in his shorts, admiring her naked body as she frantically arranged pillows on the bed.

"I wish I could get this kind of room service," he said. "How do I make coffee?"

She turned to him. "You could help."

He moved toward the bed.

"Never mind, make the coffee. It's only instant. And get dressed. Look like you just arrived, not just got out of bed." Her panic was beginning to subside as she adjusted the shams and piled the pillows on top of the bedspread. "Perfect. Now I'll take a shower. Close the window and get rid of the roach and clean the saucer from last night."

Steve put on his t-shirt, shorts, and his tan moccasins. He put two spoons of Folger's into each cup and poured the boiling water. Roxy returned from the bathroom looking more freshly scrubbed, with a light blue top over white shorts. She brushed her hair, throwing it from side to side as she stood by the table, sipping the coffee. "Looks like you were never here."

Hearing the key in the door, Roxy put down the brush and quickly sat at the small wooden dining room table. Mrs. Fisher entered with her small blue suitcase.

"How was it, Mother?" Roxy asked cheerily.

"Inspiring. Uplifting. It makes you believe in the righteousness of the Lord." She turned and saw Steve sitting at the table. She gave him a forced smile and looked at Roxy, who was bright and cheerful. She carried her suitcase into her bedroom but quickly returned with dark thunderclouds in her eyes.

"How dare you! In my own house. In my own bed . . ." She moved toward Roxy. "What kind of child are you? A child of the devil himself?"

"Mother, what do you mean? 'How dare I'?"

"What happened to my bed? I never put the pillows like that. What have you done?" She looked at Roxy and then at Steve, who quickly looked away from her gaze, feeling guilty like getting caught lying in grade school.

"Harlot. Fornicator!" she shouted at Roxy. "Daughter of the devil. Get out of my house. And get that evil serpent out of my house." She pointed to Steve and raised her hand at Roxy, who backed into the small bedroom.

"Mother, nothing happened. We were watching television," she said

"Out of my sight, harlot," she screamed again. Roxy slammed her coffee cup on the table. In her room, she quickly threw her clothes into two bags without looking at her mother. She kicked a box of books into the hallway. Steve got up to help, but Mrs. Fisher intercepted him.

"Out of my house, Satan. Out, you corrupting evil sinner."

Steve wanted to step between Roxy and her mother and be a shield to take the arrows of scorn. He was shocked at the intensity of the anger. His parents never screamed—their fights were long periods of silence. Was it about the sex? That was still the hang-up of her mother's generation . . . Roxy face was white, and her lips were tightly drawn, holding back tears. He would protect her and give her love. Roxy handed the bags to him.

"You're right, Mother. This is your house. It was never my home. I'm going, Mother, and I'm never coming back."

"Out, evil. You are not my daughter."

"You don't even know who I am." Roxy was crying. "I'm not Audrey. I'm your other daughter. The one you never wanted." She turned, sobbing. Steve led her by the arm to the car and packed it while Roxy sat in the passenger seat, crying. He put his arm around her, and she turned her head into his shoulder, her tears on his shirt. He started the car but didn't put it in gear. How could Mrs. Fisher do this to her only daughter? He wanted to go back inside and tell her mother how wrong she was about her daughter. How much he loved her and would always take care of her. He ran his hand over her hair. He would make it better. They could go back to the fraternity house, but she couldn't stay there. What could he do?

"I'm serious—I'm never going back there. Done. Never. Never." She straightened and looked out the window, taking deep breaths to control her sobbing.

"Let's go home—back to Providence. You're all I have now," she said, throwing her arms around him. He held back tears as he put his arm around her. She was so hurt, so vulnerable. He would never hurt her. He would stay in Providence. On the radio, Crosby Stills Nash & Young sang *"Teach your parents well..."*

IT'S A WILD WORLD

Roxy was moving several heavy biology books from the bed to the small desk against the window. They had been back a month, and she was getting ready for the fall semester. A small brown tensor lamp was next to Steve's manual Smith Corona typewriter on the desk. She was ready to sit when Steve took her hand.

"We need to talk."

She looked quizzical. "We do?"

"Yes." He was a little sheepish, looking down at the floor, a little boy asking for permission. He handed her the ad for the Providence police. Roxy read it, looked up at him, and read it again.

"Are you serious? Is this a joke?" She looked at him as if she were trying to see into his head.

"We talked about doing . . . When I saw the ad, I thought . . . What do you think?"

"I know we did, but this . . . It's too crazy."

"Really? I just can't watch the country be torn apart. It's our country, too." He had thought hard about it on the drive back to Providence, the memory of the bayonet point at his neck very clear. Land of the free, home of the brave. It was bullshit if he didn't do something.

Kent State had proved protesting could be deadly. He had to move forward, go for the goal.

"What do you know about doing police stuff?"

"Not much; got a ticket once. I'll be in Providence, so we can be together. The money is good. And Durk said, 'Law is what separates us from the savages. And you've got to be part of the system to change it.'" He leaned in closer to her and realized he had deepened his voice. Who was he trying to convince?

"I heard him, but what do you think you are really going to do?" She tilted her head to the side.

"I'm not really sure." He'd examined the options in his mind on the ride back from Ohio. It might be dangerous, but courage was walking to the edge of the cliff and looking over. He could handle it, but he knew that *it* was the unknown.

"Maybe I can be that conscience that Durk talked about. I might elevate the level of policing in Providence. And I would know more for law school." He wasn't going to leave her. And the idea, the thought to be like Durk and . . . He wasn't sure of the *and*, but it would be an education. Durk was so passionate about what he was doing.

"Did you talk to your dad? To anyone?"

"I know what his answer will be. Andy and I talked, but you're the one . . ."

"Yeah, but." She looked at him. "I didn't think . . . You mean . . . you. Here. Now. You will have to wear a gun and those stupid brown uniforms?"

"Yes," he said. Turning the idea over in his mind disconnected it from the reality. "It may be crazy, but I can't stop thinking about what Durk's doing. I want to get outside this Ivy League bubble. It's about right and wrong. I want to travel and see other places, but I want to stay in Providence with you. This would do both. And yeah, who knows? Maybe I could do some good while I'm at it."

She paused, turning her head to the window before looking at him. "You would do this for me?" She took his hands. "It might work. You *could* do things. You could be the conscience. You could really shake things up." Her voice became more animated as she bounced slightly. Her face was slightly flushed. "The whole system needs to be overthrown, from Nixon on down. And you could begin here and be my gallant knight, slaying dragons and rescuing damsels in distress. Right makes might." She made a fainting motion. "But you in a uniform that doesn't have a number on it?" She made a face, and they laughed.

"Maybe they'll make me chief right away so I don't have to waste time learning anything and can change things from the top." He could feel his heart beating faster. He would stay here with her. He would step over the line Colonel Travis drew in the sand at the Alamo. He would stay to fight. "And you'll be here with me." She sighed, moving her face close to his. "You're crazy, you know that. Like when you went to Alaska and fought forest fires. Crazy good—that's what I love about you. You don't just talk."

"Only crazy for you."

"And we could go to the Policeman's Ball. Do policemen have balls?" She tittered and planted a wet kiss on his lips. They became more passionate, and the clothes came off. They did not close the door. The cat, which had stayed with Andy for the month, looked at them from the top of the dresser as they fell to the bed among the flying clothes.

Steve stood at the bottom of the stairs, looking at Providence Police headquarters, which was an old grey granite building with stone gargoyles. Police cruisers were parked haphazardly in front of the station. Two police officers came down the stairs and got into a cruiser. Another car arrived. One officer exited and brought a hand-cuffed young man, his head hung down, up the steps and disappeared through the doors. Steve breathed deeply, forcing the air into his diaphragm to push back the nervous adrenaline. His hair was now shorter—not a crew cut but a neater business style, cleanly parted; a regular cut, the barber said.

He was wearing grey slacks, a white shirt, striped tie, and the camel hair tan blazer that his father had bought him before he left for school. It was the only dress jacket he had ever owned, and it had stayed in the closet for four years. His palms were moist, and his heart was racing. He felt odd looking a little preppy. Filling out the employment paperwork and taking the entrance test had been about as difficult as the driver's license exam. How did anyone not get one hundred percent on it? The department had called to set up this final interview.

Ascending the five stairs to the double front door, he held the door open for two cops before entering. Wooden high-back benches lined both sides of the room, with various people sitting on them, filling out forms. One woman was asking for information about a relative to an officer by the side door.

The raised desk in the rear of the room towered over the foyer by several feet. The policeman behind the desk looked down at Steve but didn't acknowledge him, returning to some document and keeping Steve waiting.

"Can I help you?" the desk sergeant finally asked.

"I have an appointment with Colonel McGuire. Stephen Logan."

"V or Ph?"

"Excuse me?"

"V or Ph?"

"I'm not following . . ."

"Your name—V or Ph?"

"Oh, sorry. Ph."

"Take a seat." The officer picked up the phone.

Sergeant Lyons put down the black handset and signaled Steve past the desk. "Turn left and up the stairs. Second door on the right." The sergeant gave him a long look.

Steve went through the door. Rows of dented grey metal desks were in the main squad room. One officer was sitting at a desk, hunting and pecking on a manual typewriter. Steve took in the room; it was a place where work happened, like the factory floor of the steel mill—cardboard coffee cups, cigarettes, and piles of folders. Walking to the stairs in this alien world with little color, he noticed that even the walls were institutional grey. The fluorescent light fixtures had cracked lenses or lacked them totally, and the handrails were worn brass with a shiny surface from years of hands gripping them.

Standing at the bottom of the stairs, he put one foot on the first step and again hesitated. He did not want to overanalyze; doing came more naturally to him. But he knew he was entering into an unknown world, one that would change his life. Was this what he wanted? Why was he here? Did he really believe he could make an impact? Did Roxy? While the thoughts tangled in his mind, he placed his next foot on the landing, then one foot after another, moving forward despite any doubts. At the top of the stairs, the detective offices faced him. At the end of the corridor were double wooden doors with lettering reading *Colonel McGuire, Chief of Police*.

When Steve received the call for the interview, he did his research on the chief. McGuire was appointed two years ago by the mayor after having started as a patrolman, then moving to the State Police. One of McGuire's first acts was to change the color of the uniforms from blue to brown because he liked the look—more professional.

Steve stood in the corridor, thinking about turning around and going back home. Was this as crazy an idea as all his friends thought it was? Was this about him or Roxy? Was he doing it to stay near her? To impress her? He knew he needed to prove something to himself. It was about courage and doing the right thing. Maybe the nuns really got through to him with the idea of good and evil, right and wrong. He was always attentive, but not pious. The dead students at Kent State bothered him. Bruce Miller was from the next town on Long

Island. Did he ever think he'd die at some nowhere school in Ohio? This was the right step for now.

He entered the office and faced a middle-aged woman who looked him over but didn't greet him. She was formal and primly dressed, with a high-collared blouse and cameo pin, her hair lacquered in place. She motioned him to sit in the armchair while she picked up the black phone and spoke quietly into it.

"You may go in," she said, eyeing him suspiciously.

When he entered the office, the colonel was behind his desk, his shoulders squared. His face was tanned, with a news anchor's hairstyle. Slouched in a chair to one side, with a cigar in hand, was the overweight Captain Lynch, who Steve recognized from the anti-war march. Standing to the rear was an earnest forty-year-old lieutenant with light curly hair and the name badge "Krieger."

Steve noticed that the dark wood paneling was picture-frame molding over stained plywood. There were photographs on the wall of a uniformed McGuire over the years with J. Edgar Hoover, various politicians from Rhode Island and Massachusetts, and even one with Richard Nixon.

"Why do you want to be a police officer?" McGuire asked, looking Steve over as if he were a suspect. He didn't ask Steve to sit.

"I want to contribute to society." Steve stood tall, balancing on the balls of his feet rather than a military stance. If he said he wanted to try to change things, to make the department better, he knew it was not the answer they were looking for.

"This is about keeping society safe," the chief replied, turning his eyes toward the captain.

"I realize that, sir."

"Do you?" He paused as he examined Steve. "You did well on the test and passed the physical. You graduated college?"

"Yes sir, from Brown in June."

"Do we have any college graduates?" he asked over his shoulder.

"Aside from me, sir, I don't think so. But I can check if you want," Kreiger answered crisply.

The chief waved him off. "What did you major in?"

"Anthropology, sir."

"This isn't social work.

"Fucking college kids, they did us a favor in Ohio, shooting those commie-loving kids. My men stood up and cheered. Love it or leave it." The captain lit his cigar and asked roughly, "Ever get your hands dirty, kid?"

"Sir?"

"Ever hold a real job?"

"I've always worked, sir. Worked in a steel mill." He thought that type of a real job would impress the captain.

"Sir, we may be the only police force to have an Ivy graduate on it. We could create some positive stories for how you are upgrading the professionalism of the department," Krieger said.

Steve could see the colonel take in the information as he rolled his jaw. He looked down at the folder in front of him and tapped his pen.

"Let's wait until he gets out of the academy before you start with your PR bullshit," Lynch said, pointing his cigar aggressively at Krieger The colonel turned his attention back to Steve. "Your application is in order. You begin the academy in two weeks. That will be all."

He stood up but did not offer his hand.

"Thank you, sir," Steve said, waiting for the next sentence. McGuire drew his lips together and arched his eyebrows. Steve knew the interview was over. He turned, and, as he was leaving the room, he heard Lynch say, "I don't like it."

As Steve entered the living room back in Providence, Roxy greeted him with a hug. In the maroon chair sat a tall blond girl with straight hair. She was wearing a loose-fitting peasant dress. Big boned with wide hips, very pale blue eyes, and flaxen skin, she looked like a woman who would have been coveted for her childbearing potential in the previous century. Her unshaven legs were covered in the same light-colored blond hair. She wore no makeup, and Steve could see her hands were callused from working with a rough material, like factory work.

"Steve, this is Heather. She's going to take over Andy's room. She's going to RISD."

Heather put out her strong, muscular arm and shook his hand with a solid grip.

"Nice to meet you," she said. Her slight down east Maine accent made her seem to be a true flower child straight from the country commune.

"I guess you are going for equality of the sexes in renting Andy's room." He laughed and caught Heather's eyes: unafraid and direct.

"Yes, someone who sits on the toilet when they pee," Roxy added, grimacing at Heather.

"What brings you to Providence? Rhode Island School of Design?"

"I went to the Summerhill School in England and do a lot of pottery, and I work with other materials as well. Guess I'm a sculptor with many materials. RISD will help me reach my innerness."

"We met over at the Blue Room, where she was looking at the bulletin board for roommates," Roxy said.

"What's Summerhill?" Steve asked.

"Progressive school—no classes like traditional schools. We chose the subjects that interested us. The emphasis was on learning, not tests." Her smile seemed a practiced patience.

"You just showed up in Providence looking for a place to stay? You didn't have anything arranged?" Steve was impressed with her.

Heather shrugged. "It always seems to work out." She smiled a child's smile. "My karma directs me, and I can embrace the unknown. It doesn't frighten me—does it frighten you?"

Her penetrating look was not threatening, but she created a sense of discomfort within him. He was still several steps away from embracing the Age of Aquarius stuff.

"Great," Roxy broke in. "To get down to business, it's thirty-three dollars a month, utilities included. You buy your own food. You're on once a month to clean the bathroom and living room. We have the room on the end, you have the middle one, and Cal has the one next to the living room."

"Though feel free to clean more often if you like," Steve chimed in. Roxy gently punched him.

"The room will be available on September first." Roxy and Steve took her on a tour. Heather stopped to look at the large bathroom at the end of the hall. It was painted in large red, white, and blue stripes with a chair rail of white stars.

"We're very patriotic," Steve said.

"Here's a key. There's a bed in the room but no sheets," Roxy said, giving Steve a quick smile.

"Groovy. I'll have two bags. But I always sleep in the nude." Moving quickly like a large bird, she smiled broadly at them and glided down the stairs.

The drive down Interstate 95 was a constant battle between his small VW and the tractor trailers that owned the road. Steve did not overestimate the power of his VW Bug but hung between the hulking vehicles as their wake battered the car with waves of air. The six twenty-five-cent toll booths from West Haven to New Rochelle slowed traffic to a crawl, but it was the last one in New York that signaled he was almost home. Going to see his father had been a difficult decision, but Steve had told Roxy that he needed to tell his father about the police career in person. After all, they had last seen each other at graduation, and back then, Steve had still been going to law school.

The maple trees along the Cross Island Expressway on Little Neck Bay were tinged orange and yellow from an early frost. Since he had left for college and his mother and siblings had moved to Florida, he had felt less and less connected to Long Island.

Taking the familiar exit dumped him on the stomping grounds of his youth. Borelli's Pizza was still on the corner, and Steve had to remind himself to pay attention to where he was driving. He could get lost in the memories later. The main street was unchanged—a supermarket, luncheonette, paper store, Franklin National Bank, and Persia Carpets. He remembered the neighborhood as a place a kid with a bike could conquer anywhere. The new library, a small red-brick building, had replaced the old white one-room schoolhouse building where he first fell in love with Tom Swift books.

When his mother moved to Florida, Steve stayed most of freshman summer with his father in his studio apartment, sleeping on the couch in the living room. Parking the VW in the visitor space, he approached the four-story red-brick apartment building with a quiet determination. He had made his decision, so he wasn't asking for approval. His father hadn't wanted him to go to Brown, saying they couldn't afford it. Steve had never asked him for money; he made it work on his own with jobs. He wasn't angry with his father; they never had harsh words. They agreed to disagree on things. Today would be one more time.

Greeting each other with a handshake, Steve noticed his father was more hunched. He remembered how his round, ruddy Irish face would turn beet red in the summer sun, bringing a plethora of unseen freckles to the fore. Thinning white hair and black glasses made him look like the government clerk he was.

Looking around the apartment, Steve noticed it hadn't been vacuumed in months. It didn't surprise him because his father had drifted into another world while Steve was in high school. Barely functional at work, the civil service job protected him from his lack of ambition as long as he showed up.

"How you getting on?" Steve asked, putting his shoulder bag on the couch where he would sleep.

"Aches and pain. I'm getting old," his father replied, moving to sit in the Barcalounger, where he could read and watch television. "It won't be too long."

"Right. Two years till retirement." Steve knew his father wasn't talking about retirement, but he'd been hearing the same old story for five years now.

"If I make it to retirement, God willing. I may move down to Florida, where it is warm."

"That would be good. The kids would like it."

He nodded, but Steve knew that his father was dreaming, trying to recreate the world he had lost. "What are you reading these days?"

"I just finished the Volume 9 of Durant's *Story of Civilization*. Where are you?" his father asked.

"Only on Volume 6," Steve said. "How's work going?"

His father gave him a wry smile, the smile Steve remembered from his youth. There had been mirth in his voice back then. "It's a job. I should have done better. I had the education but never the . . . Your mother thought I would do better . . . I don't know. Maybe the war put me back in the minor leagues."

Nothing new here; Steve had heard the same excuses, framed in different words, since he went to college. But his father never would talk more about the war other than to say he was in one of the waves on D-Day. He was older and better educated than most of his company. That was one of the few details Steve knew—but now that he was facing being one of the most educated on the police force, he had a feeling his father could teach him something important. If only the old man would talk.

Only anecdotes of his training time in England.

"I've got a job," he announced, figuring it was better to be upfront with everything and wanting to get it over with quickly.

"I thought you were going to law school."

"Not now. I start on the Providence Police Department next week."

He could see his father trying to process the information about what type of job in the police department would use a Brown degree. "Some type of analyst? They hire college graduates?"

"I'll just be a regular cop." Steve was sitting now, looking directly at his father, whose eyes seemed absorbed in the view out the window.

"No special program?"

"No. Just a regular cop."

"Doesn't make any sense—why go to school? You will end up a failure like . . ." Steve could hear the word *me* and could feel his father's cold disdain for a life badly led.

"No, Dad. I think I can accomplish something. It's a big commitment."

His father shook his head, looking at Steve as he picked up *Newsday*. He wore the sadness that he had worn since the family split up. Steve could feel the projection of failure on him, which he refused to accept.

"I didn't expect you to understand, but I wanted you to know." Steve looked at his father, wishing he could shake him back into life. He had tried that first summer, engaging him in political discussions, taking him to movies, even to the city for a play and Schrafft's, where his dad had taken him as a kid. He was okay for the moment but when the stimulus passed, he fell back into that other world.

"I'll buy you dinner," Steve said, standing to end the conversation about his future. "I have to go back tomorrow."

The next morning, his father was dressed in a grey suit, white shirt, and navy bow tie, ready for work at the county office. "Thanks for coming. I don't think you're making the right choice. I made some bad decisions; it didn't work out." He shook his head, defeated. "I will come and see you one of these days. Take the train up."

"I look forward to it." Steve knew they were only words.

When he was gone, Steve looked around the apartment. The kitchen sink was filled with some pans with burnt food and plates that looked like they'd been there for weeks. Cockroaches scurried away when he entered, even in the daylight. The bathroom hadn't been cleaned; it had yellow stains and smelled of urine coming from the toilet and floor. Checking the cleaning supplies from his last visit, Steve found the Comet, scrub brushes, Lysol, bucket, and mop in the same position in the closet. He set to work in the bathroom, scrubbing the soap scum and black mildew from the bathtub and washing the toilet bowl with Pine-Sol until the fresh pine scent enveloped the bathroom. In the kitchen, he cleaned the dishes and scrubbed the pots until they shone. Looking in the cabinet above the stove, he found the bottle of boric acid he had bought last time he visited. Carefully, he poured a line along the cracks in the counter, along the base of the cabinets, and under the sink. It should hold the cockroaches at bay for a month, but he needed to call the landlord to have the place exterminated again. He cleaned the floor with an electric broom and emptied all the garbage into the chute in the hallway. Domestically done, Steve washed his hands of Long Island. Although he knew that nothing had changed, he felt better for his drive back to Providence.

Little Compton Beach was a sliver of a retreat on the Atlantic, mostly known to the well-heeled of the old money set. Steve and Andy built a fire with charcoal and driftwood scooped up among the dunes. He placed rocks under the coal and lit the fire. Two coolers, one filled with beer and wine, the other with clams and mussels, were waiting for dinner. Heather, in a homemade macramé two-piece bathing suit that showed off her long, sturdy, unshaven legs, wrapped potatoes in aluminum foil, each with a different fold, and put them in the fire to roast. Andy took a Frisbee and started passing it to the girls. Roxy was in a yellow two-piece accentuating her bust, the two cups held together with a metal O ring.

They jumped in and out of the water to cool off. Steve, in blue and yellow trunks, expertly bodysurfed the waves. He wished he still had his surfboard. In high school, during the summer, he and two buddies would get up with the first light and go down to Long Beach before the lifeguards came on duty. Andy rode waves, aiming at the two girls, who screamed as they danced away from him. Steve raced to the water and grabbed Roxy off her feet and dove into an oncoming wave with her. Raising and spitting water, Roxy dunked Steve under the next wave as they laughed in the warm August Atlantic water.

When the sun began to set, they sat around the fire with towels stretched over their shoulders for comfort, not warmth.

"When are you leaving?" Steve asked, passing Andy a beer.

"Thursday," Andy replied, looking at the can and then out to the ocean.

"It'll be a great adventure. You're doing a good thing." Heather smiled at him.

"I didn't think a jungle in South America was the direct career path from Brown, but it's better than the jungle in Vietnam. I'll be doing community development, whatever that is. Or maybe an irrigation project." Andy's eyes seemed set on the horizon. "They're not exactly clear in the form letters. But definitely won't be leveling villages with napalm." Andy and Steve held each other's gaze. "You staying here?"

"Yeah, not ready to leave." He motioned to Roxy. "I got accepted and start the academy in the middle of September."

"You're serious? You're really serious? You're going through with it." Andy shook his head and lowered his chin. "Where do you think that's going to lead?"

Steve shrugged. He wasn't sure, but his new course was set. Law school could wait. He would stay in Providence and try to be part of the change.

"Talk about not wanting to get killed." Andy screwed up his mouth in mock disdain.

"Yeah, maybe I might be a little crazy."

"Do you remember that freshman game against Yale, when you . . ."

Roxy came over, smiling, to break up the guy talk.

"Better keep your hands off those senoritas." She put her arm inside Andy's. "I hear if you touch 'em, you marry them."

"So that's why the Spanish only sent conquistadors and priests." They all laughed, but for Steve and Andy, the fun was laced with nostalgia. It wasn't graduation jitters but, like tens of thousands of young men around the country, they didn't talk about the next time they might meet. Nothing was clear, just shades and amorphous shapes of things to come. When they'd arrived at Brown fresh and scrubbed, they never thought it would end this way.

The group was quiet for a moment. Steve said, "I guess it's time for real life."

"You may have graduated, but you aren't going anywhere." Roxy put Steve's arm around her. "I need you too much."

"I'll happily be a kept man, but I don't think that's what you have in mind."

"It'll work out. I'm not letting you too far off the leash. There's so much here for us." She smiled and nuzzled him.

The fire began crackling, and Andy scraped away the coals and covered the rocks with wet seaweed. He put the clams and mussels on the seaweed and covered them with more seaweed as the steam rose around him. He looked satisfied with his creation.

"Twenty minutes," Andy said to the group.

He turned on a transistor radio and Cat Stevens sang, *"Baby, baby it's a wild world . . ."*

In the apartment, Steve was dressed in his brown uniform pants and matching shirt with a beige tie and black shoes. He looked at himself in the mirror. His hair was cut very short, and his mustache was gone. Roxy came up behind him and looked at him slightly quizzically, as if she was trying to recognize him. Their gazes met and released.

"Here we go," he said, turning away from the person in the mirror.

"Yes, you are in the deep end. Do you know how to swim?"

"I guess I'll find out." Caressing her shoulder, he tenderly kissed her. He held on to her a little longer as she buried her head in his shoulder. His college days were gone, like his hair and mustache. Had it changed the way she looked at him? He turned again to the mirror and fixed the cap squarely on his head before he executed an about face, like the ROTC kids did on parade. He looked at her and remembered when they had met the year before.

Cal had brought several freshman girls back to the apartment after helping with orientation. He was regaling them with his tales of Woodstock and all the music. Roxy was quiet, taking in the shabby college apartment with amusement. Steve watched the slight, dark-haired girl with delicate features move around the apartment with a dancer's grace.

Cal was into his senior role, trying to impress the girls with his knowledge and collection of music. 'Want to hear the newest Beatles album?" He put his arms around two girls.

"I need to get back," Roxy said.

"I'll walk you back," Steve said, standing quickly. He already admired her for cutting off Cal's bullshit and followed her down the stairs to open the door for her. He wore a simple grey t-shirt that showed his smooth arm muscles.

While the dorm was only a short distance away, Steve wanted more time with her, so he suggested they walk and enjoy the warm September air. She paused and looked him over carefully before agreeing. They stopped at Thayer Market, and he bought a quart of beer with the last of his weekend money.

Walking through the stone wall entrance to Aldrich Dexter Field, the huge Meehan hockey rink loomed over the parking lot like an alien flying saucer. The small wooden building next to it, more like an old barracks, looked like a beaten jalopy next to the concrete behemoth.

"This used to be the poor farm, where they locked you up until you could pay your bills. Interesting concept." Trying to be casual, he searched for some conversation starter; his natural insecurity about girls made him stammer a bit. "Now it's the field house for the team. Football is lousy, but we're pretty good at lacrosse."

"You play?"

"Yeah. You can come to a game in the spring—athletes at Brown are not big men on campus. It's more the opposite," He was proud of how disciplined and organized he had become. It had forced him to concentrate on school.

She spotted a thirty-foot metal structure overlooking the back field. "What that? Let's climb it."

As she climbed the metal ladder to the coach's tower, her long white cotton skirt caught the wind, revealing a brief glimpse of her thigh. It caught his eyes, which had been focused on the flow of her muscles up to her tight cheeks a foot from his face.

"It's peaceful up here. You can see so much." A soft yellow glow from the flickering lights of the Colonial houses seeped through the canopy of trees. They were beginning to change costumes for the fall. As the sun set, she passed the bottle of beer to Steve. He took a sip but didn't take his eyes off her. Her dark hair moved slightly in the breeze as she lay down, looking up at the stars. He reclined nervously next to her without touching.

"Do you know what you want to study yet?" He was aware it was a lame question, but she was a freshman.

"I'm going to be a doctor," she said quickly, her voice decisive and firm.

"Why a doctor?"

She told him about her sister and the pain of watching her slowly die of cancer. Her voice quivered with emotion—bitterness controlled, but not far below the surface. He was amazed at how open and trusting she was. Despite just having met her, he felt more comfortable with her than any girl he had ever met. He wanted to reach out and hold her, but he knew that wasn't the right response.

She told him how her father had died of a heart attack when she was fifteen and her mother moved them back to Ohio and her family. "It happened so fast. From a family to almost an orphan." Her voice had gone soft as she turned to him and offered a crooked smile. He felt her vulnerability mixed with an extraordinary openness. She waited, looking directly into his eyes. "I don't know why I'm telling you this. It's not like I'm some tragic figure. It happened. I'm here." She kicked him. "Now your turn."

He told her about his family: his father's breakdown and his mother taking the kids to Florida. He smiled faintly, shocked at how much came out of his mouth. He never talked about his family, not even to his roommates. "So there we have it. Our life stories and a quart of beer."

They sat up and looked at each other in the pale light. He knew more about her in a few hours than anyone he had ever met. Was she waiting for someone to come along who she could trust and be open with? He was in unfamiliar territory, and the unsettled feeling was intoxicating.

CHAPTER 5

STREET FIGHTING MAN

The overweight captain with thin greying hair and a bulbous nose slowly scanned the call. Steve was happy to be in class but recognized the captain from the interview. This wasn't going to be easy; the captain's comment as Steve had left the interview still rankled. The captain read from a blue binder in his flat, nasal voice. His brown uniform shirt was cardboard starched. "It's illegal to transport swill and offal through the streets of Providence except in watertight tubs or casks."

Swill and offal. Steve wrote down the two apt words. It wasn't a Comparative Political Systems of Antiquity lecture at Brown, but he took notes with the same discipline. Five months after the murders at Kent State, he had changed. It was personal, but he was on the other side; some of his friends might say a traitor, part of *the establishment*. He still knew the Vietnam War was wrong and the Nixon bunch hated his generation—nothing had changed. But for him, it was time to do more, more than rhetoric and slogans. All his friends were against his decision—everyone but Roxy. If she hadn't walked into his life, he would be in a lecture hall at Georgetown Law. She was the reason he was happy and still in Providence.

"Would you define 'swill and offal'?" Steve asked without raising his hand or waiting to be called on.

The captain's mouth twisted upward, and he exhaled loudly. He stared at Steve. "You know: animal shit," he said, shuffling pages and trying to find his place to resume his lecture.

"Excrement. Both solid and liquid?" Steve persisted.

There was a murmur of laughter in the room as the recruits turned toward Steve, who was in the last seat in the second row of used schoolroom desks. Being a college graduate was one strike against him, but being from Brown was like being from another planet. His right hand moved along his temple to push his long hair behind his ear, but he realized it was no longer there. His entire appearance had been transformed back to high school, with his buzz cut and no facial hair.

"Not shit. The inside shit of animals."

"Entrails?"

"Tails, guts, whatever comes out of the inside of an animal." Blood had risen to the tips of the captain's ears, turning them rusty red. He began again. "It is one of the many ordinances of the City of Providence."

"Excuse me, sir," Steve addressed the captain, now thinking of the nun with the ruler at the front of the class. "How do we recognize if swill or offal is being transported?" He knew he should stop.

The captain's red ears brightened as he spoke. "You smell it." He almost spat the words at Steve.

"Cadet Logan." A sandy-haired lieutenant in full dress, creased as crisp as a biscotti, stepped forward and cut Steve off sternly. "It's one of the rules and regulations of the city code. But you have to learn state law as well."

Steve met the lieutenant's eyes, having made his point that he was willing to question authority. Voluntarily, he had entered this world; it seemed less alien than being in the jungles of Vietnam with fist-sized leeches, booby traps, and ambushed trails. He was here to protect people. When he was accepted, he and Roxy had agreed that he would be a force—for the better. He would do it by the book, and he would learn the book. Every night, he studied so he would know the law and the procedures cold. He was on the inside now, where Durk said he had to be. Things had to change before civil war broke out.

The captain lectured, "You will learn to subdue suspects, disperse crowds, and keep the city safe. Once you graduate the academy, you will ride with an experienced officer while you develop street sense. And I hope many of you will go on to make sergeant or even an officer of the department."

Now you're talking, Steve thought, figuring getting promoted was only a matter of time.

"Ten-hut!"

The class sprang to its feet.

"Fall out to the left."

The class assembled in close formation, two abreast. "Hut, hut, hut. Two three four." They marched out and began an easy double-time down the street.

"What the fuck were you thinking?" Cadet Tom Dylan asked as he kept an easy pace with Steve. Dylan was taller and thirty pounds heavier, with burnt orange hair and thick shoulders, and the heavy gait of someone used to running with a full backpack.

"Just trying to get my information straight." Steve's mouth turned up slightly in amusement.

"Don't fuck around with them." Dylan shook his head.

"Or what? They knew when they accepted me." Steve let the words escape between breaths.

"You're the Brown kid?"

Steve nodded.

"Last mile, sprint to the finish," the sergeant in grey sweats yelled. The cadets picked up the pace, and Steve and Dylan were soon in front of the pack. Steve began to kick the last two hundred yards, easily outdistancing the field.

"Shit, I thought I was in shape," Dylan panted as they waited for the rest of the cadets to finish.

"You are." He nodded at the line of cadets still finishing.

Dylan hesitated before they laughed.

Lieutenant Smith watched the last of the cadets complete the three-mile run. "Good job. Take five, men."

Rocky Gaeta and several other cadets came over and sat with Steve and Dylan. "Why a cop after going to college? Shit, I'd be a lawyer," Gaeta said with a *what the fuck* shrug of his shoulders.

"I may do that someday, but not now. Time for my real life."

All the other cadets were watching as the last cadet came down to the finish line, walk-running, sweating heavily. He was a 5-foot 5-inch, 250-pound Italian.

Rocky Gaeta was thin and wiry, with the street air of a wise guy.

"Hey, Meatball. Want to go around again?"

Meatball, breathing heavily, turned and glared at the group.

Gaeta continued, "If his uncle wasn't a councilman, he'd be driving a coffee wagon."

Everyone laughed. Meatball shot him a bird and fell to the ground by the group.

"Thank God we have radios and cars," Meatball said and collapsed to laughter.

As part of the ongoing training, the academy had added riot- and crowd-control segments.

"We do not expect anything like the Newark riots that destroyed large parts of that city in 1968. This city is concerned about the spreading anti-war demonstrations as well as the growing inner-city unrest," Captain Lynch explained.

The cadets drilled with longer riot batons in V-formation for crowd control and demonstrations, advancing as a V to split an imaginary crowd and forming lines to drive a crowd backward with their batons. They wore white helmets but did not have shields. In the V formation, several cadets were armed with tear gas guns that would be fired over the heads of the advancing phalanx.

Lieutenant Smith, wearing grey sweats, demonstrated the thrust to the solar plexus to disable a demonstrator. Steve tried to follow the cadets who he could tell had bayonet training by the smooth footwork and strong thrusts.

The academy days settled into a routine. The morning classes were on the statutes of the State of Rhode Island and Providence Plantations. Time was devoted to proper Miranda warnings and the mechanics of an arrest, including the paperwork that had to be typed and filed. After lunch was the fun part for the cadets: the physical and the practical.

Lieutenant Smith was in his glory, wearing his always-clean grey sweats. He demonstrated with enthusiasm how to use a slim jim to open a car door with a quick motion by slipping it down the window glass and popping the door lock.

"I'll show you the basics of lock picking tomorrow," he said as he dismissed the class for the day.

Steve, Dylan, and several cadets stopped for beers at the American Legion post near the academy. The bar in the basement never closed despite the liquor laws.

"Johnson got kicked out of the academy," Meatball announced.

"Shit, he was just the token nigger. The brass wanted to show how inclusive they were being. They weren't ever going to let him on the force," Gaeta said.

"What happened?" Steve asked. He liked Johnson, who was the other outsider. Being the token on the force wasn't easy. But now the question was moot.

"The captain sent a detail to his apartment when didn't show up for class. They found Black Power posters on the wall and some books by that Black Panther guy. Sacked him right there." Meatball turned his mouth up in mock horror. "No brains," he said pointing to his temple. "Not like the college kid."

"Fuck you," Steve said.

"I thought about college after the Army, but I wasn't much of a student," Dylan said, plucking peanuts from the open bowl on the bar.

"You in Nam?" Steve asked.

"Yeah, I was an MP. Liked the work. When I was getting out, figured it would be a good job—always need cops. And I know the town. Twenty years and full pension."

"What part are you from?"

"Out by PC—Providence College. I thought I'd go there, take some night classes or something. You know, so that I can make detective or something."

"What was Nam like? Were you drafted?"

"Hard to describe. I volunteered for the Army after high school—wanted to get out of this town. I started out as a rifleman, but walking through jungles with gooks all around was not a way to make it to retirement. A friend of mine got me into the MPs in my second tour. Guys got really fucked up over there, either afraid or not caring. Most of the job was taking kids back from the whorehouses or from fights in the bars. Good kids when they were sober. But we also had to watch out for the gooks—even our own. Never could tell when someone was a VC ready to sneak a bomb into an officer's club or mess hall on base."

"Any close calls?" Steve asked, knowing that he could have been there, like so many of his high school friends.

"Not from the gooks, other than a few mortar rounds landing on base, but some Green Berets nearly did me in."

"Green Berets?"

"Another story."

Lieutenant Smith called Dylan and Gaeta to the front of the classroom. Gaeta mugged his way up the aisle, brushing back his short black hair as if his Italian pompadour were still there. He was the street kid with the wise-ass mouth and relatives in the department. Dylan stood erect like the good soldier he was trained to be.

"We're going to review the proper technique for making an arrest," Smith continued. "Dylan, you're the officer, and you're called to the scene where Mr. Gaeta is drunk and disorderly—hard to imagine."

The class laughed as Gaeta bowed to them. Smith handed the handcuffs and a Billy club to Dylan.

"What's the problem here?" Dylan asked Gaeta.

"No problem, pig. Just having some fun."

"Fun's over. Move along."

"Fuck you." Gaeta smiled to the class.

Smith stepped in. "You have an unruly situation. If you are alone, call for backup if you are in doubt. But the criminal must respect the uniform. Proceed."

"Move it, or I'll have to take you in." Dylan moved toward Gaeta, his thick body inches away from the terrier Gaeta.

"Fuck you," Gaeta said, getting close to his face. With practiced ease, Dylan slammed Gaeta against the wall with the Billy club across his chest. With one hand, he snapped the handcuff on Gaeta's left wrist and, using it as leverage, turned Gaeta and snapped the cuff on the other wrist. Lifting the chain between the cuffs, he walked Gaeta on his tiptoes to the front of the laughing class.

Smith turned to the class. "Your cuffs, your prisoner. Nice job, Mr. Dylan. You've had some practice."

"I've handled a few drunken Marines in my day, sir."

Gaeta rubbed his wrists when the cuffs were removed, still smirking at the class. "Not the first time."

"Now Mr. Gaeta, your turn."

Gaeta grinned at the class and exchanged shouts with Dylan, who pushed back. Gaeta looked up at Dylan, who was bigger and stronger. Without warning, he rammed the club into his midsection, doubling Dylan up. "Fuck," Dylan hissed as he regained his feet and took a step toward Gaeta, who backed away and pulled a finger gun at him.

"Against the wall, motherfucker, or you die here." Gaeta's face was set, and there was little doubt he would use the gun if he had one. Steve shook his head.

"You don't agree with Mr. Gaeta?" Smith asked Steve.

"You can't shoot someone for drunk and disorderly. It's a misdemeanor."

"The fuck I can't. He was assaulting an officer. I was in fear of my life. Self-fucking-defense, asshole," Gaeta grinned.

"Bullshit. You can't just execute people." Gaeta had that know-it-all street-punk attitude. He probably cheated on exams and was a petty thief as well. Steve didn't like Gaeta. He didn't doubt Gaeta thought it was alright to shoot. Steve couldn't imagine a reason he would ever have to shoot someone. The people of Providence weren't the enemy. He was here to protect them. Wasn't that the job? It was about using the brain and sufficient force.

"Right, college kid. Maybe you can hit him with a book." Gaeta was playing to the laughter of the class.

"That's right, smart guy. I'd throw the book at him and you, too, if you shot him. You can't shoot unarmed civilians." Score one for the college kid.

"Oh, yeah? You've got a lot to learn, Einstein," Gaeta said.

"You use *sufficient and necessary* force to make the arrest," Captain Lynch said, walking from the back of the classroom. "They," he waved his arm, "must respect the uniform."

"You don't get paid to fight." Lieutenant Smith paced the cramped basement that passed as the academy's gym. The paired cadets were rhythmically circling each other, jabbing and feinting with their boxing gloves like playground boys. Their generated sweat infused the room in a thick, damp musk.

Steve continued to bob and weave like Muhammad Ali did, but knew he was playing, since he had never actually been in a fight. Moving against Meatball, he seemed to float like a butterfly.

"But sometimes, you actually have to get control of the situation. The recommended procedure is overwhelming force, but when you are one on one, you better be able to handle yourself." The lieutenant stopped some of the men, raising an elbow or demonstrating how quickly to retract a jab. He seemed interested in the choreography of his troops, correcting their footwork and their stances, demonstrating with a form that showed years in a ring. The day was going quickly since no classwork was on the agenda. Steve was energized by the physical exercise, and his muscles enjoyed the workout.

His attention was diverted when the steel door slammed against its frame. Captain Lynch had arrived and began an animated discussion with Lieutenant Smith, each of them glancing over at the cadets. Steve felt he was getting special unfriendly attention. Meatball's glove stung his cheek over his lowered guard, snapping him back to reality.

Smith's whistle was too loud for the space, but it halted all activity immediately. "It's time for the real thing," Smith announced. "We'll see who's for real." Lynch nodded for him to go on. The lieutenant's mouth was tight and controlled as he seemed to spit out the next orders.

"Dylan, fall in." The cadet stood at attention before the two officers. "Ever box?"

"Yes, sir. In the Army," Dylan said.

"Any good?"

"Regiment champion."

"What weight?"

"Heavyweight." Dylan looked the weight class, with oxen shoulders and slabs for hands.

"Logan."

"Yes, sir." Steve stepped to attention next to Dylan, who was two inches taller and outweighed him by forty pounds. He was someone you didn't want to mess with.

"Ever box?"

"Just here, sir." Steve heard the murmur come from the class, knowing what was coming. Lynch was looking for a reason to bounce him or make him quit. He wasn't going to make it that easy. He was here for the duration, and they needed to get used to it. But what else could they do—Durk said they could leave you out to dry, but how?

"Square up," Smith ordered as the cadets moved against the sides of the room to give the fighters space. "On the whistle."

The sound of the whistle was still fresh in his ears as Dylan's jab slid off Steve's upraised gloves, glancing off his head. He began circling to the right to stay away from the jab, paying attention to keeping his hands up to cover his face. The jabs were hard. Steve concentrated on catching most of the force on his gloves. He returned a jab but knew instantly it was a bad idea. Dylan counterpunched, catching him on the side of the head. The two men circled as the room chanted for Dylan.

"Come on, Dylan. Is that the best you can do against this college kid?" Lynch sneered.

Steve looked over at the fat captain. He thought it would be that easy. *He's not going to get any satisfaction today,* Steve vowed.

Dylan moved into Steve, throwing a combination to the head and body. Steve absorbed the blows to his ribs and ducked away from the head shots. But Dylan didn't let up, using combination after combination until a left hand got through to Steve's nose, snapping his head back. He felt his nose was as flat as if he had run full speed into a glass door.

Dylan delivered another left-right-left combination over Steve's flagging hands. With blood in his mouth now seeping down his throat, Steve could feel wetness running from his mouth over his cheek. He tried to focus. His head throbbed from his cortex out to his skull. He knew he was in trouble, as did the class, whose cheers for Dylan increased. They were enjoying watching the college kid get knocked around, Steve thought. He wasn't going to quit. Regrouping his thoughts, he tried to move in closer to bring the fight to Dylan but was caught with an uppercut that collapsed his right knee.

The captain yelled, "Finish him!"

Dylan moved closer, hitting Steve again with a quick combination, collapsing him to the floor.

The tiny room was a roar in Steve's head. His mind spun like a whirly from a freshman drunk. He had been knocked down before in many games, but he never stayed down. Struggling to a knee, he located Dylan, who was being congratulated by the other cadets. Regaining his feet, he swung wildly at the heavyweight, who stepped back and delivered another crushing combination. Steve fell back to a knee and another round of cheers.

"You finish it on the street," he heard Lynch yell over the cadets. "There are no rules or referees." Steve looked at the officer with his half-closed left eye, realizing this was a planned beating.

And then he snapped, like when he played in lacrosse games. He went from a rational, strategic player to an animal playing on conditioned instincts. The adrenaline exploded into every muscle. He tensed his stomach and sprang forward like a cat, catching Dylan's front leg in a single leg takedown. The surprised bigger man crashed to the floor. No rules, the captain had said, and Steve pivoted to the man's back, intertwining his left leg with Dylan's, preventing him from regaining his feet. Steve used both hands to pull Dylan's right arm into a half nelson while shoving his left shoulder into the floor. A low, guttural growl escaped Steve's throat as he drove off his free right leg while lifting on the right arm to drive Dylan's face into the mat on the floor. Cursing, Dylan could not grip with the boxing gloves. Steve pulled back and lifted his arm again, driving Dylan's face again into the floor as Dylan cried out in pain.

"Enough! Enough!" Lieutenant Smith shouted, pulling Steve by the shoulders off the prone Dylan. Steve fell back hard onto his ass, the blood still flowing into his mouth and his mind feeling like a cloudy day. He was aware that the room was quiet as he sat taking one deep breath after another. "No rules, no rules . . ." The words turned over in his mind as he looked over at Dylan sitting on a chair, head tipped back with a towel to stop his nose bleed. "I don't quit."

The police firing range was a small and tightly packed space squeezed in among other municipal outcasts like the sanitation yard and public works department at the border with North Providence. There were ten stations, and the cadets fired in groups.

Lieutenant Smith said, "Don't draw your gun unless you intend to use it. But if you must, know how to use it. Logan, do you know how to use a weapon?"

"No, sir. I have never even held a gun other than a BB gun." The response earned a derisive smile from the captain, who was watching the cadets shoot. Steve thought he was the only cadet to have never fired a weapon.

"Here is your police-issue Colt .38 revolver," Smith said, handing the gun to Steve, handle first. "It has six shots, but it's the first one that counts. Learn how to use it. You will also need an off-duty gun. Police officers must be armed at all times. Look at buying a snub-nose .38, which is easy to carry and conceal. Get over to the range and learn how to shoot."

Steve stayed back, carefully watching the other cadets shoot with two hands in a semi-crouch, tactical position. The targets at the end of the range thirty feet away were silhouettes of the upper torso of a man. Dylan returned from his range having fired six rounds from his pistol, hitting the target every time.

"You make it look pretty easy," Steve said as Dylan returned to the group.

"Steady solid position, sight over the barrel, and squeeze. Don't pull the trigger. It's the great equalizer." He looked at Steve, his nose swollen from its meeting with the mat.

"I could have used this yesterday." Steve held the revolver in his hand.

Dylan nodded. "Me, too."

"Steady and squeeze." They shot for two hours, taking turns in the ten shooting lanes.

As they came off for the day, Lieutenant Smith had targets in his hand. "Logan, never held a weapon?" he asked.

"No, sir. Not until today."

Smith held up the sheet that showed that one bullet had actually hit the paper but not the target. "You're going to need some work."

Steve was pissed at the smirk on the lieutenant's face. Yeah, they didn't want him there, but fuck them. He wasn't going anywhere. "Must be the teachers," he said.

He worked hard every night at studying the statues of the city and the state. He wanted to understand the law. He read the police procedure manual, highlighting sections like he did in college. He was going to graduate because he was going to be like Durk: some disinfectant for the department.

CHAPTER 6

MORNING HAS BROKEN

After graduating the academy in December, Steve was assigned to Brian Crowley, a career patrolman in his late forties, as his first partner. Crowley was a heavy, jowly man with black liver spots on his neck and hands. Their Ford Fairlane cruiser was several years old, with a worn driver's seat that seemed to fit Crowley, the experienced cop, perfectly.

Crowley got into his usual driver side, not even asking Steve if he would like to drive. Steve settled into the shotgun side of the cruiser, removing his cap and putting it on the seat in the middle. He adjusted the revolver so it didn't cut into his side.

"It's been a while since I had a partner." Crowley didn't look at Steve as he steered the car to his precinct north of the Capitol Building.

"Captain says all rookies will be teamed for at least several weeks," Steve shrugged.

"Yeah, but two-man cars are needed down in south or up on Federal Hill, but not up here. I've been patrolling here for fifteen years; not much happens. But for me, it's just to the end of next year; then I retire. Twenty and out. Not bad. I'll go work for my brother down in Cranston. He's got this garage and towing business. He's got the permit for I-95, so he does okay. Hang on."

Crowley pulled the police car over to the curb and jumped out, leaving the car running. He walked into a dry cleaner and emerged a few minutes later with plastic-covered hangers holding women's clothing. He talked to a couple on the sidewalk before getting into the car. Steve could see he was the cop, someone who would tell the kids to go to school or give out parking tickets if you weren't from the neighborhood.

Crowley continued, "So we figure with me knowing Providence, we can expand the business up this way. I can hook up with a couple of guys we know who have a garage but don't have the big tow rig like my brother."

He pulled over again, got out, and entered a butcher shop. He returned with several pieces of meat wrapped in brown paper. He put them in the backseat and went back to a liquor store, to come back with a bag filled with several bottles. He stopped to talk to a small lady in a grey cloth coat with a rose kerchief pulled tightly over her head. He nodded several times before patting her on the shoulder.

Crowley was just the neighborhood cop, Steve thought. This was the way it should be, the cop as a friend, the guy who keeps the order but is a good guy. Not the goons with riot helmets and batons from the demonstrations He didn't know Crowley, but riding with him eight hours a day would fix that.

"So we figure with the big rig, we can help these guys get the license for the north end of 95 as well."

He pulled into the driveway of a small house with a blue Madonna grotto in front, got out, picked up the dry cleaning and groceries, and entered the house. Was this how Providence was policed? Near Brown, the police were always seen as the enemy waiting to bust a kid for something. And down in South Providence?

"See, with the big rig, you get the truckers," Crowley continued after getting back into the car. "And they work for the big companies and have insurance that will pay. Big trucks mean big money."

Money—it always comes down to money, Steve thought. His salary was more than he had ever made, yet the cops always talked about money.

The two weeks on the job went by quickly. And Crowley was right: the district was very quiet, the way Crowley liked it. His partner told him about his four kids: the two girls were married, and now one grandkid on the way. The sons played hockey and were big Bruins fans. He introduced Steve to the coffee shop guy, the car wash owner, the candy store owner who also took numbers. His advice to Steve on how to survive the brass was fatherly. The major lesson was to be invisible most of the time. Steve listened to every call from dispatch, but most of the action was in South Providence.

"Car 24."

Crowley replied, "Twenty-four."

"That's a report of a dead body at 425 Weybosset Street. Apartment 10."

Crowley scowled. "Roger. Got it."

As Steve and Crowley approached apartment 10, Crowley said, "I hate these; never know what to say. I could hardly stay at my own mother's wake. We have to wait until the medical examiner arrives. He will take over from there. We have to file the paperwork."

As he knocked on the door, Crowley announced, "Police."

The door was opened by a small woman in her late seventies, whose face was tear-streaked.

"It's my Edgar. He's passed."

Crowley and Steve entered the apartment and followed the woman into the single bedroom. The smell of death, feces, and medication was suffocating, triggering a vomiting sensation Steve fought to overcome.

In the double bed, the dead man, in his late seventies, was motionless and gray. Crowley looked for a pulse, but it was obvious that he was dead. Staring at the corpse that was once a man, those abstract college bull sessions about the meaning of life seemed silly to Steve. This wasn't a violent death like in war, sudden and gruesome, but the man was just as dead.

"Ma'am, the medical examiner is on his way. Patrolman Logan will stay with you until he arrives."

Crowley looked at Steve, who looked back, raising his eyebrows with a "what the fuck?" question on his face. Crowley was holding his hand to his mouth, as if trying not to vomit as he ran to the front door.

"I'll meet you at the car when you're done."

The woman closed the door behind Crowley and ghostwalked into the living room. Steve spent a minute staring at the grey couch. It had gold trim, and a red bed pillow and blanket were spread over it, as if it the newly made widow had been sleeping there. The window shades were drawn tightly, bathing the room in a yellow purgatory glow.

"Edgar was a good man, though he farted too much, especially in his later years. He wasn't much of a dancer, but I made him do it anyway." Her eyes moved around the room, distracted, but her voice was firm as she spoke to Steve. He didn't think she really recognized that he was there. Photos of Edgar and the woman when they were younger were on the table by the couch. Steve still stood stiffly near the door.

"Do you want a glass of sherry?" she asked.

Steve shook his head "No."

"Well, I do. Forty-nine years with the man. I thought he would make it to fifty so we could have a big party. But no. He wasn't that considerate. Not that he was a bad man. No. He just wasn't that interested in me—well, not for the last thirty years."

Is this how Roxy would react after they were married that long? She would be controlled, the doctor—but she wouldn't cry when it was over. But what if she went first? Could he hold it together after all that time? He didn't know.

She sat down on the couch with her crystal stem glass of sherry. Another tear leaked from her eye.

"It wasn't always like that. When we were courting, he couldn't wait to get his hands on me. But men change, and women do, too." She looked at Steve, who was still standing.

"Young man, sit down here." She motioned to the side chair next to the couch. Steve was trying not to let the smell get the better of him. Taking off his hat, he sat in the too-soft side chair.

"Is your family coming? Your children?"

"Oh, they will come." She waved absently. "Probably sometime. Not the one in New York—he never comes to visit. My daughter in Fall River will be here. They will all be fussing—Edgar doesn't care now, but maybe he can do something to get his damned Red Sox to win a World Series. All he did the last few years was curse at the television every night they were on. I guess it kept him alive." She refilled her glass.

"Can I get you anything? Is there anything you need?" Steve asked, not knowing what else to say. Nobody had said anything about assignments like this at the academy. His experience with death was very limited. He had only seen one embalmed body in a funeral home. He had served many funeral masses, but the caskets were closed, and he realized that he never really thought about the person inside as he incensed the casket. He looked at his watch. How much time did it take for the medical examiner to get here? Lucky the guy was dead because he'd be dead based upon this response time.

"Thank you, young man; you are very considerate. Need? I don't know what I need. I don't know what I am going to do. My children will probably want to put me in some home so they don't have to worry about me. They never came to see us—we always went to them for any holidays, the few we ever celebrated. What do I need?" She began to cry. "I need Edgar back. I need to hear him cursing away at the Sox. I needed to die before him because I don't know how . . ." And she began to sob more. Steve took her hand, patting it.

"That's right. Let it out. You'll feel better." Steve thought he sounded like his mother soothing one of the children.

The woman looked directly at him.

"Feel better? I won't ever feel better. I may not notice it as much, not cleaning up after him day after day, but better . . ."

There was a knock on the door. Steve got up and let in the Medical Examiner, a small man with round metal glasses. He carried a medical bag, which made him look like a country doctor making a house call. He walked into the bedroom and then back to Steve.

"We'll take it from here," he said.

Steve nodded and went over to the woman, who was still sitting on the couch, blankly looking at the new man in the room.

"I have to go now. The medical examiner will take over things. Everything will be all right. Your children will take care of you."

She looked absently at Steve and gave him a polite smile. Steve stepped into the bedroom for a final look and smell of death.

Returning from the library, Roxy entered the bedroom and dropped her science books on the chair by the door. Steve was at the desk, his back to her as he worked on something in front of him. He had moved the typewriter to the floor.

"Ready for the test?" he asked, not looking up from his task.

"I guess. Bio isn't as hard as Chemistry." She walked over to see what he was doing.

Steve had spread a *Providence Journal* on the desk. There were some wads of white cotton squares, several long brushes, a long, narrow metal needle, a bottle of solvent, oil, and a wire-type toothbrush. She could smell the solvent.

"What are you doing?"

Steve was holding his blued .38 Smith and Wesson service revolver in his hand, with the cylinder open. Five bullets were on the desk, four jacketed and one hollow point. He had inserted a cleaning patch dipped in solvent through the barrel of the gun until it protruded from the other side. He then extracted it carefully. He repeated the same action with clean patches through each of the six cylinders.

"Cleaning my service revolver. They showed us at the academy," he said, not looking up.

"Do you have to do that here?" she asked, moving tentatively to the side of the desk and looking at the weapon and bullets on her desk.

"I live here; where do you want me to do it, on the campus green?" He put a few drops of oil on the moving parts and spun the cylinder, which rotated smoothly. He loaded the ammunition in the pistol, putting the four jacketed bullets in first and the hollow point last. If he needed a fifth shot, it was going to end any discussion.

"Do you have to put bullets in it?"

He turned and smiled at her with amusement. "I'd be a hell of a cop with an empty gun."

"I mean here. You know I don't like guns. And knowing we have a loaded gun in our room—it makes me uncomfortable."

"It goes with the job. I keep it out of sight most of the time." He patted his lap, and she sat on him. "I never really thought about a gun growing up—all the cowboys wore them. And I had a Roy Rogers double holster as a kid. But in real life, these fuckers are heavy. And depending on how you sit in the car, they really can dig into your side."

Her look changed to perverse pleasure. "Oh, I'm so sorry for you. I thought all you men wanted bigger guns."

"I'll give you a bigger gun," he said as he jumped up with her in his arms, swung around in an easy movement, and laid her flat on her back on the bed, holding her hands over her head. "Should I get the handcuffs now?"

She kneed him and rolled over on top of him. "No so fast, big fella. I think I need the handcuffs."

Near her, he thought how their life together had changed so much from their first date last October. The idea to go to the anti-war March on Washington was Roxy's; the decision to hitchhike was Steve's. His option offered her adventure and danger; for him, it was a practical case of money. It was a first date with a half million other people and her high school boyfriend. He had thought it was a stupid idea, but since he met her, he was having many stupid ideas.

"Are you going to the protest?" the driver with greying temples had asked as he leaned out the window of his green Volvo. The oddly sloped vehicle had a peace symbol on the back bumper.

"We are, too," the woman with short pixie hair in the shotgun seat of the car replied. "All the way to DC."

"I'm Professor Morrison Whitney. This is my wife, Priscilla. Are you Brown students?"

For the next four hours, Whit lectured about the immoral nature of the Vietnam War and the failings of the Nixon administration. He asked questions on policy and the history of the American engagement, and he seemed pleased when Steve knew the answers. Roxy chatted with Penny about the need for women and the working class to get involved to stop the war. Steve listened to Roxy as much as to Whit, wanting to know more about how she felt and thought.

Whitney exited onto 50 West, entering DC from the northeast as it turned into New York Avenue. The row houses were part of the urban decay, the fleeing of the middle class from the city to the safety of the suburbs. Penny, who had been dozing most of the trip, locked all the car doors, pushing down each button emphatically.

Steve felt a sense of siege in the city—not wholescale destruction like Newark or Detroit after Martin Luther King's murder, but one of creeping desperation and isolation. Washington had had its riots, and the toll could still be seen in the empty storefronts. Steve saw two older men in weather-beaten long cloth coats, drinking from brown paper bags—symbols of the city being relegated to the inner-city garbage heap. Steve had only seen it on TV; there weren't any riots in the suburbs.

As they pulled around the Mall, rows of police vehicles were lined up along its perimeter. Blue police barricades were being set up by men working from large open-back trucks.

"Professor, thanks so much," Steve and Roxy said almost simultaneously as they climbed out of the car.

"See you around campus. And be careful," the professor said. "I don't think this will be the Democratic Convention, but you know some of the crazy Weathermen might be here, too—or that looney Abbie Hoffman. The cops might decide to club everyone in sight."

"This march is our history." Steve stopped to look up at the eight classical Greek columns at the top of the stairs to the National Archives. "They have the Declaration of Independence, Constitution, Bill of Rights . . . Shit. All the real stuff, right here. And now here we are, exercising our rights." Amused that this was the reason he had come to Washington for the first time, he was feeling a bit awed as well. With his family, visiting relatives in New Jersey was a called a trip. Jones Beach was the only family vacation. Working in Alaska had stretched his horizons: the work had been hard and mindless, but sleeping in the open and seeing so many stars had been new to him. Now Washington. He only had read about things, but reading was not doing, being. He wanted to experience it—he needed to.

"Kenny is coming by bus with a whole group of kids from Oberlin," Roxy said with a chipper glint. "We're staying tonight in Arlington with my uncle, who works for the government, a second cousin on my dad's side." Her voice became deeper, and she twirled a strand of hair in her finger. "I can't tell you the accommodations will be great."

"After this summer, I'm sure it will be fine. How long have you been going out with Kenny?" His politeness was devouring his intestines like a tapeworm, ravenous for more, even if it killed him.

"Since senior year in high school. We did it the first time on the floor in his basement. Can't say it was romantic, but at least it wasn't in a car. I refused to be one of those girls who did it in a car—so cheap and trite."

Steve, shocked at her frankness, wondered why she was telling him details. She said it lightly. He had never met a girl who spoke so openly about sex—or about sex at all. Was she setting him up? He wasn't going to tell her about his first time in the summer after freshman year. He had fumbled around in a car and came prematurely. "Seriously?" he said, searching for some type of answer but wanting to ask more—like *why couldn't you have waited for me?* She was skipping on the Archives stairs like a child on a school trip.

"It's college. He's my high school boyfriend. I haven't seen him in two months." Steve sensed she was satisfied with his confused look, even if it was only a mask to his deeper feelings.

A boy ascended the stairs. He was five foot eight with blond hair that was short but not so short it was a crew cut. Dressed in jeans and an Oberlin sweatshirt, he was carrying a small duffle bag. Roxy ran down the stairs and kissed him before they ascended the stairs arm in arm.

"Kenny, my friend Steve. He was gallant enough to escort me down to DC."

Kenny advanced to Steve with his hand outstretched. "Thanks for taking care of her."

"Not a problem—I was going to come anyhow, and we saved on the bus fare." Steve could see the sincerity in Kenny's face and its smile and perfect white teeth. He had an openness that was different from Steve's Long Island upbringing. The urge to hit Kenny was a gust of wind as Steve steeled himself for more pain. He had never been west of

New Jersey until the summer before, when he and a fraternity brother drove to Alaska. The Alcan Highway was twelve hundred miles of unpaved road, where the only traffic was moose crossing the road.

That night, Steve debated Roxy's uncle about the global strategy of containment of communism. Roxy and Kenny sat on the couch holding hands, spectators to the event.

"You are better informed than most young people," her uncle said, breaking off the debate. "Getting involved is the only way to change things—being part of the action. But your generation seems unwilling to sacrifice like your parents did to protect our freedom." Steve didn't need to argue as he did at family gatherings where his father, uncle, and the other veterans of World War II would cite patriotism and duty. Theirs was a different war in a different time, and logic had no impact on their beliefs.

"I'll drop you off at the Key Bridge," Roxy's uncle said, looking at Steve. Her uncle gave Steve a nod to acknowledge the conversation. "Good night."

Steve looked at Roxy and Kenny, who were still holding hands.

"See you in the morning," said Roxy with a shy smile.

Steve took his sleeping bag and moved it to the far side of the room. Roxy slept next to Kenny in her sleeping bag. Steve knew he had been showing off for her by debating foreign policy with her State Department uncle. He was trying to compete with the boy she'd given her virginity to. He looked over at her, lying next to Kenny on the floor. He wanted to feel her warmth, to stroke the gentle slope of her shoulders. He rolled to his side so he didn't have to look at them, but he thought he could hear her gentle breath. Another stupid idea?

The Mall was packed from the Capitol to the Lincoln Memorial with 500,000 people. Steve, Roxy, and Kenny moved with the crowd. It wasn't so much of a march but was rather a surging, slow-moving organism that had enveloped the Mall. The excitement of the crowd on the cool autumn day was contagious. College students were mixed with forty- and fifty-year-olds and even families with young children. News reports from portable radios carried here and there said millions of people had joined local demonstrations across the nation, voicing their opposition to the war in Vietnam. Energy radiated from person to person in the form of knowing smiles and righteous nods exchanged among strangers, who felt like a family.

Steve saw a small older woman with a bright turquoise scarf wrapped around her neck. She looked like his grandmother and was holding up a homemade banner that said *Grandmas for Peace*. A father in a blue trench coat, a two-year-old boy on his shoulder holding down his Phillies hat, swayed with the movement of the march. The speeches seemed far away, but everyone broke into periodic chants of "No More War" and "Hell No, We Won't Go," and various versions of "All we are saying is give peace a chance." All sung off-key.

Steve used his strong body and hips to keep some space around Roxy, who seemed to be in danger of being crushed by the crowd. Kenny kept moving forward to get a better view of the speakers on the stage by the Washington Monument, but Roxy got swallowed by the human wave until Steve brought her back up for air. He wasn't going to leave her side.

The orderly demonstration changed gradually from angry to festive as Pete Seeger led the crowd in a more-unified singing of "Give Peace a Chance." And the crowd, still off-key, reacted with revived energy as people locked arms.

As the afternoon faded, the march slowly dissolved into groups of people along the Washington streets. The party atmosphere continued with people spontaneously sharing food or drink. Conversations from the different parts of the country intermingled with the congestion and traffic along Constitution Avenue. Kenny and Roxy were in the lead as the crowd moved past the Lincoln Memorial into Foggy Bottom. Steve slowed to observe and record his first visit to the Capitol and the largest crowd he had ever seen. When he came to college, he wasn't against the war. At his high school, getting into West Point was a great honor. But the escalation under Nixon and the reality of the draft made him realize it wasn't a war worth fighting.

"I'm hungry," Roxy announced at the top of the hill in front of a bakery. "It smells so good." She entered, followed by the two boys, and bought a *pain au chocolate*, several croissants, and two large baguettes. She ate her chocolate pastry while the boys ate their croissants.

"What's the other bread for?" Steve asked.

"I thought other people might be hungry, too," she said, scanning the crowd of people coming up the hill.

"Hungry? Want some fresh bread?" She approached a group of middle-aged women who were wearing grey republican cloth coats. They stopped for a minute as Roxy chatted excitedly with them before she handed them the last of the bread.

Smiling, she returned to the boys. "They're from Indiana." She raised her hands. "We are not alone." Steve watched her take Kenny's arm as they continued to Foggy Bottom As they arrived at the George Washington University campus on 22nd St, Kenny motioned toward a line of buses.

"That's my ride," he said with the regret of someone having to leave a good party early.

"Peace," Steve said, giving him a handshake before wandering off a distance to give Roxy and Kenny space to say good-bye. He glanced over his shoulder at them but didn't stare. The two lovers talked while locked in an embrace. At least he would have her alone on the way back to Providence. It wasn't enough. Steve had hoped he would win her, but as he watched them kiss, he knew he had lost.

When Roxy tugged at his sleeve, she asked, "How do you suggest we get back to Providence?"

Steve held up his handwritten sign on a piece of cardboard box: *Providence*. "Hope they can read." As they walked out to

Pennsylvania Avenue, which was a good place to catch a ride back to school, Steve was impressed with how many people had come to the march. If it wasn't for Roxy, he'd still be at his apartment doing the ordinary things of life. But he was here—part of the movement to stop the war, stop the madness. He felt good and was glad Roxy had encouraged him to go.

The car pulled to the side of the road on the New Jersey Turnpike near the Outerbridge Crossing exit, where Steve and Roxy got out.

"Thank you. Peace." They waved to the parents and kids from Brooklyn, who honked as they drove away in their Oldsmobile.

They didn't have to hold up their sign for long before a young couple in a Volkswagen Bus slowed to pick them up.

"We're going back to Boston, so you are on our way," the young man said. "Where are you coming from?"

"DC."

"At the march?"

"Yes, you?"

"Man, the war really sucks." The driver motioned to his girlfriend with matching granny glasses and her brown hair parted in the center with long pigtails. "Now, back to school. We should blow up the Pentagon or something. SDS has some cool ideas."

Roxy and Steve settled in the backseat, both tired. Roxy moved over and put her head on Steve's shoulder. Steve remained upright, feeling a little uncomfortable at her intimacy. He was exhilarated at the experience—so many people, so much passion to end the war. Steve felt it was as right as right could be. He was happy she had asked him to go. The experience had instilled a feeling of being part of something big. And he shared it with Roxy, which made it that much better.

"I . . . I . . . You know, I'd like to think that we made a difference in how the war . . ." he stammered.

"Thank you. You are so wonderful," Roxy snuggled closer to him.
"I'm glad you got to see Kenny. He seems like a nice guy."

Roxy knitted her eyebrows as she stared at him. "Don't you get it?"

"What?"

Roxy reached up and kissed him very hard on the mouth. "That was a good-bye."

CHAPTER 7

PEOPLE ARE STRANGE

Crowley returned to the car with two coffees, a glazed donut for himself, and a French cruller for Steve from the Dunkin' Donuts shop. Crowley balanced the coffee and donut in his right hand so he could drive with his left. Steve needed both hands.

"Car 24, Industrial National Bank Building. Report of a bomb threat."

"Car 24 on the way. Bomb? What is this, fucking Vietnam?" Crowley looked at Steve, who was surprised that there were radicals in Providence. A bomb here? Had it gone this far? There were three cars and a sergeant waiting at the front of the Art Deco style bank.

"Dispatch received an anonymous call about a bomb. We have to take it seriously. It may be those crazy Weathermen. Look for something out of place, something unusual." The bank manager arrived with the key and opened the door. He stood in the lobby but didn't proceed inside with the police.

"Weathermen? What the hell are they?" Crowley adjusted his Sam Brown belt under his protruding belly. He followed Steve behind the ornate brass teller cages.

"Weathermen, sds—Students for a Democratic Society. They're the radical fringe of the student movement. They planted some bombs in some New York police stations. And they blew themselves up a townhouse in Greenwich Village, trying to make bombs," Steve said as he looked behind a desk.

"That's crazy. Blew themselves up?"

"Yeah, and they're aligning with the Black Panthers over the killings in Chicago. Hardcore Marxists, they want the overthrow of capitalism and imperialism."

Crowley stopped looking under a desk and turned askance to Steve. Maybe that level of detail was too much because Crowley didn't comprehend any of the anti-war sentiment and certainly didn't understand why rich college kids could be against the country.

"How the fuck do you know so much?"

"New York Times." Steve smiled. "I read more than the sports pages."

"Why do college kids hate this country so much?" Crowley moved a wastebasket.

"Vietnam. It's a war for no reason, and kids are being drafted to fight it."

"But it's your country. Love it or leave it," Crowley said.

"That's the problem, Crowley: no discussion. It's called freedom of speech. It's okay to disagree with the government—peacefully."

"So what the fuck are we looking for?" Crowley edged some boxes away from the wall with his baton.

"Peacefully, I said." Steve looked around at the wooden desks neatly arranged in three rows. Peacefully. So here he was, looking for a bomb possibly placed by someone his own age who disagreed with the war in Vietnam just as much as he did. How fucking sad. And the only people who would get hurt were bank clerks just making a living. It was an inverted universe.

Steve looked behind some file cabinets and under the desks in the loan department. "Crowley, I have a question for you. What the fuck do we do if we find something? We don't have a bomb squad."

"Good question, kid." He stopped to think. "With my experience, we call for a sergeant and let him decide—that's what sergeants are for. Meanwhile, we would quickly set up a perimeter on the *exterior* of the building to make certain no civilians get hurt."

"Got it." Steve suppressed his smile. Nothing was going to get in the way of Crowley's pension. But he had to agree with Crowley. The bank wasn't something to die for.

Steve watched a white Bonneville make the right-hand turn onto Chalkstone Avenue, and a smile crossed his face. Shifting the cruiser into drive, he pulled out from the alley they had been parked in. Crowley was drinking his first of many coffees of the evening, his usual: light with double sugar.

"I'm not done yet," Crowley protested.

"I need to up my traffic count," Steve replied, knowing that Crowley didn't care about tickets as long as Steve did the paperwork. He followed the car several blocks as it drove toward the Capitol. It was headed back to college hill.

Pulling on the lever that activated the red light on the top of the car, Steve edged up close behind the car and, with his left hand, hit the siren, which gave a sharp whine before it settled into a more rhythmic doo-op beat. The driver looked into his rearview mirror at the flashing lights behind him as he slowed the car, pulling it to the side of the road. Steve put on his hat to exit the car, and Crowley fumbled to put down his coffee.

"Finish your coffee; this is an easy one," Steve said to a visibly relieved Crowley, who was still chewing his glazed donut. The red flashing lights created a strobe effect on the car windows, and Steve realized he was the uniform—another generic cop—as he approached with the black flashlight in hand.

The driver rolled down the window but didn't look up at Steve, who systematically searched the front seat with the light. He finished with the light on the driver's face. The driver was tense and nervous. Before joining the force, it never occurred to Steve that the one time most people deal with the police was during traffic stops—and fear of embarrassment was their major reaction. At the Academy, they were told that the approach to a car during a stop was one of the most dangerous actions most police officers ever encountered.

"Hands on the steering wheel, where I can see them," Steve ordered, deepening his voice a bit for effect. "License and registration." The driver took his wallet out and quickly found his license but fumbled through the crowded glove compartment for the registration.

"I know it is here somewhere," the man said, sliding along the bench seat and dumping paper napkins and a mountain of maps onto the seat. Steve kept his flashlight on the activity, his smile becoming wider as he watched the driver's increasing frustration at not finding it.

"Where are you going?" Steve asked, returning to his normal voice.

"Home," the man answered, sitting back up. "I must have left the registration at home." He gave the mess on his front seat a defeated look.

"Do you know why I stopped you?" Steve asked.

"Was I speeding?" the driver asked.

"No," Steve answered, watching the confusion on the driver's face. When he had joined the force, the idea of power was abstract. Others had power—the nuns in second grade had enough power to keep fifty petrified seven-year-olds sitting straight up in their seats. The government had power to send you to Vietnam for two years or more. Coach had power to make you do endless laps and decide if you played or not. Now he had power, standing with his flashlight over this driver, who, not knowing his offense, was probably thinking about the time and money a ticket would entail. It was the uniform, the badge, the gun—it conferred power. Before he became a cop, the uniform was a threat, just like it was to this driver. Power to take away freedom. Steve waited and watched as the man tried to process other transgressions he might have made while driving.

"I don't know?" he shrugged with the type of acceptance Steve recognized that says *give me the ticket and let me get on my way.*

"You failed to signal before you turned onto Chalkstone Avenue, Coach."

"Sorry, Officer. I didn't know that. I must have forgot to . . ."

"Coach." Steve shined his flashlight on his own face before returning it to the car. He was enjoying the confusion in the coach's face as he processed the information. He was never the coach's favorite, but Steve had earned his respect by his hard work.

"Logan?" he asked, putting his hands back on the steering wheel.

"Yes, Coach."

"How . . . I thought you left after graduation. Didn't you go to law school or . . ." His voice trailed off.

"Still in town. Getting a different legal education. I'm going to let you off with a warning, so drive carefully. Good to see you again."

"Thank you." Coach fumbled a bit with his words. "Stop by the gym; I would love to catch up," he said as he rolled up the window and cautiously drove away.

Walking back to the car, Steve realized how much a year had changed things. He had graduated and now was part of the past for Coach. Maybe when the alumni giving time came around, he would remember his name. He had kept Coach sweating a long time, but he felt a certain satisfaction at the change in power after all the years. It wasn't fear; rather, it was approval that he had wanted.

Andy would crack up if he had seen the scene. He would tell Bill later over a beer and give him something to needle Coach with during the upcoming season. It was the uniform, the badge, the gun. It was power, and now what would he do with it?

Crowley threw a black bag into the trunk of the cruiser before he took the wheel, driving away from the substation for the next midnight shift. It was an early spring night, a steady cold rain thickening the new shoots on the trees. Steve put his hat on the seat beside them and looked over the list of stolen license plates. He hadn't really listened to the announcements at roll call that night; his mind was anticipating the street. He was enjoying the night shift and being awake when most of the city slept. He was trying to become more observant: a strange car parked on a street, newspapers piling up on the driveway, garbage cans uncollected. They told a story about the people. Each night was still new, and he wanted more.

"Lousy night," Crowley said as they stopped for coffee. "No criminals work in this kind of weather, just us cops."

Steve sipped the dark black liquid. A couple of overnight parking tickets would be the excitement with Crowley. They took a leisurely cruise up and down the residential streets that were clean of cars. The houses were from the early part of the century and sat on small lots. The houses were two stories, each with individual character like round landing windows, porches with potted plants, or grottos to some saint. They were very different from the cookie-cutter houses of Long Island, where the only difference was the color of the fake shutters. They scanned the side streets looking for a vagabond vehicle, destined to make the city a little richer with a ticket for overnight parking. Steve was starting to like Providence, though he still was a stranger.

Crowley pulled the cruiser into an old factory lot that had been abandoned, circling the building to the rear loading dock. He stopped the car, put it into reverse, and backed into the dock until the cruiser was invisible. He opened the door and jumped out, returning with the black bag which he opened, revealing two pillows and blankets.

"Front or back?" he asked Steve, who was stunned.

"What?" Steve was trying the process the offer.

"All the tickets are written, and nothing happens here, so we'll coop 'til six."

"I can't do—I mean, I'm not going to sleep."

"Suit yourself. I had hockey practice 'til I had to paint a bedroom for my daughter." Taking both pillows and entering the backseat, he took his coat off and draped it over himself as a blanket.

Steve sat behind the wheel, engine idling, listening to the little chatter on the radio. The city was very quiet on this Tuesday night. There wasn't much crime fighting to be done; in fact, the major role tonight was sanitation patrol. No overnight street parking was allowed, so the tickets made for a good revenue source for the city. This spot was virtually undetectable if the captain was prowling about. Now that Captain Lynch was just promoted to captain of patrol, he might be looking for Steve—looking for a way to write him up. If there was a call, something in their precinct, Steve was answering it. Let Crowley wake up on the ride. He looked back at his partner who was soundly sleeping. He could never sleep on the job. That wasn't police work. It wasn't what he signed up for, but Crowley was a crafty veteran and knew his job too well. Steve needed to find another way.

Several weeks later, Steve had settled in with Crowley, astonished at how little police work they actually did. He spent the time telling Steve about the old days. He told Steve to stay clear of the politics and maybe they would leave him alone. He said Captain Lynch never graduated high school, which wasn't a good sign for Steve's career. When Crowley introduced him to people, the reaction was always polite but distant.

"And never give city councilmen a ticket. Just a word to the wise," was his favorite refrain. Crowley was always about what to avoid and how to avoid it.

The radio squawked, "Car 24?"

Crowley replied, "24."

"That's a disturbance at 246 Arnold Street." The voice was male, flat, and robotic.

"Roger." Steve flipped on the siren and turned the car to head in the opposite direction.

"Car 24, that's a disturbance with hammers," the voice said, still without emotion or intonation.

"Slow down; we don't have to be the first car," Crowley said as Steve pulled up to the address.

"24, we have reason to think this is a former mental patient." This time, there was some urgency in the voice.

Crowley responded simply, "Roger," but made no motion for the door. Steve was ready for action.

He got out of the car. Crowley followed him up to a single-family frame house. As they approached, they saw numerous round holes punched in the wooden door.

A small, grey-haired lady greeted them at the door. She was wearing a worn blue housecoat and slippers. "He gets like this, and I don't know what to do. He won't listen." She sounded like an annoyed parent rather than someone in fear.

"Who, ma'am?" Crowley asked, taking a small notebook from his pocket.

"My son. He's got something loose." She pointed to her head.

Crowley and Steve entered through a small foyer into the living room. A man was lying on the couch with a Red Sox cap on and a ball-peen hammer in his hand. He looked over at the two cops and stood up; he looked at the floor and ceiling before returning his eyes to the two cops in the room. He was 6'6" and over 270 pounds, with a shock of uncombed black hair greying at the temples. Crowley blanched a bit and backed toward the door.

Steve said quietly, "Call for backup. I'll see what I can do." He felt the adrenaline begin to race through his body, but he controlled it like he did before a big game. He loosened his shoulders and set his feet but kept a relaxed smile on his face.

"Aw, Ma," the man said. "I didn't mean no harm." He looked at her and at Steve.

"So what kind of year is Yaz gonna have? Think the Sox can get to the Series this year?" Steve asked in a conversational tone as he held out his open hand to the man. The man looked a little off, with that goofy type of grin that says *I'm not really here.*

"This is gonna be their year." The man smiled, handing the hammer to Steve. Taking him by the elbow, Steve led the man to the door.

"I have to take you to the hospital," Steve said to the grinning man, who nodded in agreement. "Is he on any meds?" he asked the lady.

"He doesn't like to take them. Says it makes him sleepy. But he's a good boy."

Steve nodded and made a mental note to put it in the report.

Opening the door, the street was crowded with cruisers and flashing lights as six officers followed Crowley to the house.

"Under control," Steve said, holding up his left hand.

"Cuff him," a sergeant ordered.

Steve didn't think it was necessary. He slipped the cuffs out of his belt and snapped it on the man's left wrist, twisting behind him to grab the other hand. The man became upset at the show of force.

"No, no . . ." The man pulled his free arm away from Steve.

"Don't hurt him," the little woman screamed, running from the porch before a cop grabbed her.

"Get him," the sergeant yelled, and a cop hit the man in the stomach with the end of his baton, causing him to cry out in pain. Steve snapped the cuff on the other hand as another baton landed on the man's shoulder.

"No, no . . ." the big guy screamed, standing erect, towering over the cops. "Ma . . ."

"Get him," the sergeant ordered, and the man was surrounded by cops swinging batons at his knees and torso. He twisted wildly, screaming at each blow, his arms pinned behind him by Steve's cuffs. Lowering his head, he charged at each tormentor like an angry bull. The cops closed in on him, swinging nightsticks wildly as if he were a giant piñata, until the man collapsed to the ground. Kicks and blows continued to descend, the faces of the cops becoming red with exertion, as each cop darted in and out to hit the man like wild dogs trying to get a piece of meat from the pack kill. Steve heard the sticks hit bone, reminding him of the ping of a ball off a bat.

The man had stopped moving, and Steve realized he could be dead. It was under control—he had it under control. Was he responsible for the man's death? Was this police work? He looked at the blood oozing from the man's mouth and nose onto the concrete sidewalk. Why? As the ambulance pulled to the scene, Crowley and the other cops lit up cigarettes and talked about baseball while the medics struggled to haul the battered, barely breathing, handcuffed giant onto a gurney. *What the fuck just happened?* Steve turned the scene over in his mind again, hearing the woman pleading for them not to hurt her son. What should he have done? He was angry with himself for not doing more. And the sergeant encouraged the beating. He'd ordered it.

"Whose cuffs?" the attendant asked.

"Mine?" Steve raised his hand like a schoolboy.

"Crowley, your call. Book him at the hospital," the sergeant ordered.

"Book him?" Steve turned to the sergeant, holding down his anger in a measured tone. "This man is on meds. He was under control."

"Assault on a police officer, resisting arrest, disturbing the peace . . . the sergeant will think of a few more." Crowley was smiling and began whistling. Steve was going to write the report the way he saw it. But if he went on the record with facts, the report would just be contradicted by the other cops on the scene. He adjusted the pistol on his hip. Steve should write the report that would be more accurate with the facts. The man became belligerent after he was hit. But he knew they would just trash it and write a new report. Roxy would want him to write the real report—the man was in custody and the police beat the shit out of him. The reality as a rookie, he knew that wouldn't fly. Maybe if he couched the language—"*man became belligerent after being forced to comply*"—he knew that language wouldn't satisfy anyone—certainly not what Roxy would expect—or what he knew was the right thing to do. He wasn't prepared now. Steve realized he needed a strategy, a plan.

The squad room at headquarters was a noisy, busy square when Steve entered. He could hear the humming of the fluorescent lighting. Many of the desks had simple lamps, empty coffee cups, and an odd assortment of manual typewriters: Underwood, Remington, Smith Corona. Steve sat at a solid black Underwood typewriter from the 1940s. The keys were steeply pitched and the *a* and *l* made long, graceful loops as the keys struck through the ribbon to land hard on the page. Steve typed with both hands very quickly, striking the keys hard to make a clear impression through the three carbon paper forms. At the next two desks, the cops were typing one finger at a time.

"Shit, Crowley. When you get a secretary?" Vincent Rizzo shouted as he stormed into the room. Five-foot seven with a stocky wrestler's build, dark eyes, and an in-your-face manner, his dark stubble made his face look perpetually dirty. Steve recognized him as the kid who sat on the hood of the car, cigarette pack rolled into the sleeve of his t-shirt, talking trash to passing girls as if it were cool.

"That's the college boy," a cop who was one-finger typing said disdainfully.

Rizzo looked at Steve, who was still typing.

Another cop chimed in, "Not only can he type, he can spell, too, which is more than Crowley can do."

The other cops laughed. Crowley gave them the finger and leaned over to Steve.

"Rizzo thinks he's already made detective."

"Is that going to happen soon?" a short man with a round moon face and tiny eyes asked from the front desk. He was paging through the daybook of arrests. He wrote several notes in his narrow reporter's notepad.

"Sooner than you'll get promoted off the police beat, Toad," Rizzo shot back.

"Don't see your name next to any of these arrests. On vacation?"

"Fuck off, you drunken hack."

"What was that about?" Steve asked Crowley. He watched the man meticulously go through the arrest book.

"Oh, that's Larry Sutton, who's the police reporter for the *Providence Journal*. He and Rizzo go back to high school. Seems Rizzo stuffed Sutton in a locker or some other such high school shit. Now Sutton never puts Rizzo's name in as the arresting officer. Bugs the shit out of Rizzo." Crowley smiled. Steve thought the reporter would be a good man to know.

"Look at this, eight officers to make an arrest." Sutton directed the comment at Crowley.

"He was a big guy—resisted arrest." Crowley said and walked away to get another cup of coffee.

The reporter scribbled in his thin note pad.

"The guy was sick—wasn't on his meds. Probably will end up on the psyche ward." Steve volunteered.

The reporter bit on the end of his pen as he looked at Steve.

"Sick? You a doctor?"

"His mother said he hadn't taken his meds." Steve shook his head. "Could have been handled better."

"Better?" The reporter leaned forward.

"Yeah, I think so, but who am I to say?" Steve looked down at the typewriter.

"Tell me more."

"Nothing else to say." Steve shook his head. He wanted to say more, but this wasn't the time. "You can read the report."

Steve was trying to adjust to rotating shifts. At roll call for the four-to-midnight shift, he'd already had three cups of coffee. He was trying to get used to the constantly changing sleep patterns, but he couldn't fall into a deep sleep during the day. He was looking forward to a few days off to catch up on his sleep.

The duty sergeant made his evening announcements. "Here are the stolen-vehicle sheets. Let's find some tonight. And captain wants you to report every streetlight that is out—can't have the electric company charging the city for stuff we're not using. And you guys on the residential side, we need more effort on parking tickets before Captain Lynch gets a hard-on for you."

The room filled with laughter.

"Okay, some new assignments," he started, reading pairings. "Rizzo, you have Logan."

Rizzo chortled, "I get the college boy."

"Shit, I wanted him," an officer a row back said.

Rizzo turned with a quizzical look at the officer. "What? Why?"

"The kid can type."

Rizzo looked at Steve and smiled, "I know."

Other officers chimed in. "Rizzo, you can make more than one collar tonight because the kid can actually finish your paperwork."

Rizzo made a crude gesture to the group. "Let's go, kid."

Steve nodded to his new partner. He wouldn't be sleeping on the job now. Rizzo had the reputation of being in the middle of things. Steve looked forward to more action and real police work, but he also knew Rizzo's reputation as a bully. Steve could stand up for himself, and now this was an opportunity to show the brass what he was made of, like he did in the academy.

At a small downtown coffee shop with six white plastic tables, Rizzo and Steve stopped for dinner. The waitress was in her early fifties, with thick hips and sagging breasts. She wore white nurse's shoes. Finished, Rizzo nodded to the owner as he moved to leave.

"Wait. I didn't get a check," Steve said.

"Listen, kid: You've got the uniform on; you don't pay for things." He gestured at the owner, who handed him an envelope. "They like having us around. And they know if they ain't our friend, then shit happens. Lots of things can go wrong with a business: parking tickets, trash, break-ins." He pushed open the aluminum door so roughly that it strained the arm of the door closer. Steve turned and left five dollars on the table.

In the car, Rizzo took the driver's seat.

"Let me give you a little advice, kid: You don't fit in here, so don't do anything to stand out. Keep your head down, and do your job. Say *yes sir, no sir,* and listen to the sergeants. Keep your nose clean. That's it. With time, things blow over." He was trying to make it sound like fatherly advice, but Steve was sure the message was not just from Rizzo. He had filed the report on the beating, so it could have been a harsher message. Since Captain Lynch had returned to supervise the uniformed patrol, Steve would have to keep his eyes open.

"Unit 14."

Rizzo picked up the mike. "14."

"Detectives Bouley and Jones request backup at 142 Pearl Street in 15 minutes."

"On our way. Bouley, my man, must be a drug bust. Detective is where the real money is." Rizzo put the car in gear but didn't turn on the lights or siren. He pulled the car over to the curb several doors away from the address.

Detective Bouley, a thin, wiry Doberman, was wearing a cheap blue sport jacket and blue-and-white tie. His long, thin fingers, the nails bitten to stubs, had white spots, as if they had been bleached. He exited his unmarked car on the far side of the address and met the squad car on the other side of the street.

"We've got this little shit on the second floor. I need you to cover the rear in case he tries to make like a rabbit," he said to Rizzo, not looking at Steve.

Rizzo nodded, and they took up a post at the bottom of the back staircase. There were a series of small landings on each of the three floors. Bedsheets and underwear waved from the clothesline from the window on the third floor.

Rizzo drew his gun and nodded to Steve, who did the same. He felt the revolver in his hand as he scanned the back door and the windows like Roy Rogers watching for the bad guys. He felt like he was in a TV Western, waiting for someone to start shooting. It was surreal. Feeling his blood begin to race, his mind registered that this was real life. The gun in his hand was loaded with bullets. What did he do if someone runs out—yell *stop?* Shoot? What if the suspect had a gun?

The ideas raced through his mind, but he kept his eyes scanning the windows and checking in with Rizzo to see if they should approach the rear door. He looked down at the gun in his hand. What was he thinking? Once he took the gun out, the only option was to use it. And he knew he wasn't going to shoot whoever came out of the apartment. He holstered his gun and positioned himself at the bottom of the stairs, where he could use his baton to reach anyone fleeing.

Steve heard Bouley shout "Police!" and the sound of the wood door shattering as the detectives went in the front. There was a loud crash and a heavy thump at the top of the stair as Bouley yelled, "We got a rabbit!"

Rizzo ran to the bottom of the stairs, his gun drawn and facing the steps. Steve moved to the side so that they could intercept the fleeing suspect. As the man rounded the last steps, he froze on the landing when he saw the cops. He retreated up the stairs and leapt from the landing to the ground.

"Shit! He's getting away!" Rizzo yelled. "Police! Stop or I'll shoot!" He raised his gun to shoot at the fleeing man.

"Hold your fire," Steve yelled as he sprinted after the man. Putting himself into full gear, he stretched his legs, devouring the distance. He was the cheetah with the prey in his sights. He could feel the oxygen pumping fuel through his veins as his legs burst with speed. The man kept looking over his shoulder as Steve gained on him. The man tried to cut down an alley to elude him, but Steve was on him, dragging him to the ground.

"Stay down; you're under arrest!" Steve shouted. The man rolled to his back, his black hair matted across his forehead, and kicked Steve hard in the shin and got up to run.

"Fuck!" Steve screamed as he tackled the man harder, this time driving him to the ground.

"You're doing this the hard way," Rizzo said and cracked the man across the back of his head with his stick once, twice, three times, four times.

"Enough," Steve said. He pulled the man to his feet, cuffed. Rizzo whacked the prisoner across the chest, bringing tears to his dark eyes.

"You don't run, asshole. You're lucky this rookie can run. Otherwise, we'd be calling the coroner."

Steve lifted the cuffed man, walking him back to the stairs. "You were going to shoot him." He turned to Rizzo as the rush of blood began to subside.

"Shit, yeah. He failed to obey a lawful order to stop—fleeing the scene." Rizzo shrugged as he led them up the back staircase.

"But we don't even know if he did anything." Steve felt a sense of disbelief at the cavalier answer. Shoot first, then ask questions?

"If he's running, he's guilty of something. That's all I know."

"Shoot an unarmed man in the back—how does that make it— you'll get brought up on charges."

"No grand jury is going to indict a cop for doing his job. Besides, 'unarmed'?" Rizzo stopped and turned, drawing his lips tightly together. "I've always got a drop piece."

Steve was processing what he was hearing. Was Gaeta right in the police academy—a cop can shoot an unarmed person? That wasn't right. It was against regulations. But it happened, and it was condoned—by whom?

More shouting came from the apartment, and then Bouley yelled out the window, "Got another one!" Rizzo and Steve pushed the prisoner up the back staircase. A skinny twenty-two-year-old kid with a pockmarked face was handcuffed and sitting on the floor next to the metal kitchen table. On the Formica counter was a black suitcase full of marijuana. Beside it was a briefcase filled with cash.

"That'll get these dirty hippies five years unless he cooperates," Bouley smirked. The kid scowled, but the dark-haired man kept his head down.

"Got to be a couple of kilos there, and twenty thousand in cash."

"Whew," Rizzo whistled. "Almost had to shoot this rabbit, but Rookie here chased him down."

"Fuck, he saved you some paperwork." Bouley looked at Steve, who felt like he was in a friend's apartment: plastic bead curtain separating the rooms, beanbag chairs, and a lava lamp turning over purple liquid in a languid loop. He had to make certain their apartment was kept clean. He could imagine the captain's glee if they found a bag of pot sitting on the table in the living room.

Bouley took cash out of the briefcase and put it into a paper grocery bag. He gave Rizzo a large handful of bills. Then the detective put a couple hundreds in Steve's top pocket. "Nice job, Rook."

"Rizzo, thanks for the backup." He looked critically at Steve. "Let me know next time if we have fresh meat."

Rizzo nodded.

CHAPTER 8

ONE TOKE OVER THE LINE

In the apartment, Steve, Roxy, Cal, and Bill were passing around a joint with Suzi and Liz, two close friends. They were listening to the Doors.

"Now, with Joplin and Hendricks dead at twenty-seven, what's happening to the music? The Doors are going to be on campus in a couple of weeks. We should go before Morrison is dead, too," Cal said in a slightly stoned stupor. They all nodded slowly to the idea except Steve.

"I may have to work that night," he paused. "At the concert. Crowd control."

They all laughed, "No way."

"And I'll be looking for any punk-ass kids smoking dope or doing drugs." He passed the joint.

"Yeah, you're the fascist patrol, brown shirt and all. Bust hippies and Blacks. Have you starting rounding up the Jews yet?" Cal asked.

Steve looked slowly around at the faces, knowing each one had a different hold on the present. "What an asshole thing to say. What do I do? Uphold the law? Guess it depends who I am looking at. If you see me at the concert, stay the fuck away from me so I don't crack up." He was realizing how fungible the enforcement of the law really was. Busting hippies or Blacks for drugs was high on the list. Busting stores running numbers for the mob wasn't worth the paperwork. It was exactly the immoral situation he'd hoped to find and change, and yet it was also perfectly normal.

He told himself to let it go for the night. He was relaxed with his friends, almost feeling like he was back in college. The night off felt good.

"So we get this call. Public intoxication. I'm with my partner, Crowley—who's been on the force for twenty years and is still a patrolman. Not setting any speed records with his thought process," Steve started his story, having the attention of the group.

"Is this a true story?" Suzi, a very pretty, athletic girl from Denver, asked. Steve was impressed that only a knee injury kept her from the skiing in the winter Olympics.

"Yes, it's true." Steve pulled his head back as if hurt by the question. "Crowley is a bit of an old woman at times. So we arrive in front of this apartment building at two a.m., and there is this old guy, in filthy clothes, lying on the sidewalk. Crowley says, 'Ah, shit—it's w.c. again.'

"'Who?'

"Crowley points to the man on the ground. 'We call him w.c. because he looks like w.c. Fields and is always drunk. Call the drunk wagon; we can bring him in, let him sleep it off, and feed him in the morning.' So I made the call. By the time I get back, Crowley has this old drunk sitting up against a tree so he doesn't drown in his own puke.

"When the wagon comes, the driver says to me, 'We can't take him unless you cuff him.' Crowley nods to me, I put my cuffs on w.c., and we lift him into the wagon."

Liz and Suzi were leaning forward, and Steve was enjoying their attention to his adventures, knowing he was telling them stories from another planet. He looked at Roxy, who rolled her eyes.

"Not the end of the story," Steve said.

"So what happened?"

"It was a setup. We get back to headquarters to do the paperwork, and the driver of the wagon is waiting for me. 'Come get your prisoner,' he tells me.

"'What?' I ask.

"'Your cuffs, your prisoner. You have to take him out of the wagon.' So I go downstairs and the wagon is in the garage, and about eight cops are standing around the open door. As I go over, there is W.C., all covered with greenish-yellow vomit. I look around, and all the cops are smiling. I go over to get him off the floor of the wagon, and I see he has peed in his pants; I could smell he had completed the trifecta.

"'Could someone give me a hand?' I asked the cops surrounding the door.

"'Your collar, Logan,' one of them says. 'I've had my W.C. collar. Don't need another,' another cop says. So I have to grab this guy and put him in a fireman's carry over my back, down to the detention cell with all sort of fecal matter and other stuff running . . .'"

"Enough details." Liz held up her hands. Steve saw Roxy playing with her hair as she listened.

"Well, it seems W.C. has been doing this for years—but only lately has it been three for one. And rookie cops get to have the initiations—three showers later, how do I smell?" He got up to let people smell.

"Go away," the girls cried, pushing him back with their feet, to everyone's amusement. Roxy, who was at the door, rolled her eyes at him, and they retreated to their bedroom.

"You don't need to tell these stories. I know you want to be the hero, but . . ." Roxy said as she pulled the peasant blouse over her head.

"I'm not the hero," Steve said, but he knew she was right. Tonight, he felt more like part of the group than he had in weeks. He knew the job was pulling him further and further away from his friends. And he was feeling more alone. "I'm trying to tell them how this city really is, not just up here on college hill."

She shook her head, pursing her lips. "Sure you are."

"But there is stuff. The cops beat the shit out of this mental guy. There was nothing I could do about it. And it was just plain wrong."

Roxy froze and looked at Steve up and down. "You couldn't do anything?"

"No," he said, embarrassed at his answer. "There is more shit, too . . . they just take it for granted, how things are done. I'm starting to take notes, you know like a diary . . ."

"Okay," she said, sitting on the bed and moving her chemistry book. "Nothing?" She arched her left eyebrow.

"I tried," he said, cuddling next to her. "I tried."

Steve watched a new Pontiac GTO pass a parking spot on the street below, stop sharply, and execute a perfect parallel park. He turned around to Roxy and Bill, who were reading on the couch and in the easy chair with the permanently broken springs.

"Steve, Steve? Anyone?" a man's voice called from the stairs.

Roxy walked out into the hall as Steve followed. She was dressed in a pair of shorts; Steve could see the tight t-shirt outlined her bra-less breasts.

The man, still partially concealed in the shadows, raised his sunglasses and stared suggestively at Roxy. "Now, this is worth a thousand-mile drive to see. Woman, you are a beauty to behold."

Roxy's face went dark and strained to see the young man's face on the staircase.

"You going to ask me in, or do I have to stand here and stare at your great body?"

"Tommy?"

The young man came up the remaining stairs.

"What are you doing here? Why are you here? Does Steve . . ." Roxy moved forward and hugged him tightly.

"Holy shit." Steve embraced Tommy with a full bear hug. "Is the semester over in Florida?" he asked.

"I like surprising people." He was dressed in a tight-fitting silk shirt and designer jeans and was carrying a black leather travel bag.

"Can't you afford real furniture?" Tommy entered the living room behind Roxy and stopped to critique his surroundings. "And what kind of bad acid were you on when you painted that thing?" He pointed to the flaming Miro-like mural on the wall.

"Why, why did you, when did you . . ." Steve asked.

"I had business to do. Classes can wait," Tommy said, perching his sunglasses on his head in his curly brown hair. Tanned, fit, and totally self-confident, he was wearing a Movado watch and had a gold-linked chain around his neck.

"Business?" Steve asked.

"On Long Island—back in the old neighborhood. I have some good connections in Tampa, so a little drive is worth my while. And I met a guy who has a few Providence connections, too."

"Guys, my little brother," Steve said. Tommy nodded to each of them and then reached into his black bag and brought out a bag of marijuana, all the buds still compressed. He passed it around for everyone to admire. Steve shook his head. Here he was a cop, and his little brother is selling pot. Not that pot was bad, but it was illegal, and selling it was "criminal."

"Colombian Gold—best you can get. Got any paper?"

They rolled a joint and passed it around.

Steve tried to start the conversation again. "How's everyone . . ."

"Shit. Fine; they're your brothers and sisters, too. Come for a visit. Big shot here goes off to a fancy school on a scholarship, and that's the last we see of him."

"We came to visit once," Roxy protested.

"Yeah, in that shitty old foreign car. Lucky it was downhill most of the way." He smiled a *come and get me* smile at her.

They all laughed, enjoying the weed.

"This is really good stuff," Cal said, holding in his toke. He looked up and slowly exhaled the smoke, tipping his head back so he could watch it escape.

"Any to sell?" he looked at Tommy.

"I started with a key. Not much left; I have a lid or two."

"How much?"

"One hundred twenty."

Cal left the room and came back with the money.

"Did you drop out of school?" Steve tried to refocus his question. Tommy was wild, angry with the world. "You're gonna get drafted, and you'll be smoking this shit in Nam."

Tommy looked hard at Steve. "What's school gonna do for me? I'm a poor kid from a shitty little town on Long Island like you. I'm out for myself. The war is about money—who's making the money—defense contractors—and who pays—us little guys. You smart kids up on the hill don't see this shit?"

Roxy, a little lit with the smoke, said, "It's about capitalism. Exploiting the people. You're right." She gestured with the joint. "We need justice and equality for everyone."

Tommy smirked. "Now, don't get all communist on me, femma babe. Capitalism is good—making money is good. That's why I'm here. I'm saying war isn't a great way for a little guy to make money, 'cause he gets shot doing it."

"But the capitalists will always oppress the people. Racially, socially . . ." Roxy searched for the next line.

"Anyone starving like me?" Steve broke into the conversation. He didn't want Roxy to go into a long speech that would probably set Tommy off as well. "Let's go get some hoagies and wash 'em down with some beers."

"Hoagies on me." Tommy stood, pulling out a roll of money.

Roxy seemed distracted as Tommy put his arm around her, leading to the door.

"How long you going to stay?" Steve asked, trailing them out the door.

"Just the night. Have another stop on Long Island, then got important business in Tampa."

"You've got to be careful. We put people in jail here. And I hear it's worse down south," Steve said as they left the building. He was worried about Tommy. In grammar school, he had to protect him from the bullies because Tommy always seemed to want to prove something, getting into fights with bigger kids. Now Steve was afraid he was becoming more self-destructive. "Is it worth it?"

"I'm always careful." Tommy pointed to his new GTO on the street and lowered his sunglasses. "Yeah, it's worth it."

Wearing loose, revealing pajamas, Roxy was studying at the desk while Steve was sitting propped against the pillows on the bed, reading. He came over to the desk and began nibbling at her neck.

"Go to work; I have an exam tomorrow." She hunched her shoulder with pleasure.

"It's midnight shift. I don't get points for showing up early."

"Maybe you should. I have to study. Cal got into Yale Med School. He said he would help me with the microbiology. I need an A; I want to get into a good med school."

"I certainly won't be of much help with microbiology. But I do know you can get a ticket for transporting swill and offal in open containers through the streets of Providence."

Roxy screwed up her face. "What? Stop, I need to concentrate. You're done; you come home and kick back. I still have two more years to grind through."

"You will do fine. You're very smart. And I don't just come home and kick back. I'm taking extra assignments when they offer them."

"Better than you just hanging around," she said, her voice rising.

"Maybe I can find a coaching position this spring," he said. "It would be nice to be back on the field, back on campus." He knew he wasn't explaining it well. "I'm also trying to be sociable with the guys on the force—especially my class."

"You mean you get drunk with them."

"Sometimes we may have a few too many. I'm trying to fit in. You don't understand how they look at me. The comments when they think I can't hear them—and even when they know I can."

Roxy looked at him, her eyes narrowed and her lips drawn tightly. "Sometimes, when you come home, you don't talk to me. You just sit in front of the tube. You leave when I go to bed, I leave when you go to bed and . . ." She started to speak, and the words stumbled. "And you make our friends, when you show up in uniform or they see the gun," she hesitated, "nervous."

"What the fuck? College kids . . ." He turned away, pissed that she thought it was his fault. But he knew he was lying to himself. He couldn't tell her everything because she would be angry with him for not standing up to the system. "I'm still me. If they don't like it . . ."

"They aren't going to tell you to your face. They see a uniform, not you. Now you're one of *them*. And the gun . . . people we know don't have guns. It weirds them out."

"I haven't changed," he replied with less conviction, knowing that he had been hardened by the street. He had thought he was concealing it well. "I'm not trying to freak anyone out."

"Some people won't come here anymore," she pressed. "I think you freak Cal out the most. It's almost like he's afraid of you."

"Cal. Cal? Talk about a little strange at times? He did too much acid when he was my freshman roommate. And I think the pot now makes him paranoid. But he knows I've got his back. I took him off the ledge more than once." He walked around the room in a circle, not liking the accusations but knowing he was guilty. "Taking that extra year to get the dual major in Chemistry and Mathematics before med school—he's manic crazy."

He stood for a moment at the wooden square desk covered with books. He looked down over the street, the trees still bare in the New England winter. What could he tell her? How could he explain it to her?

"I don't tell you everything. Not that I'm hiding anything." He turned and moved to the bed, where she was adjusting the triangle pillow: her nightly study spot. Her right hand was turned upright, and she cocked her head toward him. How much he loved her—it was consuming, even now, after all this time. He sat at the foot of the bed on the Indian quilt. "I don't want you to worry. You have enough on your mind."

Her eyebrows rose slightly, and she shook her head, throwing her hair away from her eyes. "Should I be worried?"

"No. Hey, this is only Providence." He forced a laugh to break the tension. What was he trying to tell her? He wasn't afraid of the street. Things could happen there, but he was ready for it. It was constantly being aware—that was it—and that was hard.

"Yeah, but you tell your stories . . ." She closed her chemistry book and called him with her finger. He crawled up the bed and sat next to her.

"I'm different from the guys on the force, almost like an alien to them. They don't understand why I'm there. But I'm not that much different. If I hadn't gone to college, I'd be one of them." He let his thoughts drift back to Long Island. His high school produced cops, firemen, LIRR conductors, and schoolteachers. Did he escape?

"You are different." She held his hand and slowly stroked it, like he was a purring cat. "You decided to make a difference. It's not that easy."

"Not easy—that's for sure. It's just that I have to be cautious with some of the cops . . ." He didn't know quite how to explain it. "Some of these guys are animals; you have to be on guard."

"How did they become cops?"

He smiled at her. "Some animal is good . . ." He poked her in the side as she wriggled away from him. "You know what I mean. You remember seeing the Chicago cops at the Democratic convention. There is a fine line between control and . . . uncontrolled." He wasn't saying it well.

"Are you making a difference?"

He held her hand more tightly. Was he? Not really. He was just a beat cop on the wrong side of the brass. Maybe one incident at a time. He was writing the reports more accurately, but that was small change.

"Not really. It's seven hours of boredom and ten minutes of police work." Some nights, maybe.

"Why don't you quit?" Her green eyes held him in that calm, steady gaze. It was so simple to her: just move on. But it wasn't that easy.

"I can't," he said. He knew she expected that answer. He wasn't going to give in because it was getting tough. He always kept his legs moving, always was the one running the hardest at the end of practice. He would tough it out. But he didn't really tell her what he wanted to, about being scared—no, concerned—and on edge. And it was wearing on him and their relationship. He didn't tell her . . . maybe tomorrow.

He reached across her body, cupping her shoulder in his hand. He ran his hand down her arm and across her stomach. She leaned into

him, bringing her hand behind his neck and up into his hair. Their
faces danced close to each other, the warmth of their breath pushing
away the thoughts in their minds. Their faces came closer together,
slowly closing the distance of the conversation.

A little animal is good.

The next morning, Steve dressed in his uniform silently, adjusting
his badge and taking his holster from the closet and putting it on.
He straightened his hat and adjusted the Sam Browne belt to secure
his handcuffs and flashlight. The ritual allowed him to change into
a cop, like putting on a costume. Walking over to Roxy, he looked
at her partially revealed breasts and started to run his hands over her
shoulder toward them.

"And if I want you to stay, to have my man sleep with me tonight,
would you call in sick and stay? No, you're too dedicated to do that.
I feel it's coming apart. I don't know what else to say. We have to
figure something else out."

Steve was a little shaken. "Sure. Whatever you need. We can
figure something out."

Roxy's face softened, and she smiled. "Be careful." She got up
and kissed him.

Steve drove his Volkswagen down past the rows of colonial-era
houses on Benefit Street before turning downtown on Angell Street
by the Rhode Island School of Design. College Hill was so different
from the rest of the city. Most kids never get off the hill—he never
did. On the simple AM radio in the car, the Doors sang about how
people are strange if you're a stranger.

He parked his car behind the police station, among the sea of
American-made cars. Entering headquarters, he passed a group
of people on the bench, waiting to find out what had happened to
a loved one. He nodded to the desk sergeant, who looked at him

blankly. Inside the squad room, Lieutenant Krieger was coming out of Captain Lynch's office.

"Logan," he called.

Steve was surprised to see the Chief's *aide-de-camp* up so late. He thought Krieger was strictly a nine-to-five guy who always seemed to be in dress uniform, ready for the next media event. He stopped as Krieger walked smartly across the room.

"Come with me." He motioned Steve to follow him upstairs to a very small office next to Colonel McGuire's office.

"Have you heard about all the problems at Central High School?"

"I read the paper," Steve replied suspiciously.

"You can't believe everything you read. There have been a number of fights over the last month. Sometimes, they have weapons. We have had to respond on numerous occasions. No one killed yet, but ugly. "

"Too much work for the day shift?"

Krieger let the comment pass, but he raised his chin, letting Steve know he'd hit the mark.

"Some people are calling for us to put some cops in the school. But the mayor and Colonel McGuire don't want it to look like we're sending an occupying army into the ghetto. A lot of these fights are between Blacks and Whites, so it would look like the cops would be there for certain reasons . . ." Krieger sized Steve up.

"And those reasons would be correct?"

"Well, yes. There are certain constituencies that are putting pressure on the mayor to do something."

"And, what are you . . . I mean the mayor and Chief planning to do?"

"You have a college degree?"

"Yeah. It's a secret; don't tell anyone."

Krieger's practiced smile turned upward around the corners of his mouth at the remark. "I'm trying to do you a favor. I want to see

the force get better—to make it more professional. I'm on your side."
He put his sincere face back on and leaned a little closer to Steve.

"So there is an idea that we could put a presence into Central
without the uniform—making it low key but taking some pressure
off the mayor without putting the colonel into an uncomfortable
position." He nodded at Steve.

"Undercover cops in the high school? I thought narcotics did that."

"No, not like that. I checked with the school board, and because of
your education, you could get a temporary teaching license. It would
allow you to be a substitute teacher."

"Me? A teacher at the high school? What are you smoking?"

"Look, Logan. This has already been discussed with the mayor,
Chief, and Captain Lynch. Instead of you getting some mindless
construction site traffic duty on your day off, you would be assigned
to Central. It would be above board because you have your college
degree and the teaching credentials. The principal is fine with it. He
would let other teachers know. The news of a cop teacher will filter to
the students soon enough. And since the kids will never know when
you will be there, they will always be looking over their shoulders.
That way, we can be there but not be visible to any news cameras."
He finished and sat back in his chair, pleased with how the details
fit together.

"Seems you have worked out all the details. I guess I don't have a
choice?" Steve was intrigued by the idea. He watched Krieger gloat
with the cleverness of his plan.

"I'm on your side. I'm trying to help you. To help the department, to make it better, and to help those kids have a safe place for
an education."

Krieger was a smart, ambitious guy, probably smarter than any
other officer. From the scuttlebutt, he knew Krieger was married to
Senator Pell's chief of staff's daughter. So he knew his way around the
upper class of Rhode Island politicians. He was solving a problem for

both the mayor and the chief—and getting the college kid obligated to him. Steve wasn't quite certain about where his unease with the plan originated, because it seemed straightforward. But he knew nothing in Providence didn't have a price attached to it.

"So when does this plan start?"

"Next month, when the kids return from Columbus Day break."

"And what do I have to do?"

"Ask for a new tie for Christmas."

There were so many areas of Providence that Steve didn't know existed. Having grown up in a tidy, grid subdivision on Long Island, he wasn't prepared for apartments in back alleys or on dark, hidden streets. He walked up an alley to a set of small wooden stairs to a second-floor apartment numbered 123½. He knocked on the door, and it was opened by a woman in her thirties. She was wrapped in a blanket, and her disheveled hair stuck out the top. Steve could see she had once been pretty, but the worn lines and blotched skin made her resemble the hag from a children's book. A torn rattan chair and single aluminum table covered with cereal boxes and empty food cans were like refugees in the kitchen. The only heat source seemed to be two open flames on the gas stove. The woman had tracks on her arm, and her heroin stupor had drained any emotion from her face. The woman barely acknowledged him as she wriggled in her blanket like a caterpillar trying to escape its cocoon.

Hearing the sound of children crying from the next room, Steve pushed the door open and saw two young kids, dirty and barely dressed, on a bare mattress on the floor. He could smell excrement. Cans of open cat food were near the children, but there was no sign of a cat. There were cockroaches running all over the apartment and over the baby on the floor. His revulsion was immediate, and his stomach pounded for release. How could this woman do this to these children? It was a new side of life for Steve—one he had never thought about. How could you not care? Become so fucked up so as not to notice? He was angry with the woman in the chair, who had barely moved since he and Rizzo had arrived. She wasn't fit to have children.

Steve turned to Rizzo, who spat in the sink. "I'll call it in. You wait here for social services."

Steve stooped to the kids, brushing away the insects. He wished he had a candy bar to share with them. How did it happen? The feeling of helplessness rose through his chest, and he felt shame as he looked at the two children in front of him. Stroking the cheek of the littlest one, he said, "It's going to be alright." He didn't believe his own words. What was he supposed to do? He wasn't social service, yet it was his call. This wasn't crime fighting, but it was still a crime. Fixing this would be better than hauling in drunks. As he sat in the car writing the details in his incident book, he shook his head. How much needed to change. It couldn't happen all at once, but it needed to change.

"Are you sure you love me?" Propped up with four pillows behind her on the bed, Roxy was looking at her organic chemistry textbook, which was open on her lap. Her red flannel nightshirt was open at the neck, where she wore the small silver locket Steve had given her for Christmas. "I'm such a bitch sometimes."

Steve put *Mr. Sammler's Planet* down on the desk and smiled at her. He should be asking that question. He had fallen in love with her so fast and completely—it wasn't anything he had been looking for or expecting when she first walked into the apartment. Now, every day, he couldn't wait to come home and be with her. He crossed the room so he could lie across their double bed and prop himself on his elbow, watching her blow stray hairs from her eyes.

"I don't think so."

"Yes, I am. It's my own, silly, immature emotions." She looked up at him. "I'm afraid that you don't love me, but I know that's a projection of me mistrusting my own emotions."

"Well maybe a little, sometimes."

She landed a kick to his side before he could react. "That's not the right answer. You have to tell me you love me, totally and completely."

"I'm madly, totally in love with you," he said, knowing that his words were not really strong enough to express what he was feeling.

"I'm afraid, I guess, because I wasn't sure what I'm feeling is really love in the fullest sense." She closed the book and fell on the bed next to him, her hair splayed in a fan on the blue blanket. "But it is. I know in my heart it is."

He leaned over her, bringing his face so close that he could feel her breath as she spoke. "Even when I point out our imperfections or express my disappointment . . ." He gently stroked her forehead and her hair, inhaling and feeling his blood rising. He was afraid of how deeply he was committed to her, but the fear was one of uncertainty, of being lost in the dense forest of love, not knowing which direction was right but moving forward, more deeply every day.

"I have never felt this way about anyone and won't ever feel this way again. Is that what love is about?" He straightened his arms as he straddled her hips, waiting, anticipating, participating.

"Oh, Steve, I know I'm insecure, but I know I won't feel that way tomorrow because those emotions interfere with my love for you, and that love will overwhelm those fears." She stopped and looked at him, bringing his hands to her lips. "I've never had such confidence in my emotions as I do in my love for you. Our love is different. It will go on for a long, long time." She reached up, opening her lips into a deep French kiss. Pulling him down, she coiled herself around him, entangling his body.

"Come to bed," she whispered.

He was here with her. They should get married. He was making enough to support them both. They could get an apartment together. Her warm touch pulled him back to her. Yes, they should. He would talk to her about it tomorrow. It would be great.

The fraternity house of Lambda Chi Alpha was inside the quad, immediately to the left of the arch. Fraternities were more of a housing choice rather than a way of life since the university could eliminate them with the stroke of a pen. The brick buildings on the quad were solid, traditional, and unexciting. They were indistinguishable from each other except for the Greek letters above the door that the administration was quick to remind the brothers could disappear with the ease of a screwdriver.

Bill and other players were drinking Narragansett beer on the raised porch at the entrance. A local band was playing the Rolling Stones' "Honky Tonk Women" in the background. The aluminum garbage can was full of purple passion—some vodka and other liquor mixed with fruit juice and Kool-Aid.

Steve was feeling out of place in the quad, where he had spent so much time over the last five years. A brother nodded to him, trying to remember who he was. Steve's short hair and clean-shaven face announced him as an alien.

Roxy was a little lit, happy to be away from the books. She was wearing a short denim skirt and a loose print top. Her hair was held back with a beaded leather band. "Let's dance. You can figure the details of our future tomorrow."

The band was a local one from Attleboro. The lead singer was doing a pretty good Jagger, but he didn't have the moves and no one cared. They played "Brown Sugar," "Wild Horses," and "Jumping Jack Flash," and the room full of college kids worked up a sweat. Couches and tables were stacked against the wall to create the dance floor. As

Steve danced, he watched Roxy swing her hips, arms, and shoulders to the music, uninhibited and relaxed. She was free, beautiful, and he was all hers. He missed the freedom of college and freedom from anxiety. Every day before he worked, he tensed not because of the street but because it was working on his mind. He had to do something, maybe just admit he wasn't making a difference and move on. Law school was still on the table. As he moved his body closer to hers, bringing his hips to hers, touching her body as they twirled, he felt himself unwind. *Just be with her,* he told himself.

They moved outside to the porch for some fresh air. Steve put his arm around her. She was flushed with the exercise and the beer. "You want to get married?"

"You know it. I'd marry you right now, but you couldn't support me." She smiled with a playful turn of her mouth, creating little parentheses of pleasure which outlined her lips.

"It makes more sense after *I* graduate, *preppy*," she said.

Steve picked up on the reference to *Love Story*, which they'd just seen. She was more beautiful than Ali McGraw, with her dark hair parted in the middle and hanging over her shoulders. "That's three years away."

"Think you can wait? We can still have sex to keep your mind off it."

Bill, his shaggy brown hair wet with sweat, was in a denim vest with silver studs. He was on the porch with two girls in long skirts and Frye boots, weaving with intoxication. The smell of pot was in the cool night air. It felt like a century ago Steve had been at his first frat party, getting so smashed he couldn't stand. But now he sipped a beer, the adult on the porch.

Some boys broke into laughter as the band struck up "Satisfaction." Steve saluted Bill with his can. He was happy, if out of place. Things would get better. The boys jumped to their feet and drunkenly sang:

I can't get no . . .

Steve sat on the wall, holding Roxy's hand and feeling more disconnected from college. He was trying to hold on, but he could feel it slipping away.

Around the table at O'Malley's, Steve, Dylan, Meatball, and others were in street clothes after their shift. There was a pitcher of beer and mugs.

"Hear Rocky is working undercover with the narcs," Meatball said. He was well-connected to the back-channel information in the department. "Heard he made a bust of some PC kids for a bunch of pot. Understand they may target Brown pushers next." He looked at Steve with a sly smile.

"I hear the chief has a huge house in Jamestown on the water and a big boat, too," Dylan said. "Not just on a cop's salary."

"He's wired. Nothing goes on without him getting his piece. He knows all the politicians." Meatball smiled. "Now, that's a smart cop."

"About those Green Berets," Steve asked Dylan. He felt Dylan was a straight arrow, someone to be trusted. He couldn't say that about others from his class. "You started the story but never finished."

"I was on duty one night on base when a few mortar rounds landed. The post sounded general quarters and everyone was supposed to get to his defensive position. This young captain had us go with him for barracks inspection. In one bunk, there were these two Berets fast asleep. Now, you think about soldiers as all spit and polish. Well, these two had been in the jungle in Laos or Cambodia or someplace else we weren't in, working with the Montagnard tribesmen. They hadn't bathed in six months, and you could smell them the minute you entered the barracks. Seems in the jungle, you want your scent to blend in with the natural odors.

"They had long hair and beards and wore calf-length leather moccasins with a knife scabbard on the outside. So this captain walks up and yells at them, 'Soldier! Out of bed! General Quarters! Get to your posts!' But neither of them moves. So this tight-ass captain walks over to one and pushes him with the butt of his rifle.

Before the captain can say a word, one of them was out of the bunk, holding a Bowie knife to the captain's throat while the other one had dropped to the floor and had us covered with his M-16, ready to waste us. All of the color was drained from the captain's face. I think he pissed in his pants.

"'In the jungle, if you touch a sleeping man, you will die. Either kill me while I'm sleeping, or leave me the fuck alone,' the beret sergeant hissed. The captain only nodded. Here, me and my partner are hanging with our balls out to these two stone-dead killers. You could see it in their eyes—the zone. They hadn't adjusted yet to being back on a secure base. These guys were the best of the best."

"And . . ." Steve leaned forward. "They didn't kill you."

"No, no," Dylan laughed. "The captain, after shitting in his pants, apologized for disturbing them and asked if he could do anything for them. They grunted and went back to bed. I saw them a week later after they had shaved, bathed, and changed clothes; they were pretty good guys, but they were trained killers. Wouldn't like to meet them in a dark alley. When you went to Nam, it did different things to people. Depended upon you, but you definitely came out changed—for good or bad."

Rizzo stormed over and sat down with them without waiting to be invited.

"Rookies night out?" He looked at the waitress, who came over. "Sweetie, two pitchers. These guys look thirsty."

He slapped her butt as she walked away. She looked back at him playfully as if he did it all the time.

Dylan began his next story. "I was at the wedding; this fight broke out. They arrested the groom for hitting his new father-in-law." Dylan added, looking at Meatball, "Must have been one of those wop weddings."

"Or some drunken Mick?" Meatball threw back.

Rizzo smiled. "Weddings. They can be pissers. Brings out the best emotions in people. Last year, there was this big wedding between this Italian girl and this Irish guy. They had it in that big hall in North Providence. It was a big wedding, couple of hundred guests. Well, after they'd been drinking a while, the two families start going at it, and the call goes out, disturbance. So the NoProvs—all five of them—get there, but it's completely out of control. So every cop is starting to find a reason to move closer to the city line: go for coffee, check on a suspicious car—we're all waiting for the call for help. But the NoProvs call for help from the Staties." He laughed.

"Shit, what do those smokies know except writing speeding tickets and acting like puppets with sticks up their ass. So you can tell we're getting a little pissed at being passed over like the ugly girl at a dance. But listening to the radio chatter, it's not going any better with the couple of Staties that show up. So the cars are moving to the border, and we have two wagons, as well. Finally, the call for help to Providence. Shit, the cavalry is on the way. We have like thirty guys there in two minutes, with sticks flying. But you know who gets it first?" He looked around at the faces at the table. "The Staties." He laughed. "We cold cocked the first two we saw, and the rest of 'em rounded up their wounded and got the hell out. Shit, it was worth the price of admission. They think they're real street cops like us." He laughed and raised his glass as the boys saluted.

Was Rizzo serious—beating up other cops for fun? How much was BS, and how much was true? Steve knew there was some truth in the story, and it made him very uneasy because there didn't seem to be any control on the violence.

Steve and Rizzo were the first at the scene of the car accident, a Chevy Corvair that hit a telephone pole. The impact had thrown the driver, a man in his mid-thirties, through the windshield, splitting his head open. The rear-mounted engine had pushed its way into the backseat from the force of the collision. There was blood on the windshield, door, seat—more blood than Steve had ever seen. The man's head, still warm, was splayed like roadkill across the hood of the car. Steve could felt the nausea, but he fought it back down his throat, the acid taste lingering as he turned to the gathering crowd.

He began pushing the silent gawkers back with his baton so that the paramedics and firemen could cut the dead body out of the car. Steve hoped he wouldn't die like that—instant, violent, unexpected. He'd rather go like the old man in the apartment.

A car stopped, and he saw Suzi and Roxy gaping at the bloody man, whose eyes were still open as if frozen with fear. Steve moved toward the car.

"You can't stop here, Suzi. The paramedics need to get in," he said.

"All right, Officer, I'll . . ." Recognition came across her face. "Steve? What happened to . . ."

"He bought it. Too much speed, too much pole. But you've got to move." He signaled with his hand as the ambulance arrived. The girls fled without waving. He knew that his presence had personalized the tragedy of this lone motorist. He wasn't just a uniform; he was part of the system. And that was still foreign to her. She saw him leave in the uniform but had never watched him in action. Could she bridge the gap in her own mind?

Several weeks later, in the living room of their apartment, Roxy, Cal, Bill, Heather, Liz, and Suzi and several other young men and women were sitting around listening to Simon and Garfunkel's *Bridge Over Troubled Water*.

Steve could smell marijuana coming from the living room as he approached the doorway, which was half open. He was in uniform, returning from work. The table had four candles flickering from two Almadan bottles and two Chianti bottles in straw baskets. A slim incense stick burned in a glass jelly jar. If the captain sent someone to check on him like he did to Johnson . . . He paused for a second.

"Police. Don't anyone move." He stood outside the door just enough to stay in the shadows. Everyone in the room froze, looking at the uniform at the door. Steve entered the room, smiling.

"Pig Alert!" Heather announced in a spacey voice. "Forgot to tell you we live with a pig."

"Fucking fascist bastard. Haven't they issued you jack boots yet so I can hear you coming?" Cal said, looking for the joint he had hastily thrown in the corner.

"You're not funny!" Roxy said, looking at some of the stunned faces around the room.

Steve fell into a chair, looking for the joint to be passed around. He felt relaxed around these friends. They knew who he was.

"You leave the door open, anyone can come in," Steve said with an edge to his voice.

"Chauvinism," Suzi said. "That's what we were talking about. Men and their power trips."

"What?" Steve tried to focus on the conversation, realizing he might be the punch line to their discussion.

"Women must demand equal rights, equal opportunities," Liz added. She was a tall, thin girl with a Miss Porter's accent. "We're not accessories; we have rights as well."

"Do you think they will go to co-ed dorms next year?" Roxy asked.

"We have the administration trying to back down from their commitment. But the faculty is with us," Suzi said with authority. "One dorm, an experiment. But that's not enough. We want our degree to be from Brown, not Pembroke—Pembroke isn't the Ivy League school. We want equal admission for men and women. We want equal access to leadership positions, more female faculty, female athletes."

"And a female lacrosse team?" Bill tried to lighten things up.

"Why not?" Liz continued, "There should be as many female athletes at Brown as men."

"I'm for female wrestlers. Mud wrestlers," Bill said, moving out of reach of Liz's punch.

"That comment shows the sexism in what men do and say," Roxy said, looking askance at Bill. "Sexualize and objectify the female. It's our civil rights movement."

Cal smiled. "Give you the pill, and next you want to rule the world. Anyone going to burn a bra?"

Liz looked down at her flat chest. "I can only contribute a t-shirt. I haven't graduated to a training bra yet." Everyone laughed, even Roxy.

"How many cops are female?" She turned to Steve.

"We have matrons for the female prisoners," Steve said. Equal rights for women, co-ed dorms. He enjoyed listening to the college debates even though it was so far from his daily life. Women cops. They'd be laughed out of the academy.

"Are they full cops? Do they carry guns?"

"Guns? Why would they want guns?" Steve knew where the conversation was going. He looked at the girls and couldn't imagine any of them wanting to be a cop in Providence.

"For the power," Liz explained, tilting her head back with the proper Connecticut Hepburn charm. "Then the men won't be the only ones packing a pistol." The girls laughed, the boys following a second later.

"And girls will be on the Supreme Court, run the university, be in the army—dream on," Bill said, not ready to concede.

"Why not?" Suzi challenged, this time getting up from her chair.

Bill playfully cringed. "In your dreams," he said as Suzi gave him a hard punch to the arm.

With the group breaking up, Steve and Roxy walked people to the stairs. Liz and Suzi gave them hugs.

"Watch it, pig. We're coming," Suzi smiled at Steve.

"Keep the door closed and the pot out of sight, or I may be coming for you." Steve said it lightly, not wanting to spoil the mood, but he was beginning to worry. They had to be more careful. He needed to tell her to clean up every day—just in case.

"That was a fucking immature thing to do. Where's your head?" Roxy said as she changed into red flannel night shirt. "You can't come in and scare our friends to death."

Steve slowly removed his uniform, hanging it over his gun belt on a hook in the closet. He was certain about the reaction his entrance had made. It woke them up.

"Just fucking with their minds. They're living in this Ivy League bubble where parents pay the bills and the kids pretend to have all the answers. Shit happens. I'm out there in that world; shit I don't tell you . . . the part of the city you can't see from up here." He didn't want to kill the mood. "Besides, they're smoking dope in my house."

"You're changing. Is this what you would have said before becoming a . . . Whatever macho right-wing crap you are learning from your tough-guy cop friends, it's making our life shitty."

"What the fuck makes you think . . . What gives you the right to criticize . . ." He looked harder at her, his voice rising in anger and resentment. It was so much easier when he was in school and didn't know as much. Seeing that junkie with the neglected kids and the domestic fights over crap . . . "Shit," he paused. "Yeah, it's shit. It's nothing like here. I'm not in law enforcement, I'm a garbage man, picking up the human garbage and keeping it away from this hill. That's what you want up here—keep the crap away."

"Want? It's what you wanted . . . but . . ."

"Me wanted? Yeah, that's right. Me. I wanted . . ." He stopped, allowing his thoughts to catch up with his emotions. But his anger and hurt were racing too far ahead. He had made the choice to stay and thought he could do something noble. Who was he kidding? He didn't want to fight with Roxy, but he was feeling isolated from everyone. "I really want to be at the bottom of the hill to catch everything that rolls down. This is a real meritocracy—except the cops have guns. Shit, I'll trade for another senior thesis. Do you have any idea how unreal this academic world is? What is the real human condition? Why are the people exploited? Why don't we all live in harmony? Why, why?" He shook his head. "I've read the books, too." It wasn't just cynicism, but he was feeling alone.

"I don't know—it's not the same anymore. It's not working." She pulled away from him, sitting heavily in the desk chair. "Maybe you should get your own place."

"Move out? Move out? Shit, the first day I landed on the street, I moved out—from this fairytale land called college. Let's debate again how things should be while we go skiing this weekend at Stowe. Now what . . ." He realized he was shouting. It had become so confused between them. They were seeing each other more in passing, without the fun of a stolen kiss in the Rockefeller Library. He wanted her to understand how he was seeing things but knew there was no way she could.

"You scare me sometimes." She lowered her chin and turned aside. "You come home, and I can feel there is something . . . you are not telling me. There's an anger you're trying to contain. Sometimes, I'm almost afraid you might hit me. I never felt that way before."

He tensed his shoulders, pulling in his stomach to control his emotions. He lowered his voice. "There's shit I don't tell you. It's the ugly side of life. You read about it or hear news reports, but it's different up close, when you're dealing with it. I'm trying to do something better. I know I chose it, but what did I know?" His voice became quieter as he looked for words. He wanted to make it all right between them. "I think I'm trying to . . ."

"But it's not right for us, for me. I have to concentrate, to study. I need the grades for med school."

Steve was not quite registering what she was saying. "What?"

"Your hours are crazy; you have a gun in the house. You come home drunk from partying with your cop friends. You scare some of our friends so much that they don't come over here anymore." She placed her hand on his cheek, holding his head still. "You should get your own place so you can come and go as you like—at least for now. Until I finish this school year."

Steve was focused; his emotions cleared from the fog of night. Roxy began crying, her soft, little tears delicate dew on her cheeks. He knew she was serious.

"I said I can't do this. I want to, but I can't. I know I pushed you . . . I thought it would be okay, that I could handle it, but it's not what I thought. I've already dealt with so much. I don't want to wonder what's going to happen every night. I don't want to guess who you are when you come home. I don't . . . I don't. Oh, Steve, it's not what I want."

Steve tried to put his arms around her, but she pulled away.

"It's not working. It's me . . . it's my fault."

She reached for her shirt and began to leave the room, but Steve held her arm. They looked at each other's eyes and hands, trembling with their pain. Roxy pulled away gently and left. Steve sat heavily on the bed, aware that she was right. The distance was growing, but he didn't want it to be over. And the captain might send visitors. He couldn't put her in danger. What could he do? The cat jumped into his lap.

"What do you think, Cyrano? Should I move out? Is this not working? Did I fuck this up? You can't read her mind, either?" He stroked the cat.

He picked up the book next to the bed: Camus, *L'Étranger.*

CHAPTER 9

WHAT'S GOING ON?

Self-conscious in his camel hair blazer and grey slacks, Steve entered the school with anticipation and a twinge of nervousness. Crossing through the Central School arch, he realized he wasn't that far removed from high school. He could see teenage defiance in some of the students' faces. He remembered how smart he thought he was when he was their age, but now it wasn't that clear. The young faces around him were sullen, not eager—more like children on the day shift in an old New England textile mill. The school was made up of three buildings. The academic classrooms were located in the old main building. The Hanley building, a 1950s addition to the 1920s original structure, housed the vocational part of the school; the gym and cafeteria were located in a third building.

In the principal's office, Steve met with Mr. Newcomb, the assistant principal, a man of medium height who sported a sharply pointed nose. He wore a green bow tie and a white shirt that looked like it had withstood several days of use already, and his tweed jacket was threadbare around the pockets. His horn-rimmed glasses hid any life in his eyes.

"I don't approve of this at all," he said, shuffling the papers on his desk. "We are educators, not wardens. I do not believe police should be in our schools. These kids have plenty of time for the police when they drop out or, God forbid, graduate." He didn't look directly at Steve, who noticed that his left arm was a bit limp, perhaps from a minor stroke.

"Many of the students have heard rumors that there may be a policeman teaching them. I'm not going to try to keep it a secret, but I'm not about to broadcast it, either. Some of our parents will be very upset about it, especially those from our minority community." There was a sound of concern in his voice before it fell into a monotone of tired resignation. "You will be substitute teaching in Ms. Gaffney's eleventh-grade English class. She called in sick for the week and didn't leave any lesson plans."

As Steve walked the dark halls, he noticed that the kids traveled in groups of either black or white. He could feel their eyes on him as they busied themselves for first period. When he stopped to look at them, they quickly turned away, except for some of the girls with teased hair who grouped in a rugby scrum and giggled. It was another side of Providence he didn't know, where the skin colors were mixed, and the kids from the bottom to the lower middle were trying to make it. On college hill and on the force, everyone had the answer—right or wrong, they had the answer. But here, he could see the girls growing into their maturing bodies and boys wanting to or maybe not become men. He stood and watched the kids move in huddles or painfully alone navigate the hallways to classrooms that held their future.

Steve spotted a short, stocky teacher in baggy corduroy pants and a white shirt rolled up at the sleeves. "Room 14?" he asked.

"Gaffney's room. Still a few more down on your left." He looked Steve over carefully. "You that cop?" he asked. "Kinda young, aren't you?"

"Steve Logan." He put out his hand.

"Dominick Zulo, but they call me Mr. Z." He stuck out his small, thick hand. Steve noticed a small anchor tattoo on his forearm. The accent was Boston, with its long *a*. "Wish they sent the whole department in. These kids have no respect for anything. When I was in the Navy, we knew what to do with trash: we threw it overboard, then you didn't have to worry about it anymore. Here, we have to take crap from the trash." He looked around with disgust.

"Don't like the job?"

"Five years to retirement. Don't get me wrong; there're a couple of good ones in every class, but it's so hard for them to stay away from trouble. What ever happened to reform school? That's where half these kids belong. If you have to start shooting, let me point out who to shoot first."

"I'll remember that." Steve walked down the hall to the classroom. It reminded him of his grammar school, which had probably been built in the same era. The room was a rectangle, with high windows, letting in plenty of air and light. The windows were large double-hung, and there was a window pole to open them at the top for circulation.

The kids shuffled in, the girls in tight dresses mostly to the knee. Steve thought there must be some type of dress code. The white boys sat in the back on the right side of the class, mixed in with the white girls. The black boys sat in the left rear. Four boys strode to the front of the class; the obvious leader of the group had a four-inch Afro, black Converse All Star sneakers, and a baggy sweatshirt. He gestured to the others to sit as he slid into his seat.

"I'm Mr. Logan. I will be substituting for the next few days for Miss Gaffney."

"You that cop we've been hearing about?" the boy in the front row asked in a loud voice, turning and mugging for his audience.

"And who are you?"

"Norvell Thompson. But you can call me Marvel—'cause that's what I am." He laughed out loud, and the class followed with a canned laugh track.

"Well Mr. Norvell, Marvel," Steve made the words rhyme as he moved closer with a twenty-four-inch wooden ruler in his hand, "when I give detention, it might be for twenty years to life."

"Oooh." Some low whistles emanated from the back of the room.

Norvell stared straight back at him, not backing down but not escalating the situation, either. Steve had thought he could connect with students right away but realized they weren't interested. He looked hard at the boy in front of him, who reminded him of his wrestling partner in high school, always showing off for the girls. But they had a relationship of mutual respect. Here, he needed to be the authority. He moved his right hand to his sport coat and tapped it so Norvell could hear the sound of leather inside the pants holster Steve was wearing. Norvell's eyes signaled that he understood.

"So I see you are reading *Julius Caesar*. Can anyone tell me what you know about Shakespeare?"

"Some old dead White guy who can't write in English," a boy said from the back of the room.

"Right on two counts." Steve could feel the group measuring him. "He was White and he is dead, and he lived a long time ago. However, he could write English better than anyone in history."

"Bullshit." Another voice came from the back. "I can't even read it."

"It was meant to be spoken, not read. Shakespeare was a playwright, the most popular one of his time." He could see them slouched in their seats, doodling on paper or with their eyes focused at the windows. "They didn't have TV or movies yet; if you wanted entertainment, you went to the theater. And if you didn't like the story or the performance, you threw rotten vegetables at the actors."

That remark seemed to stir their primal destructive urge.

"No shit," a heavy girl wearing too much makeup said through her chewing gum. "Like what kind?"

"Depended upon what was in season: cabbage, onions, you name it. They didn't have to wait for ratings."

"I'd be throwing shit at my TV if I could hit some of those stinky-ass actors." Norvell was back into show form.

"So what happened in *Julius Caesar?* Can someone tell me the story?"

A wiry kid with dark curly hair combed in a sixties pompadour spoke up. "This Roman guy, he wanted to take over, but the other guys didn't like the idea, so they iced him, but they didn't get all his guys so they got hunted down and got popped themselves."

"Succinct plot summary, mister . . .?" Steve waited.

"Quinn, Larry Quinn."

"Thank you, Mr. Quinn." Steve was standing in front of the room, rocking in his athletic stance.

"Weren't those Romans like Italians?" a dark-haired boy asked.

"Shit, where do you think Rome is? Connecticut? Dumbass White boy." Norvell was pleased with himself. The boy jumped up out of his seat to rush toward Norvell. Immediately, Black and White boys jumped up, each staring with fists clenched.

Steve struck the heavy ruler hard against the steel desk, shooting a bolt of noise through the room. The boys turned as Steve slowly walked down the aisle between the two groups, his shoulders back and the long ruler in his hands. The boys eyed him and each other as they returned to their seats.

"Well, Norvell? Can you tell me about the characters in this play?"

"There are these guys: Cassius—like before he became Mohammed Ali—and Bluto and Anthony—can't forget the wop. So they get together and murder this Caesar dude to take over his empire."

"Brutus. Bluto is a cartoon character."

Norvell shrugged, unconcerned.

"So how did it go down?"

"That's where this shit gets hard. The guy can't write in English that anybody can read."

"Actually, you should read it out loud to really understand it. He writes in verse, so you need a bigger vocabulary than *WTF?*" The class giggled quietly.

"Yon Cassius has a mean and hungry look; he thinks too much, such men are dangerous." Steve pointed to a serious, skinny kid two rows back. "Watch out for the skinny kid who don't talk too much; he's looking to knock you off."

Norvell shot a look at the kid, who cringed a bit, and the class laughed.

"Why did they want to murder him?"

"Grab his stuff, I guess."

"Well some might have, but not Brutus. He thought he was defending Rome."

"That's in Italy, honky." Norvell turned to the class.

"So what happens next?"

"They all start fighting and killing each other."

"You missed the turning point: when Antony delivers his funeral speech and turns the mob against Cassius, Brutus, and the other killers. *Friends, Romans and Countrymen, lend me your ears. I come not to praise Caesar but to bury him.*"

The bell rang, and the kids sprang out of their chairs. Norvell got up and, with a flourish, led the Black boys to the door. He turned and nodded to Steve before he exited into the crowded hall. The white kids followed. Steve watched them go and for the next week tried to explain the mayhem and murder of Shakespeare to them. He found himself enjoying the give and take with the kids. It was better than on the street—he wasn't the same kind of enemy here. Yes, he was the authority figure, but he had something to give them. Shouldn't he be able to do that on the street? In the car, the police responded to problems only after they happened. Here, maybe he was trying to keep them from happening in the first place. It was another place to make changes.

Roxy's face was ashen, and she was running her finger around the edge of the jelly glass filled with wine when Steve came home after midnight. She did not move from the chair when he entered the living room. She wasn't reading or studying but looking at the mural on the wall.

"They were here," she said, her lips tight as she turned to Steve, who was still in uniform.

"They scared the shit out of me—all of us."

"Who, they?" Steve was looking forward to three days off with her.

"Cops. *Your* cops."

"What?" Steve didn't understand. "What do you mean?"

"Two fucking cops came to the apartment about seven tonight. Said they were doing a routine inspection." She took a sip of wine but still didn't move from the chair. Her face was dark, and her voice was hard.

"Was the place clean?" Steve felt a small panic coming over him. "What did they want? What did they ask you?"

"There wasn't any grass around, if that's what you mean," she said. "Clean?" She looked around the living room of salvaged furniture and a cable spool coffee table. "Debatable."

It was the captain. Since Captain Lynch took over patrol, he was paying special attention to Steve. Now, in his home, he couldn't relax. Now Roxy was a target?

"What did they say? Exactly."

She sipped the wine, looking up at him. Her eyes were fierce, like at the demonstration, and he could tell she felt violated. "They asked who I was. Who lived here? How long did we live here? They looked around the living room, walked into the kitchen. I didn't like the way they looked at me. So much like . . . like I was a suspect or something. I didn't want them in our home."

"Did they go into the bedrooms? Talk to anyone else?" He needed to know what they knew, what they were up to. They had probably talked to the tenants downstairs.

"Heather came in, and they stared at her breasts. Fucking pigs." Roxy said, refilling her glass. "What did they want? Why?"

Steve knew the why—it was an accusation. She knew why—it was about him. They were checking up on him. The captain was building a file. Now it would read "Lives with dirty hippies." He could feel the anger building in him. *Fucking do the right thing. And what does it get you?*

He took Roxy's hand, which was limp in his grip. She was angry with him; she blamed him for being frightened, intimidated, invaded. He hadn't thought about it before, about the captain's reach. How could he have missed the signs?

"I'm sorry," he said. He forgot how intimidating the sight of two uniforms at the door was to ordinary people. He pulled her from the chair into a bear hug, trying to make it go away, to take away the fear and the anger. But her arms were limp.

"I'm going to bed," she said, her voice quiet and controlled.

"That's a good idea," he said. He would follow shortly, but first he had to think this through a bit more. He would make it up to her. He had a few days. Where does it fit with the puzzle? How was he supposed to keep her safe if he was at risk, too?

CHAPTER 10

ALL ALONG THE
WATCHTOWER

Rizzo steered the car along the industrial area on Allens Avenue by the docks, the pungent smell of low tide rot blowing in from Narragansett Bay. Rizzo eyed the hookers who ducked into the darkness of the doorways and alleys as the police cruiser appeared on the street. He drove slowly to allow all the girls and their pimps time to see the car pass. Steve saw a late-model Lincoln parked up against a building, dark but for a lighted cigarette dancing like a pixie in the windshield.

Turning the corner, Rizzo gunned the engine to pick up speed. As he cleared the warehouse building, he turned off the headlights and made a hard right into an alley that was barely wide enough for the car. Proceeding slowly, they crept along so the tires were noiseless. Steve strained to find figures in the faint light of the flickering neon signs. Coming to the end of the building, Rizzo stopped the car and rolled down the window, listening for sounds and voices.

Steve watched as a car approached and two girls, dressed in revealing tops and panties, approached the passenger side window. He could hear the high pitch of a woman's voice but couldn't make out the words. Rizzo drummed his fingers on the steering wheel, waiting. One woman entered the car, and it disappeared into the darkness. Steve thought they might have gone parking behind a building on the docks or into the park. Several women's voices, conversationally bored, came from directly in front of them.

Without warning, Rizzo gunned the cruiser from its hiding place, springing forward like a giant cat, across the street and up the entrance ramp to the loading dock. He turned on the lights, hitting the high beam, freezing three women in the harsh light illuminating their black bodies. Jumping from the car, Rizzo shouted, "Freeze!"

One girl ran quickly to the end of the loading dock and jumped into the darkness. The other two stood frozen, silhouettes in the head-lights. Steve was out of the car a step behind Rizzo as he approached the women. He checked the surroundings for their pimps.

"How's business?" Rizzo asked the older woman. Thick, with bright red lips, Steve thought she was in her mid-thirties, past her prime for the business. But her full breasts, pushing hard against the red corset with a deep cleavage, made her look attractive in the darkness.

"Slow. And you cruising the streets don't help," she said, sticking out her chin at Rizzo.

"You know who I am?" he asked. She nodded. "And you know how I work?" Again, she nodded. "Okay." Rizzo motioned her to go with a nod, and the woman quickly disappeared into the darkness. The other woman, glassy eyed with fear, looked young to Steve.

"You're new here. What's your name?" Rizzo demanded.

"Pearl," she said, searching for the name. Steve guessed the girl was only eighteen or maybe younger, like one of the kids at school. What was she doing out here? Her body was full-figured, and her arm had a white vaccination mark. Her white sheer bra, nipples erect in the cool night air, was partially covered with a thin white negligee.

"You know who I am?" Rizzo barked, pushing the girl to the car. "Hands on the car." Steve had to suppress a smile since there wasn't much clothing to search, but Rizzo reached for the girl's breasts and popped them out of the bra as bills fell to the ground. "I'm Rizzo. You ask the other girls. You can be my friend, or you can do it the hard way. Understand?"

The girl nodded while she looked at the money strewn at her feet.

"So when I need information, you remember me." He pushed her down so her head was facing his crotch. She looked up hesitantly before she reached for his zipper. After she pulled it down, he pushed her so she fell back against the car.

"I don't need nothing from a street whore," he said roughly while pulling up his zipper. "You remember me." The girl scrambled on her knees, collecting her night's earnings.

Rizzo backed the car into the street. "They've got to fear you, know that you can take away their living or their freedom anytime you want," he said, looking over his newest snitch.

Steve understood Rizzo was about power and money. He liked the fear in their eyes and their shuffling deference to his power. It wasn't about protecting the people. These shakedowns were disgusting, but there wasn't anything he could do. As a detective, Rizzo would have even less supervision than now, which was a frightening thought. Steve thought Rizzo—divorced twice—wanted a woman only for sex or to serve him. Steve was struggling to understand it. There was good and evil, but here it was grafted onto each other so that it was hard to tell it apart. He had thought it was easy to understand when he started, but now it was murkier. There was all this brutal shit, but that was just the symptom of the overall corruption—no one was accountable. Where do you begin?

Rizzo drove into the parking lot of a warehouse complex. A small lit sign that read *Mickey's*, large enough for its purpose, was in front of a steel door. He parked the cruiser in the fire lane and got out. Steve followed. As Rizzo pushed open the door, a wall of music assaulted them. The bar was dimly lit and crowded. Rizzo and Steve made their way inside, and patrons moved away or allowed a path to appear and then close behind them. Steve's eyes adjusted to the low light, and he slowly surveyed the scene. The patrons, some in halter tops and skirts, and others in jeans and tight t-shirts, were all men.

Rizzo kept plowing his way past the bar to a small door next to the men's room. He rapped on the door with his baton and pushed his way in. A tall, thin man with bony features and long, thin fingers sat behind his metal desk. His short, cropped hair was grey at the temples, and he had an Italian *cornicello* on a chain at the open neck of his nylon shirt. He looked at Rizzo and didn't try to hide his disgust as the sides of his mouth turned. Steve closed the door after them, but it did little to deaden the music.

"Hey, Smitty. Looks like business is pretty good."

"Just making a living." Smitty had a frozen smile and was staring at Rizzo like an unwelcome relative.

"If you call being a butt-fucking faggot living."

Smitty didn't change his expression but opened the center desk drawer and took out a large manila envelope. He handed it to Rizzo, who opened it and thumbed through the cash inside.

"It's all there. Now, would you tell the captain to stop ticketing my customers on side streets? Shit. There is no one working on the docks at night."

"Tell them to park legally. Or we might get you a deal on the lot on the corner."

"No thanks; I can't afford any more of your overhead. Jimmy will set you up with a drink before you leave," Smitty said. Steve heard the sarcasm, but it seemed to escape his partner.

"Your choice." Rizzo turned, and Steve followed. As they walked through the bar, a large man with rouged cheeks and red lipstick slid off a barstool and looked Rizzo in the eye.

"I love a man in uniform," he said and petted Rizzo's sleeve.

Rizzo pushed the man's hand away with his stick and continued to the door. Steve saw the man smile to his friend as if he were going to collect on a dare. A low laughter came from the crowd as they exited.

Back in the car, Rizzo muttered, "Those fags make my skin creep. Every time I have to make this pickup . . ."

"They think you're their kind of man," Steve smiled. It was nice to see Rizzo not in control.

Rizzo scowled and turned hard down another deserted street.

"Now, at this pickup, I never mind staying to have a drink at the bar."

There was a sign ahead that read *Alley Cat Club* in the shape of a buxom girl bending over.

The thickly tattooed bouncer at the front door stepped aside as Rizzo entered with Steve following. The cashier, wearing a pink negligee that revealed the outline of her breasts, gave Rizzo a peck on the cheek as he walked in. She smiled at Steve to demonstrate she understood the game, and Steve caught her eye.

A short girl with very large breasts was dancing on the semi-circular stage in the center of the room. A row of chairs hugged the apron so that men could reach the dancer from below to put money in her garter. The dancer's pole gleamed in the spotlight as the girl encircled it with her arm and spun around it on one foot, slowly lowering herself to the ground until she was on all fours, facing the three men sitting at the edge of the stage.

Steve watched Rizzo take in the scene as several girls quickly hovered around him like bees. He moved through the room slowly, looking at each man, some sitting at tables or others in booths along the wall, with a partially clothed girl next to them. The men averted their eyes or were too drunk to care.

As he passed the small green door to the girls' dressing room, he asked a large blonde dressed in a secretary's skirt and a deeply plunging blouse waiting to go on stage, "Is Lily working tonight?"

The girl stopped for a moment, sizing up Rizzo before replying, "Yeah. She dances after me." Rizzo smiled at the girl before entering the small office.

The shock of the bright light caused Steve to blink as he got his bearings. The small office had a metal desk, metal filing cabinet, and three *Playboy* centerfolds taped to the wall.

"How's business, Frankie?" Rizzo extended his hand to the middle-aged man with a mole on his left cheek. Frankie stood and extended his hand.

"Could be busier. Need more of you boys to stop by after work. I got a nice crop of new girls—some even from Boston. Great place for a promotion party," he said, nodding to Rizzo. Reaching into his desk, he handed the white envelope to Rizzo, who put it into his jacket pocket without checking the contents. As Steve watched the exchange, he guessed that they had been doing business together for years. How much this time? Steve was realizing there was organization to the pickups, and Rizzo was one of the trusted. This is what Durk was talking about. But Durk had help, which Steve didn't see happening in Providence.

"Now I need a little closer inspection of the merchandise," Rizzo smiled.

"Knock your lights out," Frankie said.

Steve and Rizzo re-entered the bar, which was beginning to fill with the evening crowd. The girls raced to the door at each arrival, looking to hustle a table dance. A tall girl with bleached platinum hair completed a split on stage and swiveled her hips until she was flat, then slithered across the stage like a blond anaconda. She allowed dollar bills to be stuffed in her G-string as she passed. Rizzo followed her serpentine movements and offered her his hand as she stepped down the stage steps. The next girl, a small brunette, finished putting quarters in the jukebox and stepped up to the stage in a babydoll blue camisole as "Satisfaction" began to play.

"Buy you a drink, Lily?" Rizzo asked politely.

"A VIP drink?" she smiled at him.

"Only the best for you, baby." He took her by the arm, leading her to the steps to the private VIP rooms upstairs.

Steve stood there, unsure of what to do next. The girl on stage threw her blue panties at him, and he caught them instinctively. He politely placed them at the edge of the stage. The girl danced toward him, shaking her breasts rhythmically to the music. Steve watched them and looked at the girl, who was no more than nineteen. She caught his eye with a practiced vulnerability. He wondered how her tight body would feel under him. VIP room—did that come with the job? To touch her, feel her body on his, have a little fling? Roxy was the second girl he had ever been with, and his only real relationship. He shook away the thoughts—it came with the job, temptations. He wanted to give her some money but was aware of the eyes on him.

He backed away from the stage and took up a less-conspicuous station by the front door. He watched the girls approach the men around the stage, taking them by the hand to darker parts of the club while he waited for Rizzo to achieve satisfaction.

The racial tension at Central High School had not improved since Steve had begun teaching two days a week. When he entered the teacher's lounge, the three teachers by the door went silent. He found that when he made small talk, the teacher quickly exited to attend to other pressing duties.

"Ready to quit your night job?" Mr. Zulo came over with a cup of coffee. "Get you a cup," he said, pointing to the hotplate on the counter.

"Never during the day. With all I drink at night, it's eating a hole through my stomach."

"Never mind these shitheads." Mr. Zulo motioned at the two teachers sitting at a table. "Most of them don't know what's good for them. I've been trying to get them to form a union for years. Maybe a half a dozen of us care, but the rest? They say, 'We're educators, not factory workers.' If you ask me, we're in the warehousing business. What do you think?"

"It's tough. I think I might be getting through to a couple of them."

"Maybe for a minute, but it doesn't stick. That's what's so damn frustrating. You think they see the light, and the next day they come in, and you know the bulb needs to be replaced again."

"It's the times; nobody wants to trust authority. I was just there, and look at me now." Steve felt he connected better with the kids than Zulo did because he respected them. Or was he just kidding himself and projecting how he dealt with high school? He was close to their age and remembered the difference a teacher could make in a class. Zulo looked him over critically, like a recruit, and patted him on the back. "You're okay, kid. Who you subbing for today?"

"A math teacher today, Mr. Bozo. If that was my name, I would have changed it," Steve said as he headed for the door.

"When you meet him, you know that it fits."

"Hey, teacher man." Norvell was walking down the hall with his swagger and troupe of followers, including a very tall, large kid.

"Norvell," Steve acknowledged. "How's your Shakespeare coming along?"

"Sucks. Coming to the basketball game tonight? See, my man Marvin," he motioned to the big kid, "do a little schooling on Pawtucket. Better get to see him while he's cheap. He's goin' to the pros. Big bucks."

"And you are his manager?"

Norvell puffed up more. "I'm just giving him trusted advice."

"I'm teaching a math class. You should get to one so you can count all that money."

"I can count." Norvell was offended.

Steve looked at the big kid, who he seemed to hang on every word Norvell said. Maybe he appreciated the protection and smarts Norvell seemed to offer.

That night, to Norvell's surprise, Steve climbed the wooden bleachers and sat down next to the students. The sounds of bouncing balls and hoots and insults ricocheted in the packed gym. Students from both schools were huddled in prides, ready to pounce on any opposing weakness. The stamping of feet on the old bleachers caused the structures to wobble like an old man.

"You got money on the game?" Steve asked, knowing Norvell was uncomfortable but proud that the cop was sitting next to him.

"I'm not a gambler, I'm a businessman," he shot back. "But if I was making book, I'd take Central and give you ten. Marvin is that good."

"So what kind of business?"

"Money business. Ya know, buying and selling."

"Buying and selling what? Stuff that falls off the truck?"

"Man, don't insult me," Norvell said, opening his mouth and raising his eyebrows. "I'm an entrepreneur."

Norvell nodded at Steve as if the two of them were on the same page. Maybe they were, Steve thought. Norvell was smarter than he let on, quick with numbers, and had enough schooling to talk over most of his crowd. If he stayed out of trouble, he could go far.

The whistle blew, and Steve stood to return to the floor with the other teachers. "Tell your friends to keep it in line. Or I'll have to be back up here. Don't fuck with me."

"No need for that shit. This game won't be close enough to have a fight. Besides, I already covered all my bets." Norvell smiled and nodded as Steve returned to the hardwood, standing by the door with several other teachers.

On the opening tip, Marvin put home a mighty dunk to the roar of the home crowd, and the game was all Central, who beat the opposition by eighteen points.

"You covered the spread," Steve said as Norvell exited the gym.

"Told you my boy Marvin was money. Now we're gonna do a little partying."

"See you in math class, Mr. Entrepreneur," Steve said, but Norvell just smiled and shook his head to the amusement of his crew.

"That's a report of a rape, 125 Benevolent Street," the dispatcher's flat voice said.

Cars quickly responded to the call. "Car 12 going. Car 20 on the way. Car 15 on the way."

Steve picked up the microphone. "Car 24 on the way." And he moved the car from park, heading up Olney Street toward college hill.

"Why the fuck did you do that?" Crowley asked, still holding onto his second cup of coffee. "It's out of our district. Not our call."

"Yeah, but I might be of some help up in my neighborhood." He knew that Suzi lived on Benevolent Street, but he didn't know the number. It was probably Brown students involved, and he wanted to be able to help.

"Not our call. You know the captain gets pissed when you cross town for a call." Crowley said.

"It's adjacent, okay? Not across town." Steve saw Crowley roll his eyes, but since Steve was driving, he didn't have much choice.

Steve hit Waterman Street and gunned the cruiser up the hill, all siren and lights. It was past three in the morning on a Friday night. Campus was relatively quiet, but he was already working the situation in his head. Was it a grab-and-drag rape or drunk kids, too much touching, not enough no, and next thing rape. It wasn't like south Providence, where someone gets pulled into a vacant house or pushed into their apartment.

As he pulled up to the two-story wood frame house, he recognized the building that had been divided into student apartments. The blue and red lights of the police cars colored the night. A crowd of students from adjacent buildings was gathering on the sidewalk. Steve opened the front door and slid past two cops. The first floor was divided into three apartments. The door on the left was open to a studio apartment. Two cops and a sergeant were talking to a girl sitting on the bed. On the walls were posters of album covers: Jimi Hendrix, the Doors, Beatles, and Che Guevara, his dark eyes surveying the scene from under his beret. The girl was a familiar face, someone Steve had seen but didn't know. He wondered where she was from and what she was hoping to do. Her face was round and puffy from crying. Her mousey brown hair was tangled and damp. She wore a loose-fitting cotton blouse and pajama bottoms. When she came to Brown, she was probably at the top of her class, all achievement and promise. Steve thought of his freshman class—and the kids who washed out trying to be the best and hating their failure. Drunk too many nights or high, they disappeared over the years. Not saying goodbye, just never returning. Roxy was an A all the way and killing herself for the grades. He was in awe of her determination and jealous for more of her time.

A sergeant was questioning her. "Did she want to press charges? Is this the guy? When did it happen?" Steve could hear her unsteady voice slowly enunciating words through a thick haze of liquor.

"He did it. I didn't want him to, but he forced me," she was saying. More cops were arriving to gawk at the poor girl. Steve felt sorry for her. These guys would make her go over the story again in even more detail, asking about where she was penetrated, how it felt, did she know him, did she enjoy it? They would write the report, and the day shift would make her relive it all over again. There was not a woman in the mix.

When she was sober, would she want to go through it again and again? She would be embarrassed. She was in pain—anger pain, existential pain. And the system would only generate more. She would drop the charges, frustrated with the callousness of the state. How could he change it? Wouldn't it be better if the girl could speak to another woman? It was how it was, the brass would say. But why couldn't it be changed? He was angry, but there was no place to channel it right now.

A thick-set boy with hair hanging like a beaded curtain around his ears and a small goatee sat handcuffed in the hallway. He was wearing a green t-shirt and boxer shorts.

"I didn't do anything. She's crazy. She's just pissed off 'cause I want to break up."

"Sure, Romeo," another cop said.

A strong odor of pot drifted down the stairs with the plaintive sounds of an off-key Donavan. Two cops followed the smell upstairs and banged on a door. The hapless folk singer with shoulder-length dirty blond hair was brought downstairs in shorts and sandals.

"Man, I wasn't bothering anyone," he said, looking confused at the interruption of his concert. The cops were laughing at their bust. Another hippie busted; one more for the good guys. Steve was disgusted, knowing there was nothing he could do to help the girl. He wanted to take the girl to Roxy and Heather and let her sleep it off so tomorrow she could think straight. He hated the leering cops on principle. By the time she went through her story for the fifth time, she would realize that it was better to let it go.

"She was asking for it," Meatball said, walking down the hall. "College sluts."

"Asshole." Steve moved toward him. "She's got a right to her body. What if she was your sister?"

"My sister wouldn't be drunk with some low-life hippie. And if I caught her, she'd be crying more than rape." Meatball laughed with the audience of cops.

"You're right. She wouldn't be in college because she was already knocked up," Steve said.

"Logan, you scumbag." Meatball pushed forward toward Steve, who squared off against him.

"She deserves some respect and privacy, just like your sister would. Look at this fucking circus." They stood facing each other as more patrol cars arrived. Steve pointed at the cops arriving to gawk. "This is so fucking sick."

Crowley was standing with several other cops by the squad cars, smoking a cigarette. The student crowd across the street was thinning out as the cops milled around without any real purpose once their curiosity was satisfied. Steve saw Liz and Suzi watching from the sidewalk. He was just another uniform to them. It was uncomfortable how people looked past him when he was in uniform.

Captain Lynch arrived, driven by a patrolman. The older policemen moved to the side or slipped away to their cars, knowing they were far out of their districts. The captain stopped and looked at Steve as if making a mental note. Steve did not back down from the stare, knowing that he couldn't hide his presence at the scene. It was the right thing to do, to be here. He was sorry he couldn't help the girl.

"Let's go. Nothing we can do here," Steve said to Crowley as he walked to the car.

Taking his cap off, he stood at the car door, surveying the college neighborhood. How different it looked tonight. He was seeing it for the first time: small single-family homes squeezing in kids who lived on munchies and beer. A pizza joint and a package store—what else does a college neighborhood need?

It would be nice to be back in school. As he turned, he met Suzi's wide eyes as if she had just seen a ghost. She had seen him in uniform many times, but not in action, with a car, one of them. He touched his forefinger to his eyebrow in a small salute and entered the police car. To her, he was one of them. But he had never left the hill. It couldn't just stay like this, but where to start? He couldn't just let it pass, not this time. Did he have the courage? Courage for what? He wasn't afraid, he was . . . what . . . unfocused? He would talk to Roxy. They would work it out. He had to believe that.

Over the next weeks, Rizzo, with his perfect flattop haircut, was Steve's regular partner. Steve was becoming immune to the crude jokes and comments about hippies, blacks and broads. Rizzo was quick to jump on any call even if it wasn't in their territory. And the brass didn't seem to care.

"Car 28, family disturbance 201 Ford Street. Take a CCR of 278 at 10:58."

"Roger." Steve hit the siren and lights. He pulled up to a three-family floor-through wooden house with wide grey asbestos shingles that were chipped at the corners. Steve and Rizzo entered the left door, leading to the upstairs apartments. He could smell the cooked garlic and heard Louis Prima singing from the second-floor apartment as the old stairs creaked under his feet. The shouting and screaming were coming from the top floor. Rizzo took two steps at a time, knocking hard on the door with his baton.

"Police. Open the door."

The door opened a foot, and a small woman in her early twenties looked at the two cops like uninvited cockroaches. Her face was flushed from shouting; her unwashed, stringy black hair was wet with sweat. Rizzo kicked the door wide open with his foot. Inside the apartment were about thirty people, all arguing heatedly. A short Italian in his late twenties with a gold chain around his neck came to the hallway from the living room.

"Who called you fucking pigs? That old witch downstairs?" the woman screamed.

"Angela . . ." the husband screamed at the girl. "What the fuck?"

Rizzo pushed the woman back into the apartment as he entered the small foyer.

"Shut up, you fucking whore. You answer *my* questions," he ordered, leading with his chin. Steve hated the way Rizzo talked to people. It was time to defuse the situation, not throw an accelerant on it. Steve was sick of Rizzo screwing with other people. The change had to come from the top. Steve imagined the captain was like Rizzo as a young cop—aggressive, demeaning, and ready to use force first. That was how you got ahead in Providence.

"Get the fuck out of here," the girl screamed as she tried to push Rizzo back to the door. He shoved her hard against the wall, knocking to the floor a plastic crucifix that had been holding a dried palm frond. He turned to look at the room of people and screamed, "Shut the fuck up!"

Some who had seen the two cops enter stopped arguing and began moving toward the foyer. The small woman sprang back like a fighter off the ropes and unleashed a roundhouse punch directly to Rizzo's nose, causing his head to snap back, spraying blood on the rose wallpaper. Stunned, Rizzo was still for a second before he turned to the woman, raising his baton to crush her skull. Her husband jumped forward, blocking Rizzo's arm as it came down.

Steve tackled the man, hitting him hard in the midsection with his shoulder before the man could throw a punch at Rizzo. He drove the husband to the floor in one motion and pinned the husband's arms with a double bar arm wrestling hold, immobilizing his body so he could cuff him. A hail of plates and glasses showered the room, greeting the backup units as more cops charged up the stairs swinging clubs.

Steve and the man were being hit by wildly undirected police batons and flapjacks as the cops swung furiously at anyone who moved.

"Take it easy," Steve said into the man's ear. "We'll figure this out at the station." He felt the man stop struggling and, with help from another cop, got the man to his feet. He hustled him downstairs to the police wagon as more adrenaline-filled cops crashed up the stairs.

Rizzo, with a little blood on his face and nose, came charging downstairs and rammed his baton hard into the cuffed man's midsection. He hit him on the knee, spilling him to the ground, and, as he tried to get up, Rizzo hit him again across the back, dropping him to the ground with a grunt.

"Fucking shit." Rizzo was breathing hard. "Fucking shit!" A fresh trickle of blood ran from Rizzo's nose. "Fucking shit. Hit a cop." The cuffed young woman screamed a litany of obscenities at Rizzo as she was put in the back of a car and driven away.

Rizzo watched the car turn the corner and then whacked the husband again with his stick. Detective Bouley and his partner arrived in an unmarked car. Dylan and his partner arrived with the wagon but made no move to assist the man.

"Easy, man. The girl hit you." Steve put himself between Rizzo and the prisoner.

"What are you, a fucking priest or something?" Rizzo glowered at Steve, pushing him to the side as he hit the man again.

Bouley looked down at the handcuffed man. "You hit a cop? You don't hit cops, you piece of shit." The man looked up, a bit dazed. And Bouley kicked the man in the ribs, dropping him to the ground.

The man looked fearfully from Rizzo to Bouley. "Don't let them hit me," he pleaded to Steve.

"Into the wagon." Steve grabbed him to put him out of danger.

"Fuck you, Logan. I'm not done with him," Bouley said as he hit the man in the ribs with a blackjack.

"Shit, man. Enough. He's cuffed." Steve shielded the man with his body.

"Get out of the way. Gimme that cocksucker." Bouley tried to push Steve away, but he kept his body between the prisoner and the detective. Bouley tried to swing around Steve, but Steve was quicker. He didn't like Bouley and hated his sadistic approach to being a cop.

"Son of a bitch, I gonna teach you." Bouley grabbed the front of Steve's jacket with both hands. Steve clamped his hands on top of Bouley's and began forcing him to the ground. Eyes locked, he could see Bouley's surprise. He was losing this battle, but the rookie was learning to fight back.

"Enough. Let's get this scene cleaned up." A sergeant barked the order. "Logan, stand down."

Steve released Bouley, having made his point.

Bouley grabbed the prisoner roughly by the back of his shirt and slammed him face-first into the back of the wagon.

"He probably could use a little tuning up," Bouley snarled, turning to Rizzo and the other cops.

Steve was ready to have it out with Bouley right there. This was his prisoner; if Bouley wanted an arrest, he should get it himself. But the scene was now full of cars, with a sergeant and a lieutenant having arrived. He knew he wasn't going to win this battle, but it didn't change anything. It was fucking wrong, and Rizzo had started the whole damn mess. But he wasn't going to be responsible for what was about to happen to the prisoner. His cuffs, his responsibility. He turned to Dylan. "Give me your cuffs."

Dylan hesitated before throwing them to Steve. Steve pinned the man's arms and put Dylan's cuffs on him before removing his own.

"Your prisoner, Dylan," Steve said.

Dylan shrugged and shook his head. Dylan was a good soldier, and Steve didn't want to put this shit on him, but he didn't trust Bouley.

"You shitting me?" Bouley looked fiercely at Steve and then grabbed the man and again slammed him hard into the side of the wagon. "This guy wants to see the park. Let's take the scenic route," he ordered Dylan before he got into the wagon behind the prisoner.

As Dylan closed the door, Steve heard the man grunt again in pain as he was hit.

More police and prisoners poured from the building as several more wagons arrived. Steve looked over the chaotic scene, knowing it was his call and his paperwork. He wasn't going to let this one slide.

Later that night, the station room was packed when Steve arrived with Rizzo after a stop at Rhode Island General. Most of the officers involved in the fight were sitting at typewriters, hunting and pecking their reports. Looking up and then quickly back down at their reports, no officer spoke to Steve. Foley made eye contact with him and slowly shook his head as he returned to typing. The steady clicking rhythm of keys and ringing bells filled the unusually quiet room.

Steve rolled the form into the typewriter and filled out the date, time, and call number. He looked at the paper, the anger still roiling inside. He took several deep breaths to calm himself before he began.

> *Loud noise call. Upon reaching the residence, a female responded to the door. The female refused the officer's request to enter the premises upon which the officer forcefully opened the door pushing female occupant against the wall . . . .*

Rizzo read Steve's finished twelve arrest reports and then his injury report. The nose injury would give Rizzo sick leave for a couple of weeks with pay. He said nothing to Steve but dropped the report in the basket at the front desk as he left to change into civilian clothes. Rizzo was still angry, but Steve could hear him laughing as he boasted about the number of collars he would be credited for. One step closer to detective.

The prisoner was in a holding cell downstairs after Bouley's handiwork. *The perpetrator fell down all three flights of stairs trying to escape from the police* was the wording of Rizzo's report that Steve typed. He did not go downstairs, having seen enough tuned-up prisoners.

Steve typed up a separate report which followed the facts. Someone had to do it. It disgusted him the way bullies like Rizzo liked to beat on handcuffed prisoners.

"Logan!" the desk sergeant yelled into the room. "Captain Lynch wants to see you."

Steve turned around and went to the captain's office. It was dark and filled with stale cigar smoke. The captain was sitting at his desk, and a single green desk lamp shone on some papers. Steve waited by the door as Bouley rose from the seat next to the captain. Exiting, he eyed Steve and mouthed, "Fuck you."

"What was that shit tonight?" the captain demanded. He was twirling a yellow pencil between the fingers of his left hand.

"Sir?"

"Cuffing and re-cuffing the prisoner?"

"I used sufficient force to make the arrest. The prisoner was in my custody and was providing no resistance, as you taught us at the Academy. When I turned him over to the wagon, I transferred custody to the wagon so I put the wagon cuffs on the prisoner."

Lynch glared at him and took the cigar out of his mouth, as if he knew the answer to his next question. "Why did you do that?"

"I knew the condition of the prisoner when he entered the wagon, but I had no control over him afterward. I passed along custody; he no longer was my prisoner. It is in accordance with police protocol as you taught us at the Academy."

Lynch bit harder on the end of the cigar. Smoke came from his nose as the tip of the cigar burnt a bright red. Lynch began slowly, "Logan, legally and technically, you are correct." He paused. "But that's not how things are done around here. This isn't book learning." He glared at Steve, tapping the ash from the cigar without breaking eye contact.

Steve held his look, trying not to reveal that his somersaulting stomach made him feel like he was before the principal in grammar school, Sister Mary Bertha. Steve stood tall at attention, trying not to show any weakness. Technically, he was correct. He was following the rule book. The captain didn't have many options.

"Dismissed," Lynch snapped without removing the cigar. Steve saluted, pivoted smartly, and walked straight through the squad room, his shoulders square. The typing stopped as he passed. He was pissed and angry.

He sat on the wooden bench in front of the locker to change into civilian clothes. He put his pistol and holster into his tan canvas gym bag and was removing his shirt when a sharp blow to his left shoulder knocked him into the locker. Another blow, aimed at his head, glanced off his forearm as he raised it to deflect the blackjack. *What the fuck?* The locker room, hit from behind; would they really do that? His mind raced, trying to put the facts in order. Cowards, not willing to face him. He'd had locker room scuffles after intense practices before, but always face to face. He tried to see his attacker, but a boot landed against his rib cage, forcing a cry of pain from his lips. There was more than one, and he was on the ground.

From his side, he swung a clean leg sweep, catching one of his attacker's heels, causing Steve to fall back into the lockers on the other side of the bench. Could he reach his service revolver? Another blackjack blow to his back and then his arm caused him to curl more into a ball to protect himself. This was no college-boy argument. These were professional thugs. Why didn't he see it coming? He was pissed at himself. He never imagined that they would go this far.

"Fucking cowards," he screamed at them. "Come face me." He struggled to his feet, keeping his face in the locker for protection. His kidneys and buttocks were taking the blows. He was the tough guy when he played football in high school, never backing down from even the biggest linemen. Stay low and keep your feet moving. He wasn't going to give them the satisfaction of quitting. He kicked back hard, knocking the bench against the lockers. They vibrated and rang with a hollow, bell-like sound. The loud noise caused his attackers to pause, looking at the door, and Steve kicked hard like a mule, finding the knee of one of the men, who loudly cursed.

Another blow across the back of his legs with a baton caused Steve to crumple back to the ground. *Stay down,* he told himself. He wasn't going to win this one. With his right hand, he fumbled in his gym bag, looking for his gun belt.

"We protect our own, asshole." It sounded like Bouley, but even Steve's hearing was cloudy. "Don't get in the way again."

Steve felt the handle of his pistol and slowly surrounded it with his fingers. *I should finish it right now. They have it coming.* He knew he couldn't do it. It wasn't who he was.

"What's going on in here?" He heard the deep voice of the patrol sergeant.

And there was silence—that silence that existed on the force. He imagined the looks that were exchanged between the men as they looked at him, still on the ground. The college boy better understand the rules. Don't stand in the way, don't buck the system. He waited, and the silence remained. Hurting but more ashamed, he slowly pulled himself to his feet and finished dressing in civilian clothes. They had made their point, but it didn't change anything.

"Holy shit," Steve said later, slamming his hand on the steering wheel of his car. "Holy shit. You do the right thing and you get fucked." He had followed his instincts, not that it helped the poor bastard in the wagon. And he stood up to that prick Bouley, just to be ambushed in the locker room. He sat forward in the seat to keep the welts on his back from touching the seat. He would play along with them for now, but they had just changed the rules.

He drove up the hill, realizing he fought battles without a strategy for winning. What was his next step? Where could he go in the department? Not the chief. Steve wanted the satisfaction to remain, but he knew he had to be careful now. Now *they* thought he was afraid, and that was good. He would talk to Roxy—they would think it through.

Reporting to work the next shift, Steve was assigned a walking post. Crowley drove him in the patrol car north toward an area stated for redevelopment but currently wasn't much more than the remains of factory buildings in various stages of decay. Steve rode shotgun as Crowley drove slowly up north Main Street.

"How's Rizzo?" Steve asked.

"She broke his nose, stupid bastard. But he's on paid sick leave for three weeks." Crowley nodded with a smile. "And tonight you get punishment post. That's Providence justice."

"I'm sure he doesn't want the street to know he got creamed by a chick," Steve said as he got out of the car. He enjoyed Crowley as a partner, even if he was a lazy cop. Their relationship was professional, and Crowley didn't avoid him. Steve trusted him not to fuck him over.

"I understand you met the enforcers."

"They have a name?"

"Not technically."

"Fucking cowards." Steve turned to Crowley, who continued to look forward out the front windshield.

"You're a good kid, so don't take risks. It's not worth it. Nothing's gonna change, believe me. They can burn you whenever they want— little dope found in your locker, planted at your apartment, slow radio . . . All sorts of shit can happen."

Steve liked Crowley. He breathed a little more easily. Crowley was looking out for him, and he appreciated that. "Thanks."

Crowley said change was impossible. That if Steve continued the crusade to change the things that he'd talked about, the enforcers would escalate the situation for him. He had to be smarter than them. He had been keeping records but not systematically. Now he would, and he would have to push in farther.

It was a cold March night with a light drizzle. Steve adjusted his gun and radio and pulled the collar of his coat up around his neck against the raw air. Walking along the desolate abandoned warehouse area, he had never given any thought to punishment posts. It seemed to be a waste of manpower since no criminal would be in this part of Providence on this shitty night. Any good scrap from these buildings had long been stolen. But he understood Lynch's logic—Steve had broken an unwritten code. He had not participated in savagely beating a man who *almost* took a swing at a cop because the cop was about to rearrange the man's wife's head with his baton. Steve had taken the man down, fought him into custody, and brought him to the van, but vengeance needed to be extracted somewhere. Steve had stood up to the sadistic detective. Steve hadn't stopped them, which he knew was the right thing to do, but he hadn't participated, either. And that *wasn't how things were done around here.* But it was wrong and had to move forward . . .

The new brick building next to Wriston Quad was graduate center lounge, an open room with sofas and cushioned chairs, the university's answer to the coffee houses on Thayer Street. Roxy, Liz, Suzi, and Bill were sitting on two sofas as Steve returned with two pitchers of beer. Several weeks had gone by, and he could comfortably sit again. He hadn't told Roxy the truth, insisting the bruises were from breaking up a fight in a bar. He waved off her concern, and she didn't press him.

"The woman is the stronger sex," Suzi said, her light-brown hair pulled back in a ponytail. "We have always had to be because we're the ones who carry on the species."

Steve saw a thin young man sitting with a group of students. In the darkness, he couldn't be certain but the look and shape . . . He looked like that sneaky Gaeta. Was he working undercover here? Who was the target? Could it be that he was being set up? Or Roxy?

"If that's so, why do guys do all the fighting?" Bill asked. He looked like an auto mechanic with thick arms and strong rounded shoulders and a hell of an attackman.

"Men start wars; they should fight them. You men are just little kids. I can beat you up. No you can't, yes I can . . ." Liz mocked, turning her head on her long, thin neck.

"It's you men who made up rules to control women through religion, law, and physical power." Roxy was adamant and animated. "Western society is afraid of us and terrified of our sexuality."

"Not me. I like your sexuality," Bill protested.

"Pig," Liz said, smiling at him.

"Laws kept us from voting, inheriting property. It's all the male insecurity, and we want equal rights." Roxy's eyes were lit with the fire of another cause.

"But the male provides protection. We're the ones they send off to war," Bill said. "Not that many of us want to go to Nam."

"And you still need us for procreation," Steve added to stir the pot.

"I'd just need to cut off a penis and keep it in a drawer for when I felt a need for it," Liz said, rolling her eyes at the general laughter. "Well, it would be easier than these complicated relationships and dealing with you men."

"It might shrivel up a bit," Suzi laughed, bringing her hands in closer and closer together.

"You know what I mean, It's better than . . ." Liz flushed, and the other girls laughed.

"Masturbating. Come on girl, say the word," Suzi encouraged.

"Yes, that word. Oh, my mother would die." Liz led them in laughter.

"Guys do it all the time, right?" Roxy turned to the boys.

Steve met Roxy's eyes, and they lingered for a few seconds, exchanging a moment of awkward silence.

Cal moved to the upright piano and started playing show tunes. First he played "Getting to Know You" then moved into "Oh, What a Beautiful Morning." Roxy joined him on the bench, playing "A Few of My Favorite Things" while the kids sang the words they knew and hummed the rest. Cal followed with "Camelot," and Roxy answered with "Some Enchanted Evening," which Steve sang along with. He still found Roxy's intensity intoxicating. She was never lukewarm; she was either passionate or totally disinterested in a subject. Whether she was protesting the war or advocating for equal rights for women, she was never on the fence. And she had discovered how to have greater influence the longer she'd been at Brown. Whether it was equality like eliminating the Pembroke diploma or establishing co-ed dorms, he knew she'd be relentless. He was still her security, but their fire had dimmed.

Looking around the room, he could hear students fervently rearranging facts and solving the problems of the world while sitting in the safety of a college campus. Pontificating about equal justice as written by the great philosophers, their ideas were dreams, lofty dreams. Don't bother with the boring details or getting your hands dirty. He had protested the war but now was trying to do something more. He was once part of this world—he had enjoyed it, believed in the completeness of it. But his world had moved on to deal directly with the unpleasant truths of the grownup world.

The welts on his back still ached. He wasn't nostalgic, but he had a sense of satisfaction at having made the transition from the lounge to the street. A smile reached his face as he thought how the captain expected him to back down. But now he had to be careful. He wasn't going to give in. He was more determined now to figure out the puzzle like the one Durk had to do. He set his teeth tightly with a slight shake of his head. There was a way.

"I didn't know you could play the piano," he said as the group settled back into their final beer.

"Audrey and I used to play all the time. My father would sing along, making up words when he didn't know them." She was smiling at the memory, but the smile faded. "I haven't played since she died." He squeezed Roxy's left hand, and she covered his with her right. They would have the night together.

As they were leaving, he motioned Bill to come close. He saw Gaeta, who did not seem to recognize him. Now he was worried.

"See that skinny kid with the Bruins jersey on?" Bill nodded. "He's a cop, working narcotics. Tell people to steer clear of him." Now he would be on guard, even here.

Steve hung out at O'Malley's after the evening shift. Dylan, Meatball, and some of the other guys from the Academy were regulars. Steve didn't know if he could trust them.

They talked about high school rivalries and Red Sox heroes. Steve drank with them but wasn't really a part of the conversation. They weren't his memories—being a Yankees fan wasn't going to win him any friends. These guys were his age, sharing the same dangers and boredom on the street, but he wasn't one of them. He was an outsider. He could talk sports and be diligent about the job, never trying to take credit for the increased production of his partner. But he wasn't one of them, and they knew it. Some envied his education; some resented it. Not being from Providence didn't help either because he had no back channels like Meatball did.

They knew how the captain felt, and about the locker room. So he was marked. Each of these guys would have to make their own decision on right or wrong. Steve had made his decision.

"Sorry about the other night. Didn't mean to put you in a tough spot." Steve said to Foley as they were leaving.

Foley shrugged. "You were following procedure."

"That's not how the captain sees it."

"What are you trying to do, get yourself killed?" Foley stopped in the night air.

Steve looked him straight in the eye. "Some of this stuff is just wrong, and it doesn't have to be. A little sunlight is a great disinfectant."

"What the fuck are you talking about?"

"I mean all this shit—the tuning up, the payoffs, the special favors. We work for the people, not the brass."

"Too much beer, man." Foley opened the door to his car. "You are trying to get yourself killed. It's bigger than you."

Getting into his car, he couldn't remember how many pitchers of beer they had consumed. Crossing town, he rolled through each red light, confident that he couldn't get a traffic ticket in Providence.

Stumbling up the stairs to the apartment, he dropped his keys twice before he opened the door to the bedroom, aware that he was making too much noise. Falling heavily into a chair, he tried to take his shoes off, but his revolver bounced on the wood floor. Roxy sat up with a start, turning on the small reading lamp next to the bed.

"Sorry. I was trying to be quiet." He tried to enunciate the words, aware he was slurring.

"It's four a.m. again, and you're drunk," Roxy said, flipping off the light and lying down. He quickly stripped off the remainder of his clothes, getting into bed beside her. He felt an erection as he touched her back. He nuzzled up to her neck with kisses as he wrapped his arms around her, reaching for her breast. Pushing his hand away, she flipped to her stomach. He gently stroked her back, following its curve to the tight round mounds of her ass, which he caressed, running his finger between the cheeks. He continued to probe lower to her vagina, parting the lips with his finger, looking to stimulate moisture.

"Okay. You won't let me sleep," she said, turning over on her back. "Come on." She guided him into her, but as he built a rhythm, she was passive, waiting for him to come. When he finally exploded inside her, she pushed him off.

"Sleep it off," she said and turned again to her side with her back facing him. He lay on his back, knowing that he had fucked her but they hadn't made love. Why didn't she didn't want him? He needed her so badly. This wasn't what he wanted—he thought he would be her hero. He should tell her more, the anxiety bordering on fear that he kept hidden in his macho shell. He wasn't going to let them beat him. And now he felt he was a stranger even to her.

He touched her shoulder as he cuddled to her back. Then the beer captured his brain, and he fell quickly to sleep.

At the next roll call, Steve thought he would still be on foot.

"Logan, you lucked out tonight," the sergeant said. "You ain't walking. You're sitting. Captain wants these reports typed up by morning."

He handed Steve a large pile of handwritten documents. Steve looked at the sergeant, who shrugged.

"Better than freezing your ass off."

Steve retreated to a desk at the far side of the room to be away from the door, the booking desk, and anyone coming in to do a report. The office was better than the stupid punishment posts where no one was alive but little animals scurrying in the darkness. Maybe learning to type in high school was the great skill his father told him it would be. He put an incident form in the black manual Underwood and began filling out the report.

239 Williams Street. 12/12/71—Dangerous conditions, disturbances. Police responded to a call at residence. Found house and steps badly maintained. Tenants caused disturbances and potential fire hazards observed.

249 John Street. 12/21/71—Police responded to call of loitering and possible drug dealing at the location. Hazardous conditions and violations of occupancy laws observed. Landlord not in residence.

239 Williams Street. 1/4/72—Call for illegal gambling ring, potential numbers operations being run. Numerous suspects fled upon arrival by the police.

249 John Street. 1/18/72—Disturbance with weapons reported. Upon arrival, police observed a suspect fleeing the scene. Observations show property in disrepair and potential fire code violations.

249 John Street. 2/28/72—Accompany fire department on inspection of property. Numerous fire code violations. In addition the property is an active nuisance and the scene of illegal gambling and drug activities.

Steve finished up the reports and approached the desk sergeant. "A lot of activity in Fox Point," Steve said.

"The Portuguese. Always arguing with each other. Using those knives. They should go back to where they came from."

"Up by me. Don't remember any calls," Steve said, knowing that he paid special attention to any calls on the hill. It didn't fit the normal pattern, which was mostly breaking and entering or family disturbance calls.

The sergeant shrugged. "I only remember the important ones."

"What calls?" the little round newspaper man asked as Steve was returning to the squad room.

"Nothing. Just some disturbances in Fox Point," Steve said, turning to Toad who was leafing through the day book, looking at the arrest records.

"What's different about them?"

"You ask a lot of questions."

"Of course I do. I'm a newspaper man. Larry Sutton, *Providence Journal*." The man stuck out his hand.

"Steve Logan."

"The college boy. You were partnered with Rizzo the night the chick broke his nose?"

"Yeah. You've got your facts straight. We met a while back."

Sutton lit a Lucky Strike. "Yeah, I keep track of Rizzo. He's still the bully boy he was in high school, but now with a gun."

"Not your favorite cop?"

"Tough to have a favorite in this town. I've been covering the department for five years, and I'm still amazed at what passes for normal."

"I've had to get used to a new normal in my life."

"We should have coffee. You'd be an interesting story."

"Not exactly what I need right now."

Sutton nodded and handed Steve his business card. "Maybe coffee."

Steve put the card in his pocket. "Yeah, maybe coffee." This could be useful.

On his way home, Steve turned up Benefit Street toward the college. The street was very much the same as it had been in the eighteenth century. Sturdy clapboard colonial houses stood side by side, the front doors located right at the sidewalk. Each had a different historic plaque with the house name and the date it was built. The sidewalks were still brick, and the street lamps were electric replicas of the old gas lanterns. Freshman winter, Steve had walked down the street in the snow and felt transported back to the American Revolution.

Coming to Waterman Street past the court house, he took a sharp right and headed back to Fox Point. It was the long way home, but he had to take a look. He drove past 239 Williams Street: a modest two-story house with clapboard siding on a corner with several apartments. He turned the corner. 249 John Street. It backed up to the house on Williams Street. It was also a wood frame three-story floor-through apartment building. There were no signs of activity. One block away was the new university parking garage. He didn't remember many incidents here, so this was making him think. Who would be interested in a couple of nondescript rental properties? There was more to the reports he had typed. He tore a page from his incident book and wrote down the house numbers. He would check the call log. It didn't add up.

"It's me, not you. When I met you, you were so different from any boy I knew. You were smarter and fearless. Not that you aren't now. But I was more . . . more . . . scared, frightened. Being away, here, for the first time, with all these rich Ivy League kids. You made me feel safer." Roxy was wearing a blue flannel shirt, her hair pulled into a ponytail.

"I'll still protect you," Steve protested.

"Yes." She tossed her head at him. "Because of you, I don't need so much protection. You've helped me grow up. More than ever, I know what I need to do and what it'll take to get there."

He nodded in agreement. "You do, and you will."

"And you—what are you becoming?"

"What do you mean? I'm here to . . ."

"What about those dreams to see the world? To write in a little café in France, to climb Mt. Kilimanjaro, to travel?"

"All still there. When we get married after you graduate, we can . . ."

"Do you hear yourself? I didn't come to Brown to find a husband. That was another generation. I've got plans and a medical career. I'm not going to be anyone's housewife. And you're too young."

"But you said . . ."

"I know me more now. That was high school speaking. And I thank you for it." She was holding his hands in hers; he looked down at her short nails and the rough skin she'd gotten from lab work.

"But I know that there are . . ."

"We need more space. Your hours are . . . I want to concentrate more . . . I don't need to hear any more stories about arresting people . . . poor drunks. We're living in two different worlds now."

He retreated behind a tight smile, hurt but knowing that the threads between them were frayed. While he wanted to deny the reality of it, he sometimes felt awkward with their friends. He hadn't told her about the locker room because he didn't want her to worry. He wanted her love, not her pity.

The arguing went on for several weeks, but it was the silence that got to him. He would come home after the midnight shift, have a few beers, and watch old movies in the living room until Roxy turned out her study light. He lay in bed next to her, wanting to touch but not knowing if he could. He was a stranger in his own bed. Love—he had never thought about love ending; rather, it was just going through an adjustment, growing into something more profound. He realized that she felt more secure working in the bio labs, doing experiments. It was the world she wanted to be in. He wanted it to always be them; he couldn't imagine it differently. He couldn't let it just slip away. Maybe this job was changing him more than he realized. He needed to do more. He turned his back and fell into a fitful sleep.

He'd been dreading this moment for weeks, but he knew that their relationship had changed. He was more on edge, more disconnected from her daily life, her studies. School seemed more trivial to him now, but she was even more driven as the courses got harder. And work had changed. He noticed the way conversations stopped or quieted when he was around. It would be safer for her. The captain would certainly send another detail to check on him—when, he didn't know, but he was sure it would happen. And with the grass, it would be an easy bust. It would be better if he moved.

She was right: their lives didn't match, so dating rather than living together would make more sense. He had no desire to date anyone else. He knew he was rationalizing because he loved looking at her while she slept. He would come home in the morning and watch her, peaceful, as her chest rose with each breath.

Steve finished putting his clothes in black garbage bags. He stacked several boxes of books and his lacrosse stick and gloves by the door. Roxy was sitting on the bed.

"I'll leave the albums." He motioned to the stack of records against the wall. "Since you have the stereo."

She nodded.

"I'm invited to listen to them whenever I want, right?"

"You still have your key," she said, her eyes slightly moist. "It's just temporary, until the end of the year." She shifted her weight as she moved to help him carry a bag. Steve sighed heavily, picking up his bag and nodding to her, his lips tight.

"Are you still going to come to the Gloria Steinem lecture with me?" she asked. "It's Thursday."

"Yeah, I'm on midnight. You won't mind if I come in uniform?" He smiled crookedly, forcing her to smile, too. It was just what she needed, bringing a cop to a campus feminist speech.

"Great. I'm sure the girls won't mind as long as I keep my Chauvinist Pig on a leash," she said, smiling.

Several days later in the squad room, Steve reported for duty. Was it going to be another night on punishment post or desk duty?

"Logan, walking post 12," the sergeant said in his clipped official cadence while looking at Steve.

"Yes, sir."

As they walked to the patrol car, Crowley said, "A step up for you this time—Atwells Avenue. At least it has people on it."

Crowley drove from the station to the Italian area on Federal Hill.

"Couple of things," he said in the fatherly tone he had begun using. "I'm not going to jeopardize my retirement, but a couple of pointers in this neighborhood." He pointed to Spatuzzi Bakery.

"Vincenzo gets in about four a.m. to do the baking. So when you need to warm up, go around to the back door; follow the smell of the bread. Knock. Also, there are two restaurants that always have someone lurking around." He pointed to a store with few windows and a brick storefront with a *Vending Machines* sign over the front door. "Make certain you check that one on all sides for any sign of break-in."

"Who wants to break into a vending machine store?"

"For a college kid, you aren't very smart. That's Patriarca's place."

Steve leaned back, the side of his mouth turning upward.

"Raymond Patriarca. Head of the New England mob. That's where his family operates from."

"Here? In Providence?"

"Easier to do business. Overhead is lower, I guess. The brass upstairs makes all the decisions and the big money."

"But," Steve hesitated, "who'd want to break . . . I mean, mess with them?"

"Still not very bright, college boy. The Feds. Upstairs wants to know if the Feds are bugging the place again. Just let me know—I'm just the messenger boy. I don't know shit and don't want to know shit."

He was getting tired of Crowley's career advice on how to avoid the brass and any hard police work. Steve didn't want to be like Crowley, working toward a pension without getting hurt.

There were a series of shops with windows and recessed doorways where Steve could stand and see the street without being seen himself. After twenty minutes of watching the rhythm of the neighborhood, he walked the street slowly, practicing twirling the baton like an old-time beat cop, looking into each of the different stores. There were two jewelry stores, several clothing stores, and the bakery.

He stopped at the butcher and watched the live chickens as they pecked for lost scraps in their cage. Hanging in the window were large round provolone cheeses, *prosciutto di parma,* genoa salami, and other staples. It brought back memories of visiting his Italian grandfather in New Jersey. Now he just needed the rag man with his horse and wagon.

A liquor store, a fresh-pasta store, fish market, several restaurants, hair salons, and pizza joints filled out the blocks.

He walked around the Vending Machine store. In the back alley, there was a thick steel door. Smoked windows were ten feet high off the ground in the side alley. Steve shook the door; it seemed padlocked from inside. He completed his sweep and walked down to the next alley, which was filled with the smell of garlic and tomatoes. A late-model car had been parked behind the Italian restaurant. The windows were steamed up, and he could hear grunting and groaning. He tapped on the window with his flashlight. No response. He tapped harder. The window rolled down, and a young Italian man with his shirt off looked up at the flashlight. Steve shone the light at a young Italian girl, holding it on her bare breasts.

"You gotta go. Can't stay here," Steve said, quickly moving the light in an act of modesty as the girl tried to find her blouse.

"Do you know who I am?" the Italian man asked aggressively.

"No, but you can't stay here."

"Fuck. You don't know who you are messing with."

"No, but you can't stay here." Steve stood tall and used a modulated voice.

The man got out of the car and took a step aggressively at him. The girl had pulled on her blouse.

"Shit, you fucking rookie shit. You don't know who you are messing with. Fuck. My old man doesn't pay you guys for this kind of shit." The man was not much older than Steve, with wavy black hair and a slightly pocked face. He had a thin mustache, like an old 1930s movie star.

"I don't know anything about that," Steve replied, trying to keep his voice calm as he braced himself for a physical confrontation. The baton was in his right hand.

"Fuck you don't. You stupid moron. But the brass sure as shit does—and they will shove it up your ass."

"Get back in the car, and take your girlfriend somewhere else," Steve ordered, firmly but not harshly.

"Girlfriend . . . Shit," he smiled and lowered his voice. "She's just the waitress. I thought I'd bang her and be gone, but you fucked it up."

He reached into his pocket, took out a roll of bills, and put $100 into Steve's pocket.

"Now you know who I am, so no misunderstanding next time." He got back into the car. "And you didn't see nothin' tonight."

Steve watched the man drive away. He slowly walked down Atwells Avenue, shining his light into some of the stores. He knew the mob had influence, but to him, they were just stories. Now, he knew more. The mob had ties at the highest level of the city. Steve was looking at just the daily corruption, the payoffs. But this was bigger and more dangerous.

At four a.m., the thud from newspaper delivery trucks dropping bundles of the *Providence Journal* on the sidewalk was the only sound. The cold concrete had penetrated his shoes, and he wriggled his toes to improve circulation. Without gloves, the tips of his fingers had turned a pale pink.

He walked around to the back of a two-story wooden building and knocked on the door. A middle-aged man in a white apron opened the door and let him into the bakery. The ovens were hot, and the smell of freshly baked bread enveloped him. The baker and his helper were rolling dough, patches of flour on their aprons and faces. Sheets of stainless steel baking pans filled with different shapes sat on the counter, waiting to enter the hot womb of the oven.

"You new here?" the baker, a small wiry man, asked with a thick Italian accent.

He put a hot, hard crust roll in front of Steve.

"Just from the oven. Better than in the old country. You are still a young man. I don't know much; I'm just a baker, but you have to remember family and hard work. And always, always be honest with your family and friends. Let me tell you a story."

The room was warm, and the smell of baking bread was comforting. Steve leaned against the wall, knowing this was going to be a long fight. The warm roll melted in his mouth, releasing his tension and warming his body. He watched the baker work methodically on the dough until he slipped the long baking sheets into the oven. The man sat next to Steve.

"There were these two brothers, Luigi and Giuseppe. So one day Giuseppe says to Luigi, 'Luigi, my brother. I need some money. Can you help me out?'

"Luigi says, 'Giuseppe, you're my brother. I trust you. Open the top drawer. There is one hundred dollars.'

"Giuseppe says, 'Oh Luigi, you're truly my friend. I'll repay you.' Some time passes, and Giuseppe comes to Luigi and says, 'Luigi, you're my brother and my best friend since we are children. I need some money. Can you help me out?'

"Luigi says, 'Giuseppe, you're my dearest brother. Of course, I'll help. Go to the top drawer.'

"Giuseppe goes to the drawer and opens it. He says, 'Luigi, Luigi. There's nothing in the drawer.' Luigi comes over and looks in the drawer and then looks at Giuseppe. 'What, you forget to put it back?'"

He paused. "Always remember to put it back in the drawer."

The baker beamed and turned back to his oven. Steve looked at him gratefully as he ate a second warm roll. It wasn't that simple for him anymore. He had faced up to the captain, but now he would continue to pay for it. This baker and all the other small-shop owners deserved honest, competent police. Was that too much to ask? He didn't know if it was possible. Who could he trust? Maybe Dylan—he was a stand-up guy, but Dylan was getting married and seemed he was getting comfortable in the system. Maybe others?

Crowley was interested only in getting to retirement, as were most of the older cops. They had made their peace with the system. Everyone had their little spiff. But there were so many people who were part of the system—how many, he didn't know, but it was becoming clearer to him.

The baking bread created a warm embrace. He would be visiting the baker and listening to his stories more often. And he would find out more about how Federal Hill tied into downtown.

C H A P T E R   1 1

IF YOU COULD
READ MY MIND

Steve was invited to the weekly basketball game with some of the former cadets at Dylan's elementary school playground only when they were short on players. Steve wasn't a good player, but the wisecracks created some sense of camaraderie. There were a lot of deliberate hard fouls aimed at him, but Steve shook them off or returned them in kind. The exercise took the edge off with some guys, but none of them wanted to be seen as his buddy. He knew he was marked, and the upper ranks were still trying to figure out what to do with him.

"I heard the teaching gig is over," Dylan said as they walked from the court, his red hair slick with sweat. He picked up his Red Sox sweatshirt and draped it over his shoulders.

"Yeah, last week. Krieger called me into his office. He said some teachers objected to a cop with a gun in the school. Also some shit that a White cop was trying to entrap the Black kids."

"Right, like you'd be that smart," Dylan said.

"I was beginning to enjoy it. Getting to know some of the kids—they're not as tough as they think they are. It was a break from this shit, and the money was okay."

Dylan punched him in the arm, and they squared up into boxing stances, exchanging a few slaps between feinting and ducking. "How'd Krieger take it?"

"He's smart; made it look like the mayor's idea. I don't think the chief ever liked the idea. He probably wanted uniforms there. It was another political clusterfuck. So they declared the project a success because there wasn't any bad press."

"He owes you one."

Steve, Dylan, and a few others from their recruiting class sat on the courtside bench with some beers.

"Hear Thompson wrecked a cruiser drag racing a State Trooper down 95. Fucking captain is ballistic." They laughed. "It's gonna be a month of paperwork, which will keep the captain off our asses for a while."

"You ever think about where this is going?" Steve asked Dylan as they walked to the parking lot. Dylan had put on some weight since the Academy—too many donuts and sitting in a car for eight-hour shifts.

"No. I'm trying to live," Dylan said. "Better here than in Nam. And as a cop, twenty and out with full pension. I'm married, so we'll have a bunch of kids, a house in West Warwick, and a small boat to go fishing on Narragansett Bay. What could be better?"

Steve smiled at him. "I could think of a few things." Dylan had gotten married in February. Steve was the only one from the team not invited to the wedding. Even Dylan needed to think about his career first.

"Me, too, but I'm not good enough to play for the Sox." He smiled.

"Does any of this stuff ever bother you?" Steve asked, not wanting to be too direct.

"Like what?"

"You know, the stuff you see or don't see happening around here?"

"I try not to give it too much thought. Not my business."

"But does it bother you?"

"I learned in the Army you can't buck the system, so why beat your head against the wall? I'm a good soldier. Nothing I can do to change it." He shrugged noncommittally.

"Something strange happened when I was on desk duty. I was given a bunch of reports to type up from handwritten notes. And there were a series of incidents in Fox Point that didn't make sense. Like a half dozen calls in a couple of days, including Fire Department reports. When did we start writing their reports? Do you remember a lot of calls?" Steve looked at Dylan.

Dylan thought. "No, not really, but sometimes the shifts blend together. Whose notes?"

"Not sure. The captain left them for me. No one signed the reports. So I went by the houses, the locations, on the way home. Four houses, back to back, close to the university."

Dylan said, "Leave it alone. You know you don't like the smell of it. It isn't the kind of question you ask around here. You didn't see it."

Steve thought Dylan was basically an honest cop who might care. "You think that it could go as far up as . . ."

"You're talking upstairs stuff—big money. Way above your pay grade. I hear serious money is being made in real estate by certain people. Redevelopment. It depends upon who you know. It's more than the weekly scat."

"Yeah, but who?

"That's what you don't want to know. You heard about curiosity killing a cat?" Dylan got into his car.

"This is big stuff. We could break it wide open."

"We? Not me. Leave it alone, Steve. You have enough problems. You didn't see nothing."

Steve knew it was there. He had hoped Foley was cop enough to help. He could use a partner to watch his back. But it wasn't to be.

Steve stared at the green faces, hundreds of them on the bare oak floor of his apartment. Picking up each pile of Franklins and Grants, he stacked the bills like playing cards and put them into white legal envelopes writing the time, place, and amount in his florid Catholic school script. Ten thousand dollars, almost his annual salary accumulated over the months. His father had never seen this much cash.

He carefully concealed each envelope in a book and arranged them on the pine shelves held up with cinder blocks. *War and Peace* had five envelopes in it; *Sun and Steel* and *Plutarch's Lives* had four; *The Quiet American, Slaughterhouse Five,* and *The Feminine Mystique* each had three, and so forth.

Looking around his studio apartment, the only improvements he had made were bedsheets on the windows to keep the sun out so he could sleep during the day. When he had been partnered with that bastard Rizzo, the money flow had increased. He was trying to fit in—if taking the money was fitting in. Running out of hiding places, he needed to make another trip to the bookstore.

His plan wasn't fully formed yet, but the direction was clearer. The brutality and money came from the top. The money was part of the proof, but he needed more—that would be the hard part. Being a cop at first was a grand adventure, but now he would have to step up his game since the captain had raised the stakes singling him out for punishment posts. Most of the cops just did their job—at least the job as it was defined. But it had to change. He wanted to discuss it with Roxy; she would pick holes in his thinking.

She had altered the course of his life. He knew love could do that, but this was more than love. She was the reason he was here, counting money—not that she knew about the money. They had questioned law school after Kent State, but he took this different path. Now he had this new plan that they needed to discuss. It would put them back on track.

His unmade bed was a thick piece of foam covered with grey sheets and a thin blanket. In the galley kitchen at the end of the room, his plate and cup from dinner were in the dish rack, waiting to be reused tonight. He always washed his dishes immediately to keep the cockroaches at bay.

Stretching his arms over his head, he bent forward and placed the palms of his hands on the floor, keeping his knees locked. He dropped to the floor and counted out fifty push-ups, followed by a quick fifty sit-ups.

Today, he was working the four to midnight shift. And now he was playing their game; they thought he was whipped. And he was getting more of the rewards.

Walking to the closet, he took the brown uniform shirt and pants from the dry cleaning bag—no more t-shirts and jeans. Handcuffs, extra bullets, ticket book, black flashlight, Billy club—he went through his checklist. Even now, the clean-cut face and crew cut in the bathroom mirror was a stranger. If the Vietnam War wasn't going on, would he be here? How had it come this far so fast? Being sucked into the machine was creating a different Steve. He would carefully fight back every day, or they would own him.

After work, he would stop by to see Roxy. She'd be up studying, probably just back from the library. It was still their apartment despite what had happened. He still had things there, including his stereo and albums. But it wasn't over. They just needed more space. He needed to tell her what he was thinking and planning. At least she was in less danger without him living there. Now that he had some money, maybe they would travel when school ended: Europe, Paris.

It was Thursday, so he could ask to spend the weekend because he had a lot to tell her. But he was getting ahead of himself. He should have questioned the New York cop about how he dealt with the looks, the low whispers, and the distrust. He was tense, not knowing if he was being set up. And he didn't trust his antennae. He would always be the college kid, the outsider, and Captain Lynch still hated his guts. But there was some color on the pieces. Big money was being made up on Federal Hill and steady money from scat around town. There was something about real estate, but he didn't know what.

In the coffee house on a second floor overlooking Thayer Street, Professor Whitney was sitting on a low chair in the far corner. There was a plaintive folk singer on a low stage, singing to the empty house in the early evening.

Professor Whitney stood to greet Steve. "This is a pleasant surprise. I thought you were off to law school."

"Thanks for meeting me. I am, in a way," Steve smiled as they sat down.

"Going to night school?"

Steve was amused. "Yeah. Sometimes double shifts."

Whitney looked confused by the statement.

Steve smiled, guessing what Whit's reaction would be. "I'm a cop."

"What?"

"I'm a Providence cop."

Whitney leaned forward, looking hard at Steve as he seemed to be processing the information. Steve smiled because he knew it was not what Whit expected to hear.

"A cop? In Providence? Here?"

Steve nodded.

"I never—no one ever." He was mouth moved sideways, searching for a response. "You don't go to school here to become . . . Whatever made you . . ."

"You said you have to become involved to make a difference."

"Yes, but that was theory. I mean, this is . . . Well, I mean this is different."

He took out an unfiltered Gaulois cigarette and offered one to Steve, who declined. The professor blew perfect smoke rings as he thought.

"So you've acted on the theory, not just read the books. Brown students protest and then go to grad school or back to their inheritance." He tilted his head at Steve. "Interesting. Different. But Providence—it's such a . . . a low-class . . . What you must have to deal with. Do they even know how to . . ."

"It's a different city up here on the hill. But that's not why I asked you to meet me. I need help or need to know where to go for help."

"How can I help?" He picked a piece of tobacco from his mouth.

"This police force is corrupt, like in New York. Maybe up to the top. I don't know, but I see it all around. You've read about the Knapp Commission in New York. I met Sergeant Durk during the strike, at the teach-in. He said you have to change it from the inside. It could be the whole city; I don't know."

Steve took out a stack of envelopes.

"People give you a hundred bucks to not see things. Not for not doing anything—for not seeing things. The money is bigger on the top of the force, where they can actually do or fix something." He took a quick look around, having given it much thought while walking the punishment posts. He didn't trust anyone on the force and wanted to know his options when he spoke to Roxy.

He spoke more quietly. "Now, I know Brown has some big political connections. If I could get this information to the right people . . ."

"I'm a political science professor, not a politician. I know the theory . . ."

"Yeah, I know the theory too, Professor. But now I can name names. This isn't textbook out there. I'm not the most popular guy on the force."

"But what do you want me to do?"

"You have access to people. I need to know, need help in how to get this information to the right people. To people I can trust."

Whit paused and looked Steve over intently. "I'll see what I can do."

Steve finished a coffee in the Blue Room and walked through campus, past the statue of Marcus Aurelius on horseback, toward Thayer Street. There were signs on both sides on the path and a crowd of students around the Soldiers Gate. The signs said *Save Fox Point, Stop the Greedy Landlords,* and *Help Fox Point.* Steve saw Roxy in the crowd, which had gathered in front of a platform made of milk crates. They stopped milling as a tall man in long grey robes, with a full, bushy beard, took the megaphone. It squealed when he tried to speak. He looked at it and started again.

"Students, thank you for being here and allowing me to interrupt your studies. I'm Father Hugo Schmidt. I'm a Franciscan friar from Brazil. My parish is in Fox Point, a short walk from here. We need your support. Our parish is mostly poor Portuguese immigrants who work hard for their dreams. God has a special place for the insignificant, the unimportant, the defenseless. The poor have a special place in God's eyes. The spirit of the church is the line to universal salvation and eternal life, but our temporal role is to assist the helpless in their rights to dignity and justice.

"We need volunteers to help us with English and to fight the greedy landlords who are trying to drive them out of their homes. We need volunteers, and we need money. I know we're not in church, but," he waved a battered bush hat, "I have brought this hat from my home in Brazil, and it will have to do." He smiled at them, a St. Francis beatific smile, waiting for the birds to land on his outstretched arms. "We thank you for your support—and you are all welcome at Sunday Mass."

Steve moved to Roxy's side. She put money in the hat and looked at Steve, who reached into his pocket for a ten-dollar bill. With Roxy pleased at his gesture, they exited through the gate. Steve wondered if this Fox Point issue didn't tie into the reports he had typed. "What was that about? Are you getting involved in another protest?" Steve asked.

Roxy said, "The landlords in Fox Point are raising the rents to drive the immigrants out. Where will they go? And where would the country be without immigrants—it's not fair."

"That doesn't make sense. Who do they think will replace them? Millionaires or poor college kids? It's not a great area." Steve found there were no incident calls related to the reports he had typed. Was there a connection?

"I don't know. But Father Schmidt believes in the liberation theology that says the church is morally and socially obligated to actively help the poor reach economic and political equality."

"But you're not Catholic. I am."

"It doesn't matter." She looked at him with a little girl's serenity and trust in how tomorrow will be better. "I can't just study. We can all help, even if in little ways."

"Can I buy you dinner tonight? We can go to the—"

"Sure," she said. "But it will have to be early. I still have work to do."

"I'm off Saturday. Want to go to Newport?"

"Yes, that would be fun."

Steve approached University Hall, the original college edifice that sat on the Brown campus, formerly known as the *College in the English Colony of Rhode Island and Providence Plantations*. The history of the school, its connection to the Brown family and their involvement in the slave trade, and the school's name were hotly debated subjects by students and faculty while he was at school.

Dean Donald Toll IV sat behind an antique desk from the 1840s. His office was appointed with pieces from the two centuries of university growth. He was dressed in a conservative grey Ivy League suit. Steve entered the room dressed in khaki pants, cream shirt with blue knit tie, and his camel hair blazer. Professor Whitney was sitting in a wing chair to the side of the room. There were two guest chairs in front of the desk.

Dean Toll stood. "Mr. Logan. Please come in and have a seat. Professor Whitney has told me what you've done with the fine education you have received here." There was a sneer in his Boston-accented voice. "And now you are having problems. Obviously, you are not currently a member of the university community, but as you are an alumnus, I'm willing to listen, but I am not certain what help I can be."

"Sir, thank you for seeing me. I'm asking for advice as well as help. I've been a police officer since graduating last year."

Dean Toll leaned back in his chair and looked to the side, not directly at Steve.

"I've learned a great deal about the real world, especially about Providence. It's not what you see from the Hill."

Dean Toll cocked his head.

"It *is* a different world down there."

"Yes, I know."

"Well sir, the police force is full of corruption, from the ordinary cop taking a free meal to protecting the New England mafia from the Feds. I think it might go all the way to the top. Brown is sophisticated, and you and the people here know all the politicians, so I thought you might be able to help or point me in the right direction to get help. You see, my plan would be . . ."

"Young man, while I might admire your idealistic instincts, this is not anything that the university would want to be involved with. We have a good relationship with the Providence community. We have worked hard over the years to maintain that relationship so that our mission of educating young minds goes undisturbed. We do not get involved in local politics. It cannot result in any positive outcomes for the university."

"But I'm talking about big-time things here. Things that are wrong, that shouldn't be going on. Something should be done."

"I'm certain there are, and I agree that someone should look into such things, but it is not the role of the university to be involved. That is all we're discussing here."

"Well, I thought you might be able to help. To steer me in the right direction . . ."

Dean Toll tilted his look down at Steve, the sides of his mouth turned tightly upward. "Perhaps you should talk to the U.S. Attorney or the FBI. This would be in their jurisdiction."

Steve had thought that there would be more encouragement. "I thought I might get some introduction or some help in sorting it through."

Dean Toll stood abruptly. "I am so sorry, but the university cannot get involved. I sympathize with your experience but really can't help you." He ushered Steve to the door. "I am so sorry to cut this meeting short, but I do have a pressing appointment."

As Steve was leaving, Toll flung a final dart. "If you go to law school, I'm certain you could learn how to address these types of issues."

He shook hands and pushed the door closed, but it didn't close all the way. Steve paused by the door.

Dean Toll harshly asked Whitney, "What possessed you to think the university would ever want to get involved with the local police? We have an agreement with them—we police ourselves and cooperate with them. We have significant expansion plans that require the cooperation of city officials."

He paused, correcting his tone to more conversational. "I mean, if we start stirring things up, it wouldn't be good for our students. Do you know how many of our students could be arrested on alcohol and drug charges alone?"

Steve heard a note of surprise in Whitney's voice. "No, but I can imagine."

Toll continued, shuffling some papers. "We can't do anything specific, but we need to create some distance from the university and that kid. Is he one of those wild-eyed radicals—SDS? You know that type. I don't want a trail leading back here, back to the university. You understand? How do we let that type into this school?" Steve heard disgust in the Dean's voice.

Steve turned and left as Whitney opened the door.

Another domestic-disturbance call, the third one of the night. Saturday nights were like that: too much time together with too much alcohol, and soon people were at each other, throwing obscenities and physical objects. Steve had already learned that you never knew what you were walking into. Crowley was affecting his limp up the dimly lit stairs to the two-family house, allowing Steve to take two steps at a time. Steve had noticed Crowley was slow to take calls or show up on scene when he didn't have backup. Only months to retirement.

"Police. Open up," Steve said.

"Don't you go near that door." He could hear the man's angry voice, followed by some curses and a hard slap, sending a body against a wall with a thud. The brass doorknob turned, and the door began to open. The man's voice screamed again.

"I told you not to open that door."

Steve heard the sound of a strap, and a woman cried out in pain. He jammed his baton into the partial opening before it could close. The man pushed hard against the door, once, twice. Steve timed his push to when the man had let up pressure for another push. Ramming his shoulder into the door and driving with his legs, the door exploded inward, throwing the man back down the hallway as the door slammed against the wall.

Steve saw a woman in her early fifties, with a doughy face and arms like water wings, looking dazed. Her sleeveless yellow housedress looked stained with mustard, coffee, and red wine or blood. She was seated on the floor near an aluminum kitchen chair.

"Get up," Steve ordered the man as he grabbed the three-inch-wide leather belt from the man's hand. "Get against the wall." The man, dressed in a blue denim work shirt and white painter's pants, had several days' growth on his face and thick, bushy eyebrows. His eyes were bloodshot and angry.

"What's the problem here?" Crowley pushed past Steve now that the danger was under control.

"This bitch is a . . ." the man started, but Steve pushed him against the wall with his stick.

"We're not talking to you."

"He hit me," the woman said. "He goes crazy. I burnt the meat, and he threw the dinner at . . . Then I tried to clean it up but . . ." Her words were slow and slurred.

"Okay, ma'am. Are you hurt?" Crowley asked. It was another domestic disturbance, which meant lots of paperwork if the EMTs were called.

She lowered her head, crying and revealing a large red welt on her neck.

"Let's go, buddy. We're going for a walk," Steve said, taking the man by the arm. He didn't understand the wife beating, girlfriend beating—the violence and ferocity of it. And the way the women would take it.

"No, no," the woman protested. "I'm not gonna press any charges."

"'Course not." Crowley said in disgust, passing by Steve and out the door. "Let's get out of here."

"Buddy, take a walk. Cool down," Steve told the man.

"She better have this place cleaned up by the time I come back, or else . . ." The man turned back to the woman.

"Or else what?" Steve said putting his face inches away from the man.

"I'll teach her to . . ."

"Teach her, tough guy." Steve rammed his stick into the man's solar plexus, causing him to double over. "And you'll use this?" Steve held the leather belt up for the man to see before he slapped the man hard across his back with it. Again and again, Steve hit him, driving him to the front door.

"No, no! Don't hurt him. He's all I got," the woman cried and screamed.

Steve drove the man down the stairs with blow after blow from the belt. Pushing him up against the front porch, Steve put the belt in front of the man's face.

"Don't make us come back, because if we come back, I won't be so nice next time. You'll get a little ride around town that will make even your teeth ache. You understand me?"

The man nodded in agreement and began walking down the darkened street. Steve returned to the car. Crowley sat in the driver's seat, lighting up a cigarette.

"You going to write it up?" Crowley asked with a look of satisfaction on his face.

Steve could feel the adrenaline slowly subsiding as his heart rate began to drop. He didn't mean to lose it, but the asshole deserved it. Why beat on a woman? He didn't get it. *He* was judge and jury tonight. Was this how the system worked—simple, effective? The man wouldn't forget him and might think twice next time. He had won a tough game, but the nagging realization that he had crossed a line lingered.

"Yeah, I'll write it up." It meant *domestic disturbance, husband left the premises*.

Steve and Roxy rode in the green Volkswagen on Bellevue Avenue in Newport, leaving the Gilded Age mansions. Steve had proposed the day trip from Providence. "Can you ever imagine being that rich?"

"Rich—is that an objective? Not for me," he said.

"But having an army of servants for your every whim. Even someone to dress you?" Roxy shook her head slowly.

"I can always be there to undress you," he said with a smile.

"You know what I mean—having so much money that this is a summer cottage. So unfair. Did you see the size of those safes during the tour? For the silverware?"

"But look what happened to them—their homes are all museums now. They can't afford them anymore. Help is not quite so cheap. I don't think I could ever be that rich." He turned pensive. "There are better ways to spend money than on parties."

"I'd like to try it for a while, you know. Being rich. Maybe not forever, but it would make things easier."

"When you're a doctor, you'll be set for life."

"Ten years from now," she exhaled and stared out the window. "I guess so."

"I'm working; we could find a nicer apartment. Get some real furniture, a place where you could study. We could even go somewhere on summer break. Europe, maybe Paris. We could find a little hotel on the Left Bank. Have coffee with writers at Café Du Magots. Find some paintings from an unknown artist in Montmartre. I get paid vacation now." His love for her was a constant ache. He'd do almost anything to make it work between them.

"It would be wonderful to see Europe."

"I'll buy you fresh *pain au chocolate* in the morning, and we can eat wine and cheese in the evening along the Seine."

"Now you're dreaming, but keep it coming." He saw a sparkle in her eyes as she thought about the offer. Why not? He had the cash. And it would be a new beginning for them.

As they reached the row of restaurants along the water, Steve parked the small car.

"Supposed to be the best seafood."

"It's so different down here. A world away from Providence."

"Once upon a time, a world away from everywhere. Only the rich need apply, unless you were a servant," Steve said.

They entered a nautically themed restaurant with rope handrails on the pier. Because it was early spring, it was not crowded. The table overlooked the harbor, which was filled with a mixture of fishing boats and a few pleasure-sailing vessels waiting for commissions.

"I've been looking at law school again. Maybe Boston; that way, I can commute. With my schedule," Steve said, trying to judge her interest. "I could go full-time in the day and still work. That way, I would stay in Providence but not just be a cop. I'd be back into the academic area, so we could be more in the same . . . have study dates again."

"Can you afford it? It would be good for you. You can't waste your life being a cop."

"Only nineteen and out," Steve smiled.

"What?" she said.

"Only nineteen more years, and I retire at full pension. I'll be only forty-three. That's how my one partner thinks. What do you say?"

She smiled at his little joke. "Yeah, right. Nineteen more years in Providence?"

He shrugged. "They have lobster on the menu. You ever have it?"

"Yeah, we have it all the time in Columbus. Generally with mayo. What does it taste like?"

"Never had it either, but it's supposed to be the best. When in Newport, eat like the rich people."

"Okay," she said and turned serious. "You know how much I want to get into a good med school. To be a doctor who discovers cures for people, who doesn't let people die young." Her hair fell over her left eye as she shook her head. "I don't want people to be left alone. I will not let good people like my sister die." Her eyes became misty.

"I know you do." He reached for her hand, but she pulled it back.

"What are you doing with your life? Are you becoming one of them? Have you given up on your other dreams?"

"I'm trying, but it is more complicated than I thought it would be." Next time, he would tell her about the money, the locker room, and his plan. Tonight was about them.

"I will help. I will be a doctor. You *should* go ahead with law school."

"I can wait to apply, see where you get in, and find a school close by. Until then, I can work and save money." He wanted her back with the unconditional first love they had. It was what he wanted, but they had to get to the next phase of love, where it broadens and deepens. He needed her thoughts as much as her touches.

"Don't put your life on hold for me," she said, reaching across the table and touching his hand.

The waiter arrived at the table with two whole lobsters, which looked like giant orange insects on plates. He put a plastic bucket containing two bibs and nutcrackers on the table. Steve and Roxy looked at each other and broke into giggles that they tried to subdue.

"What do we do now? Are there instructions?" She was choking on her giggles. "Ask for a side of mayo?"

Her smile banished the tension.

"You are my life. I'll do anything for you," he said.

"I know. Let's keep talking. I would love to see Paris."

Driving back to Providence, the A M radio played Creedence Clearwater Revival's "Who'll Stop the Rain?"

CHAPTER 12

I'M NO FUN ANYMORE

"You really fucked up again. No one has done this walking post in years. What did you do this time?" Crowley asked, letting Steve out of the car.

"Ran some Italian guy off who was trying to fuck a waitress behind the restaurant."

"Guess he was connected."

"So he said."

"You won't run into anyone here. At night, nothing's going on." Steve looked out over a stretch of barren land and three empty buildings with no windows or roofs. "I'll bring you coffee at two and four. Pick you up at seven. Captain Lynch is sending you a strong message. They're out to get you, kid. I think the dicks may be on you at home, so watch yourself. They protect themselves. If you're a threat, they will eliminate it." He nodded to Steve in his fatherly fashion. Steve thought he looked tired, as if weary and counting the days until retirement.

Steve acknowledged that Crowley had gone as far as he could in counseling Steve. He wasn't going to provoke the captain. "Some days, it's your turn in the barrel," Steve said. Crowley looked at him with puzzled eyes.

"Long story," Steve said.

Walking the barren landscape, a Grateful Dead song came out as a whistle. He knew he was tough enough to endure this type of harassment shit. His wasn't going down without a fight. But it was the stuff that they could do and not knowing who might be coming. He was glad that Roxy was safer. Were they going to set him up, plant shit in his locker? He didn't use the locker room anymore, and it was beginning to worry him. Did Crowley know more?

It wasn't his smartest move, staring down the captain. He thought he had put it in the past, being compliant and not putting up any more fights. But tactically, he hadn't thought through the consequences. The isolation in the station house was growing, as if he were infected with a disease. It wasn't any overt act, but conversations were shorter, the group at the bar was smaller. No one wanted to cross the captain, especially not for him. That was clear. The captain was making life hard for him, but so were the lifers. He understood the facts and had less and less to lose now. It was bigger than just the dollar payoffs for not seeing things. He and Roxy would get back together and . . .

Maybe Lieutenant Kreiger—now Captain Kreiger—could help. He'd done Kreiger a big favor, taking on the school assignment. Maybe he'd arrange a transfer, or at least turn down the heat. He stood in front of the abandoned building and looked up North Main Street as it rose up the hill. "I will get by. I will survive." The words came out quietly.

Driving his green car with a peace sticker on the back bumper after his four to midnight shift, he slowed down for red lights before driving through them, making sure no cars were coming. He knew it was bigger than just the payoffs—it had to reach to the top. He would have to do more digging and take some chances. Talking the plan over with Roxy would help him sort out his strategy. He drove to his old apartment and looked up at the window. The light was still on in Roxy's room. She was still studying so it might be a good time to talk. Pulling over, he climbed the stars, knocked on Roxy's bedroom door, and then opened it with his key. No one was there. He went down the hall to the living room and put on some water for instant coffee. He heard stirring in Cal's room and voices, male and female. Steve listened and then moved to the door and opened it violently. Roxy and Cal were in bed, naked.

"Shit, fucking shit. What the hell!" Steve roared as he looked at Roxy. "What the fucking . . ." He moved aggressively toward Cal, clenching his fists. The rage had overcome his confusion as the adrenaline pumped into his muscles.

Cal stood up, his eyes wide and his mouth pulsing and pleading, "Steve . . ."

Roxy shrieked, "Steve! No!"

Steve hit Cal with his closed fist, knocking him back across the bed, blood spattering from his face onto the wall. He drew his off-duty .38 and jumped over the bed toward him. Cal didn't move. Putting the gun in his face, Steve was trying to process what he saw before him. Betrayal, treachery, the snake. Never did he dream, think . . . Tune him up the way Bouley would, teach him a lesson he would never forget. Maybe he should pull the trigger and end it here.

Roxy scrambled on all fours to grab and hold onto his arm, but she was unable to move him.

"No, no. Steve, it's not what you think," she cried.

Steve looked hard at her and turned the gun to her. His hurt and confusion froze his ability to think. He looked into her pleading eyes. What could he do? He looked back at Cal, who had retreated to the wall, curling into a tiny ball. Steve stepped toward him, watching him duck his head in fear of another blow. He hit him with an open hand, ready to pistol-whip him. He should have let him jump off that fucking ledge all those years ago.

But he turned and slowly walked to *their* room. Wave after wave of guilt mixed with anger tossed his mind. How did it get to this? How did he let it . . .? Ambushed, alone . . .

He sat heavily on the bed and looked down the barrel of the .38 in his hand. End it here. What was the point? He didn't belong in either world. His life had all come apart. Noble idea—a bunch of crap. It seemed like a good idea to shake things up from the inside. Now what was left for him? Roxy ran naked down the hall to the room and jumped on the bed behind him.

"It was nothing." She was still crying. "We were studying, and then we got high. Steve, I love you."

"Yeah, sure. You and everyone in the world loves me. I'm quite the package these days." He studied the gun in his hand. In the mouth and it was done. Ended here on their bed, where it all started. She would have to clean up the mess and have one more death to carry around.

"No. I mean, forgive me." She wrapped her arms around him and began kissing his neck. He could feel the warmth of her body penetrating him. Her scent, so soothing, held him. How did it happen—why did he let it happen? If he hadn't moved out . . . He should have fought harder to stay. He looked at the muzzle of the gun pointed at his face. Would it make a difference to anyone? It just hurt so much.

"Yeah, I forgive you. Sure, why not." He let his arm and gun drop limply in front of him. It happened. He let it happen. What should he have done? With Cal, with Cal—that fucking snake. How could she? He was to blame. He never should have moved out. Give her space. Fuck it.

He tried to get up from the bed, but Roxy clung to him, silently pleading with him. He gently removed her arms from his neck, looking at her tear-streaked cheeks and her face covered with pain. He stood and slowly walked to the door. Turning to Roxy, whose eyes were pleading for forgiveness, he felt the fracture in his heart, the betrayal, the loss of his world. She was the only girl he had ever loved. He would never love like that again.

The cat's eyes were on both of them, but he could see and feel nothing but pain. Moving through the door, almost sleepwalking, he entered the hallway. Heather opened her door, dressed in a sheer nightshift. Her eyes met with his, and she mouthed, "I'm sorry you are hurt."

Steve nodded and sprinted down the stairs as Roxy sat on the bed, crying.

The next day, Steve was working the midnight shift. Having consumed a quart of Wild Turkey the night before, his head was pounding when he rolled out of bed at noon. Pulling on some gym shorts and a grey t-shirt, he stretched, trying to chase away the image of Roxy naked in Cal's room. How did it go so wrong? Lacing up his sneakers, he started at an easy pace toward the athletic fields. A few laps would sweat the alcohol from his system, he thought, but the image of the two of them kept returning.

He sped up the pace, pumping his arms hard, almost in sprint mode until his stomach began to spasm and his throat burned. Stopping, winded, he folded in half and nearly collapsed as the alcohol and eggs from the night before poured out his mouth in yellow waves, each one slightly less intense than the one before. He breathed through his nose, pushing the air down into his diaphragm while the yellow acid smell of his vomit caused dry heaves. He took a more leisurely pace back to his apartment, and after his shower, his body felt cleansed, but the images still turned over in his mind.

Retrieving his service revolver and holster from the hook, he threw them in his blue gym bag with his nylon windbreaker and badge. The police firing range was in the basement of the small shed next to the academy. Since graduation, Steve had tried to go once a week to shoot. Having never handled a gun before joining the force, he wanted to be good, and the only way he knew to get better was to practice. He called Tom Donohue, the range master, to make certain he would be there this afternoon. It was never crowded except before recertification.

Having the range to himself, he put on the sound control headset and settled into the second of five practice slots. With a box of one hundred rounds, he set the target of a man twenty-five feet away. With his loaded .38, he looked over the sight of the barrel, seeing Cal's head at the end of the range. Squeezing off six rounds in rapid succession, the bullets smashed into the paper.

He reloaded and pumped twelve more holes at the torso before pulling the target back and replacing it with a new one. Now he saw Roxy, and he slowly tried to plant bullet after bullet in the target, not wanting to spoil her beautiful face but to needing to inflict as much pain in her as she had in him.

His anger flew with each shot, but he knew it was his own pain that he was projecting on the target. With the third target, he could see himself, Roxy shooting the bullets at him, wounding him in the arms, shoulders, and head before putting six bullets dead center on his heart. When he finished the box of ammunition, he holstered the gun and removed the headset.

"Look at you," Donohue said from behind him in the observation booth. "You usually barely hit the target. You've been practicing?"

Steve felt self-conscious at the hatred he had just leveled at the targets. "No. Guess I was concentrating better. I wanted to hit what I'm aiming at."

Coming on duty on Rizzo's day off, Steve was partnered with Crowley. After coffee, they took a leisurely drive through the district, writing parking tickets for cars left on the street overnight. The parking fine revenue was worth over a million dollars a year to the city, and Captain Lynch was on a tear to break the record this year. They were also counting street lights that were out; it was going to be a night of high-value police work.

"Car 28, report of a fire. 288 Thompson."

"Roger that," Steve answered. He was at the wheel so Crowley could doze after a long day at his tow-truck job. He pulled the car to the front of a two-story wood frame house that once was a single-family residence, but Steve guessed it had been cut up into numerous illegal one-room apartments. Black smoke was coming from the front window on the second floor, and several people in nightclothes were milling about in front of the building. Steve and Crowley got out of the car, but there was no sign of the fire department.

"Old Mr. Novak is still in there." A stooped grandmother in a stained blue bathrobe pulled on Steve's arm as he reached the curb. "He's on the second floor in the back. He can hardly walk anymore." Her eyes were wide, staring the house as little red flames licked near the roof.

"You live here?" he asked.

"On the first floor. I bring him soup and do some shopping for him." The intensity of the smoke pouring from the building increased. The color was getting darker.

"Where the fuck are the firemen?" Steve asked Crowley, who was busy pushing people back onto the sidewalk.

"Fuck," Steve said. "Second floor in the back . . . How many apartments are there?" he asked the woman.

"Two on each floor."

"Fuck it," he said to himself, looking at Crowley, who didn't move to help. He sprinted for the house, holding his black flashlight in front of him. Entering the door, the wall of smoke slammed into his face, absorbing the light from his beam like a black hole. He crouched to a half run to get to the stairs, which were thankfully in front of him. He touched the railing. The wood was still cool, so he used it as a guide to the second floor. The dense smoke drove him even lower to the ground.

"Mr. Novak! Mr. Novak!" he yelled, looking for some sound to guide his direction as he felt the steps level off at the second floor. The heat from the fire felt like the blast furnace at the mill in Ohio. It caused sweat to pour down his forehead. He coughed but yelled again, "Novak!" He hoped the man hadn't already died from the smoke.

"Here, here." Steve could hear the whisper from his left. Now in a duck walk that he had last used in football practice in high school, Steve pushed forward, repeating the man's name and following the sounds. When he reached the room, it was not totally filled with smoke yet, so with his flashlight, he found the man lying on a bed.

"Can you walk?" Steve asked.

"No," came the feeble reply. Already, the visibility in the room had been cut in half, and Steve felt his throat burn from the smoke. Having never been in a fire before, he searched for the flames. He was certain the century-old house had a kindling point where the entire place would burst into a giant funeral pyre for them.

Grabbing Novak, Steve slung the old man across his back, holding Novak's head in his right arm and his feet in his left. Returning with a quickened duck walk, the pain in his knees cut into his lower back. He realized he was now racing against his own ability to consume oxygen as the thick smoke caused him to cough and gag.

Carefully, he felt for the stairs with his feet, not wanting to fall down the flight. He wondered what Roxy would feel if he never came out again, if he died a hero trying to save a man. She would cry, but would she understand? Would he rather die here than have to go back and face her again?

He coughed again, gasping to hold onto consciousness as he slowly descended the stairs, the old man on his back, pain beginning to cut into him, but he refused to quit. There was noise in front of him, and he quickened his pace down the stairs, sprinting in his own mind to the finish line. Two large figures in masks and black coats were at the door; they grabbed his arms and pulled him and Novak out into the clean night air. He looked up at the firemen, giving them a weak smile.

"Little smokey in there?" the fireman asked, pulling on his oxygen mask as he led the hose team into the house. A medic came over to Steve and gave him an oxygen mask of his own. The street was now filled with fire trucks, police cars, and a crowd of people from the neighborhood. The flashing blue, red, and yellow lights from the vehicles bathed the scene in a cacophony of colors. He stared weakly in the truck mirror at his raccoon mask of soot. He closed his eyes; he wanted to see her.

The sounds of the fire grew with crackling and shouts from the fire captain. The hose brigade beat a hasty retreat as the captain directed the fireman to wet down the adjacent houses. Yellow flames shot from the front windows, black smoke pouring out from every crack in the building. The firemen poured water on the lost house to contain the damage as the sounds of collapsing walls sent fire flares high into the sky. Steve was transfixed with the power and the speed of the flames.

"What the fuck were you thinking? That's not our job," Crowley said as he drove Steve to Rhode Island General for a physical.

"Guess I wasn't thinking," he said, but he was only thinking of Roxy.

The International House of Pancakes, with its bright blue roof, was a stroke of genius when it opened on Thayer Street. It was the only place near campus to get food after midnight that didn't have wheels on it. It was full of bleary-eyed students or stoned kids with the munchies. Two weeks had passed since that night with Roxy and Cal. He had stayed away, but he couldn't not see Roxy. The shock was gone, the pain continued, but was it under control? Not wanting to lose her, he was beginning to blame himself for not seeing what was happening to them. But to do it with Cal? They sat in a booth in the small end of the restaurant, eating pancakes.

"I know it's going to work out. I mean, I'll wait and wait," he said, trying to convince Roxy that he was past the pain of that night. "Look, we'll get married when you graduate, and then we can move. I . . ."

Roxy's face was drawn; there wasn't any sparkle to her eyes. "I don't know. I don't know. I'm confused. I need more space; I need to figure out who I am, what I am . . . I need . . . time. I don't know what happened. How can you say you still love me after . . ." Inverted parenthesis formed as she drew her eyebrows together.

"No, I mean, fine. I'm not trying to . . . I'm trying to understand. I'm trying to give you space. I did what . . . I don't know what I'm saying. I'm trying. I'm here for you. I won't leave you. I miss you."

"Are you listening? I don't know. I still have eight more years before I'm a doctor. It's what keeps me going. You have to understand—watching my sister change from this wonderfully supportive person who I could fight with about clothes on the floor to a shrunken shell who I loved more each day. I couldn't wait to see her, yet I hated the idea, knowing how powerless I was. I'm closer now. I'll do it. You are, I'm . . . It's different. When you're in that uniform, I can hardly look at . . . You've become part of them . . . I don't know if it's you or me."

"But you, you . . . I mean, we talked about . . . You thought it would be . . ." Steve understood but didn't want to accept the distance. She needed him less as her confidence and maturity increased. And he was trying to dig in, to stop her love from slipping away, but he was only making it worse. He knew she felt guilty, but what could he do?

"I don't know—it's not the same. Things, you need to be going somewhere. To have bigger dreams than marrying me. I need to do this on my own."

"Would you have told me about Cal?" he asked, looking hard at her to try and see behind her words.

"I don't know," she said, cocking her head to the side, a dark cascade of hair covering one eye. "Would you tell me? Did you ever cheat . . ."

His mind raced to that day with Annie Chamberlin, blond, Main Line. It was in her dorm room last fall. They had met in class. She was a year behind him and when he saw her struggling with a box going into her dorm, he had gallantly carried it to her room. They had flirted over the years, but when she closed the door, stripped off her Lacoste shirt, revealing her small, white breasts, and kissed him hard on the lips, pushing him back onto her single dorm bed, he was shocked. But he returned her kisses, her expensive perfume filling his head as his guilt mixed with the unexpected desire. When his fingers touched the soft wetness between her legs, his penis hard with expectation, he stood up abruptly, leaving Annie on her back, glaring at him. "I can't," was all he said as he pulled his shirt on and raced down the stairs to the open air.

Steve was beginning to tear, sensing she was feeling guilty about her betrayal. "Yes."

She stopped and stared hard. "Yes, what . . ."

His heart was racing with fear as he tried to decide what was the right answer. "Yes . . ." He hesitated. "Yes, I did," he lied, hoping she would feel better about her guilt. But the moment the words left his mouth, he knew it was the wrong decision. Her face, which was turned quizzically to him before, now had sharper edges around her mouth and eyes, as if chiseled by a master sculptor.

"Who? When?"

"Annie Chamberlin." He compounded his mistake, hoping she could imagine how it could happen. But he was wrong again.

"How could you? That pushy bitch. Would you have told me if you hadn't? How could you?" Her angry tone cut deeply into him. He was trying to make it better, not worse. She gathered her books, blinking her eyes as if to hold back tears.

"We need to talk. There is something I need to tell you. My day off is tomorrow." He realized his plea was badly timed.

"That's not a good idea. Not now. I'm so . . ." She got up, and he sprang to his feet, putting his arms around her, hugging her tightly, but she went limp and pushed him away.

"This weekend? I'm not working Friday night."

"We'll see."

He watched her go out the door and realized that she was gone. Did it die or just slowly ebb away? He knew he couldn't put the magic back in the bottle, but maybe he could recapture or reinvent them. She was still young, hadn't seen the real world. Maybe . . . he was trying to think of a way to recreate himself for her. Bigger dreams? She was right, but now, on the force, he was living in the present. He had bigger plans and nothing to lose.

He should have told her more about his plans and what he was trying to do. She would be proud of him. But the time to tell her had passed. She would see it as a desperate attempt to look heroic. He needed to do it, not just talk. Now, he needed to stay here in Providence with her but without her. He would let her set terms, he would be patient. He looked at the empty cup of coffee, knowing there was no refill.

Several weeks passed before he saw Roxy again. They walked down Hope Street toward Fox Point as the neat historic houses around the university changed to two and three-family working-class rentals. Fewer people were on the street, and broken glass and overflowing metal trash bins reinforced the changed social status. Experience had taught him that the population was transient and distrustful of the police.

"Thank you for coming with me. I was a little nervous going alone," Roxy said, holding on to his arm in a playful way. He smiled, feeling a genuine warmth return from her. The weeks had passed in painful silence since their meeting at the pancake house. Without her, he was very alone.

"No problem," Steve answered; pleased she had asked him to join her. He didn't want to miss an opportunity to spend time with her, even if it meant listening to the Brazilian priest again.

"It should be interesting. They're trying to organize a community-wide boycott, something to really punish those greedy landlords. If the merchants complain, then they will know it's real," Roxy said.

"As long as it's not violent," Steve said, hearing himself speaking against a protest he would have joined as a student. "Captain Lynch doesn't like protests."

She looked at him and shook her head.

They entered the one-story wood storefront that was being used as the parish hall. The room was set up with bare metal folding chairs, the type he remembered from his grade school auditorium. He had liked volunteering to help the custodians clean up after school events, folding each chair exactly, getting into the rhythm of putting them back into the rolling rack until the auditorium was ready for gym class.

Metal venetian blinds covered the windows, concealing the group from the casual passersby. Steve knew he had passed the building a hundred times, but it had never attracted his attention or interest.

The room was filled with Portuguese working men and women of varying ages, dressed in thick clothes against the cold air. A group of young students in a variety of pea coats and watch caps, long hair, and boots, leaned against one wall. Steve and Roxy were to the far side of the hall—Steve's clean-cut look stood out in the crowd. He held onto Roxy's arm a little tighter.

"The time has come for increased action," Father Schmidt said in his booming missionary voice. "We can no longer tolerate the actions by these capitalist landlords. We must fight back."

"Alleluia," the room responded in almost complete harmony. Father Schmidt changed to Portuguese, and the crowd was wrapped around his words. The students were looking toward the door, so the priest switched back to English.

"The landlords are doubling the rents when they come up for renewal. Sometimes tripling to say get out, get out. We don't want you. We must organize our protest to put pressure on it where it hurts the most." He motioned to his pocket. "Right here."

Doubling the rent—it didn't make sense unless the landlords would get a better return. Basic economics. Steve wondered if the series of bogus calls—the reports he had typed—were related. How? He would have to figure it out.

"Right on," a young man said from the side.

"But Father," a woman in her early forties, her face creased with worry and poverty, asked, "What do I do when they come and tell me to leave? Where do I go?" Her pleading voice had a sense of desperation.

"You will not be dispossessed," Father Schmidt said in his Portuguese/German-accented English, raising his voice on the last syllable. "We will protect you."

"We'll protect you with force." A young man raised his arm in a clinched fist salute. "Fox Point is our home."

"*Sim, Sim, nosssas casas.*"

A number of the other men raised their arms and nodded adamantly.

"We'll burn 'em down before we give 'em up," a couple of the young college students shouted, jumping to their feet to show their support.

The priest held up his hands to quell the restive gathering. "We don't need to resort to violence *yet*. But we can appropriate their property for the good of the working man. We can demand justice from the ruling class by overthrowing their privilege." The priest continued with his speech about how God was with them in their struggle against oppression.

Steve leaned over to Roxy. "Isn't that kid with the green cap the head of the SDS chapter? What's he doing here?"

She looked at him. "They want to overthrow the capitalist imperialist government in Washington, but they want to begin it here."

"This is Providence," he said. "Nothing big starts here. They'll just create trouble."

"They will stand with the working class."

"Like me?" He was amused at her touting the pseudo-Marxism of the priest.

"Aren't you the establishment now?" she asked, looking back toward the priest, who was wrapping up his speech.

"We will begin the boycott on Sunday after Mass. No more purchases from the local merchants. We will be organizing van trips to the Star Market each week. We will also run a food coop out of this parish house. We'll make it hurt them."

"Hallelujah," Roxy said, standing as the crowd chanted. Steve surveyed the parish room, filled with a revivalist energy to take on the landlords. *What am I doing here?* he thought as the puzzle turned over in his mind. It was as if he were undercover and learning about a protest before it began, but the reports and Fox Point stuck in his mind. If the community was coming together to protest, then there had to be a pattern—someone was looking to push these people out. He would dig deeper.

The bell on the beige rotary phone rang loudly next to the foam mattress on the floor, rudely waking Steve.

"Hello."

"Is there a street address that goes with this number?"

"Huh, who?"

"I know you don't live in that walk-up, so do you mind giving me the address?"

"Tommy?"

"Shit, you're detective material."

"Yeah, why—where are you?"

"I'm in Providence, and my dime is about to run out. Address?"

"485 Waterman Street. Apartment 2R."

Ten minutes later, there was a pounding on the door. Tommy took off his sunglasses as he entered the darkened apartment.

"Living like a vampire?" He walked to the window and opened up the bed sheet curtains, letting in streams of light. Tommy looked around the bare apartment with the desk and chair, foam mattress, and milk crate dresser-bookshelf combination. "They don't pay you to be a cop?" He sat in the only chair. "Shit, I bet your prison cells are better furnished than this."

Steve was still in his athletic shorts. "I haven't gotten around to decorating it yet," he apologized, realizing how Spartan the place really was. He only ate there and did his one hundred push-ups and sit-ups every day.

Tommy was tanned and dressed in a green silk shirt and cream linen trousers. The size and weight of the gold rope chains around his neck had increased. His dark curly hair had some blond highlights, and he wore a gold ring with diamonds on the middle finger of each hand.

He began to move around the room nervously. "Not even a stereo? The divorce must have been a . . . the bitch get everything?" He looked at Steve contemptuously. "Shit, I have a sound system that could blow you through the wall—big KHL speakers and a thirty-five-inch television. Get dressed. I need something to eat, and this apartment is starting to depress me."

They got into Tommy's new maroon Monte Carlo SS. "This thing can fly. Four-fifty-four V8," Tommy boasted. "You still drive that insect?"

"Yeah, gets me to work. What brings you to Providence?" Steve asked the question but really didn't want to know the answer.

"Business. A friend from Long Island put me in touch with a kid at Providence College. Gonna meet him this afternoon. Come along; I could use the company."

Tommy pulled the car into a parking lot near the diner on Admiral Street.

"Tommy, I shouldn't be doing this. I should be busting you."

"Relax, brother. Nothing's gonna happen. And if the shit goes bad, you get to bust these kids and become a hero."

"That's not what I mean. You got to get out of this business."

"Who am I hurting? It's supply and demand. If I don't sell it, someone else will."

Steve was trying to be the big brother, but Tommy had always lived on the edge. "That's not the point. You know it. Cops are busting kids like you all the time. You'll make a mistake, or someone you're selling to will and they'll nail you."

"Look, I'm making great money, and I deal only with friends or friends of friends. Be cool. You just sit in the booth. If these kids know I'm not naked, they won't try anything stupid. Now look mean."

They entered the diner, and Tommy eyed the room, quickly picking out two nervous college kids in a booth by the window. Steve chose the last booth in front so he had his back to the wall and could see the parking lot. He could feel his .38 dig into his side as he slid into the seat.

A tall, thin boy with acne on his face and bushy brown hair nervously approached them.

"You Tommy?" he asked with a thick Long Island accent.

"I said you couldn't miss me." Tommy looked around at the few working-class patrons. The boy sat. "My name is Willie, you know Hank. We went to high school together in Lynbrook. He told me . . ."

Tommy cut him off. "Enough information. You cool?"

The boy looked hurt.

"Business." Tommy lowered his voice. He looked conspicuous in this place in his Florida clothes

"Yeah, sure."

"Okay, listen. I'm going to the men's room. You go back to your friends and come back to me alone." He gave the kid a hard stare until the kid nodded and got up.

Tommy watched him talk to his friends. He looked at Steve. "Watch my back."

He got up casually with a gym bag in his hand and walked to the men's room to the left of the counter. The tall boy followed with a backpack. Several minutes seemed like hours to Steve, who was watching the parking lot and the diner.

If there was a sting, he would have recognized it by now. He knew most of the cops by sight. And Gaeta was doing the undercover college thing. Steve had seen him up at Brown again, and he'd heard he'd made a bust at PC.

He shifted nervously as the waitress refilled his coffee and scanned the parking lot again, trying to look down the street to see if any cars might be parked out of view. Tommy came out and motioned him to go as he dropped a twenty-dollar bill on the table for the two coffees. Getting into the car, Steve saw the two college kids with their backpack exit and scurry excitedly back toward campus. He checked the street; no one followed.

"Easy ten grand," Tommy said, driving back across the city with Steve directing.

"You got to stop." Steve was emphatic. He was afraid for him, knowing how they treated drug dealers in Providence. But he knew there was this burning anger in Tommy that was always just below the surface. Tommy always was showing Steve his money, his clothes, his car. Steve had tried to reason with him, but the money now possessed him. Money—it just wasn't that important to Steve. He had a bookcase full of it.

"I'm not hurting anyone. Just supplying pot the market needs."

"Yeah, maybe. But now you're in my town, and it's not a good idea."

"And why is it illegal? Someday it will be legal again. It's a weed that makes people feel good. And in the meantime, I'm going to get rich." He smiled with satisfaction, but Steve was not pleased with the answer. He knew Tommy would fly into violent rages as a kid. Now he seemed consumed with money.

"Staying the night?" Steve asked as they returned to his apartment.

"Not in your shithole." They laughed. "No, I think I'll start back to Tampa. Maybe I'll stop somewhere on 95 past New York. How's this cop shit going for you?"

"I'm not the most popular guy on the force. It's a regular thugocracy—tough to compete."

"You gotta watch out for yourself. No one else will." Tommy shook his head and took a small bottle of white powder from his pants. He did two quick snorts with a small spoon.

"What the fuck, Tommy?"

"Just a little coke. It will keep me going till Virginia." He looked around Steve's apartment again. "What a waste. You gonna do something with your life?" He motioned around the room. "Expensive education and all?"

"Yeah. I got to clear up some personal things."

"Forget it. No bitch is worth it. There are so many of them out there. Come visit; I'll show you how to live." He smiled. Steve smiled too; Tommy was always the ladies' man.

"Tommy, be careful." He was worried Tommy was spinning out of control; coke was hardcore. "And put something back in the drawer."

"Huh?"

"A story this Italian baker told me—you got to put something back. I'll tell you the whole story next time."

"Steve, thanks for the backup. I really appreciate it." He offered him five hundred dollars. Steve refused the money.

"What's a big brother for?" he asked, wondering when he would see Tommy again. He looked around the room. Tommy was right: it wasn't much to look at. It was time for the fourth quarter, and he had to dig deeper. The pieces were there, and now he had to concentrate on putting them together.

CHAPTER 13

DOCTOR MY EYES

"Is the university buying more buildings in Fox Point?" Steve asked, sitting in the coffeehouse that he and Whit liked to use for their meetings. The professor continued to absorb Steve's point of view, which was so different from anything he encountered on the Brown campus.

"I'm sure they are always looking for property." He smoked his Galois while he drank his espresso. "The long-range plan is always expansion. We have the medical school beginning. And I'm sure they want to expand the science and engineering sections. I even heard they want the Bryant College property."

"And they're offering top dollar?" Steve didn't think the professor knew much, but he did hear things.

"I don't think everyone would agree with that assessment. I understand the relationship is a little strained right now."

"You mean people won't sell at the offered price?"

"So I understand."

"But the university has friends?"

"So I understand."

"Do you know more?"

"Is this an official interrogation?" The professor shifted in his chair uncomfortably and looked around the room.

"Sorry, Professor. Guess I fall into professional mode." He sipped the coffee. His face relaxed as he took a deep breath. "I can't seem to fit it all together."

"Is that part of your job?" Whitney asked. "Or are you looking into things on your own?"

"I told you what the department is like, but is it the entire city, even Brown?"

"Are you surprised? Do we need to discuss the nature of virtue or the venality of politics and politicians? I may be too idealistic about how the system should work, but for how it actually works, follow the money." Blowing small smoke rings from his cigarette, the professor tilted his head back so the rings rose to the ceiling. "I've never had to look at corruption this close. Ancient Rome is easier to dissect."

"Doesn't it bother you to know that you could do something about . . .?"

"Bother me, maybe. Do something? I'm afraid I'm too comfortable to want to rock any boats. Sign a petition, participate in a march—all protected by tenure. *You*, however, there might be hope." He took a long drag of his cigarette. "You read about the cop Serpico, who's been helping Durk and the Knapp Commission?"

"No." Steve shook his head. Between the job and Roxy, he had stopped reading the paper every day or even watching the news.

"He was shot in the face during a drug bust. There seems to be suspicion that he was set up by other cops. In fact, his partners didn't even call for help; it was some guy who lived in the building."

"Is he dead?"

"Somehow, the bullet missed anything vital. He'll live, but no one will ever know the true story. You understand what they can do—cops can get killed on the job. You understand what you are doing?" The professor raised his eyebrows while letting out a stream of smoke from the side of his mouth.

They shot a cop. Actually pretty easy. He thought about the number of times he was first up the stairs or the first into a room. *Bang.* He would never know what hit him. All the more reason for secrecy. But he could see it happening.

Whit passed Steve a business card, face down on the table. "Why *did* you become a cop?"

Steve read the card and nodded appreciation.

"I ask myself that more each day. Not to change the world. Maybe to make it a little better. Maybe to prove to . . ." He hesitated, not wanting to bring Roxy in as an excuse. "Prove to myself that I wasn't B.S.—like most college kids."

"How is it turning out for you?" The professor leaned in again, and Steve shifted his shoulders backward.

"Not exactly what I thought. I've got a few ideas. But we'll see how it works out."

"One word: Serpico."

After the professor left, Steve looked over the card, thinking hard. If he took this step, he couldn't go back. But go back to what? Things had to change and he might be able to help them, even a little bit. He dropped the change, into the pay phone and closed the door.

"U.S. Attorney's office," the voice on the other end answered.

"Yes, Agent Adams, please," Steve said.

At the Blue Room, the small café on campus, Bill and Heather, in a cotton dress and headband, were sitting with Steve in a booth.

"Life gets weird as you get older. You think you know stuff, but you don't." Steve shook his head.

"You took the jump off the cliff without looking how far down was. You regretting it yet? Ready to do something saner?" Bill's curly black hair was uncombed and his long mutton chops, as usual. Steve liked Bill's steady presence in his life. Their upbringing on Long Island was similar. Bill was one of the few people he felt comfortable talking with about the job. "I was thinking about Roxy. I don't know how, where I screwed it up. I stayed around, didn't go to law school. Finally have a little money to treat her better, but everything is worse. How do I get through to her?"

He looked at Heather.

"You can't make people love you; it comes from within. And we change. You've changed, and so has she. She's not the young, vulnerable girl you met. She's become a woman." She smiled as if she had said something profound.

"No, but I'm the same guy."

"In your head, but not in your outer being. Your karma is disrupted, more aggressive, more demanding."

"She means you're more of an a-hole than you used to be," Bill said, cutting her off with a chuckle.

"Fuck. That's a lot of help."

"Roxy is searching, too. She's growing, expanding, discovering her womanhood—we all are and always will be changing. Trees grow through rocks, looking for the sun, light, and air," Heather said with a practiced patience.

Steve looked at her, not on the same wavelength but happy she was listening. "Yeah but, but sometimes it's hard."

Heather stroked his hand gently with her rough potter's hand. Steve gave her a weak smile. She was beautiful as a night sky—ethereal and beyond comprehension. Her warmth was genuine and an antidote to the cruelness of the street.

"But it's not that simple anymore. I have to make some decisions. Decisions about . . . things. About her and me." He became pensive, thinking about the card the professor had given him. Now there wasn't any excuse. "Stuff I can't take back."

"You have to do what's right, what will ease your karma." Taking both his hands, she looked intently at him without blinking her pale blue eyes. "You'll do what's right because that's you."

Her eyes were calm and almost peaceful. She radiated a security he hadn't felt in a long time.

"You guys hungry? I could really go for some Italian," Bill said. Heather nodded with some excitement.

"I know this great place on Federal Hill. All the mafia guys eat there," Steve said as he pulled his hand away from her. "It's got a great history. It once had this big plate glass window so you could see the tables and the people eating. One day, a guy gets a phone call. When he goes to the booth by the window, two guys with shotguns kill him right through the window. Classic mafia hit. Right out of the movies. Now it's a brick front with some high windows for light."

"Cool. You know all this history stuff." Heather jumped up, her long arms wrapping a scarf around her bare shoulders.

Steve thought for a minute and patted the waistband of his jeans. "Let's stop by my apartment on the way. I forgot my wallet."

Picking up some bills and a letter in the mailbox on the way up to his apartment, there was a thick envelope marked *Peace Corps* that he slowly turned over in his hands. He opened the package, and all the paperwork was confirmed. Andy had written several times saying how much he loved the Peace Corps. Putting the package of material in the drawer, Steve pulled out his off-duty gun.

What the fuck am I doing? he thought, tucking the gun inside his waistband. *I'm going to dinner with friends, and I'm carrying a gun.* He paused and looked critically at himself in the mirror and shook his head. *What the fuck am I doing?*

He had made his decision, but now he had to carry it out. He didn't have a plan when he joined the force, but now it was clearer what he would do. Roxy would see—she would be proud. He returned slowly to Bill and Heather, who were waiting in his car.

"All set. Let's eat."

Sitting in the small carrel on the third floor of the Rockefeller Library, Steve looked east at University Hall, waiting for the midnight closing of the Rock. He remembered many nights spent fighting to stay awake after practice to finish a paper. Dressed in a t-shirt, jeans, and a dark blue windbreaker, he looked like a typical student carrying a small backpack. With the closing call, he slowly exited the Rock, waiting at the foot of the stairs until all the students had dispersed in different directions back to their dorms and apartments. Tonight was the night. He had been watching and waiting for weeks, trying to get up the nerve, but it would be tonight.

He walked slowly past Van Winkle Gate across the front of the green, looking for any straggling students. Ascending the steps to Manning Chapel, he concealed himself behind one of the Greek columns, waiting. His heart was racing, knowing that he was about to cross another line. It would be a perfect time for a cigarette, he thought, even if he didn't smoke. Saturday night was the right night—campus security would be busy with loud parties and drunken students.

Looking around one more time, he crept deliberately in the shadows to the door of University Hall and slipped out a gas credit card, quickly opening the door's nineteenth-century mortise lock. Entering the dark hall, he closed the door behind him, froze, and listened while his eyes adjusted to the dark. He held the dark oak banister and cautiously made his way up the stairs to Dean Toll's office, guided by his small pocket flashlight.

The door was locked, but Steve again used his academy training to open it. The office was how he remembered it, but this time he was the one making the decisions. When he had been there the last time, there was something about the dean that he didn't trust. Was he developing cop instincts? Body language, tone of voice, or maybe the way the Dean hurried to get rid of him—a piece of the puzzle was here.

Quietly, he jimmied open the top drawer of the desk. It contained papers, correspondence with faculty, and antacids. He wasn't sure what he was looking for but was confident he would find something of interest. In the credenza was an invitation to a golf tournament, tickets for a benefit at the Hope Club, and assorted student files.

The three metal file cabinets against the back wall were locked. Steve took a lock pick from his bag and, holding down the pins, quickly popped each lock. He opened the first top drawer and pulled out folders. Disciplinary Files. Motivated by curiosity, he opened the first to find the names of four football players He knew two of them, but they all had been caught cheating on an Engineering 6 exam—wires and pliers—one of the gut courses that Professor Hazeltine taught. How could they screw that up? All failed. Next one: two fraternity boys, Delt's Angels who were caught pissing on students who passed under Wayland Arch. In spite of Steve's nervous rush, he found himself lost for a minute with guys he knew. Just some Saturday night fun. He wondered how they ever got caught. He began thumbing other disciplinary files but had to stop himself. This wasn't what he was here for.

The next cabinet had fundraising returns and a list of big donors. Looking through the folder, there were many letters expressing extreme displeasure at the school strike last spring and the new co-ed dorms. The writers refused to contribute to the annual drive.

He heard a creak, maybe a step, so he switched off his flashlight and waited. A person in the building or just the old building groaning from age? He waited. What would he do—fight, run? Breaking the rules was new to him. He moved to the door and waited, his ear against the door. He felt his waistband and touched his off-duty .38. What good would that do? He held his breath until it was quiet again.

In the third file cabinet, a folder marked *University 2000* drew his interest. Inside a legal folder was a lot map of the East Side areas, shaded in different colors. An area of Fox Point was shaded in grey. Next to several lots closest to the university were numbers: 15k; 25k; 15k. The lots on Williams Street, John, Benevolent Street, and Thayer Street were cross-hatched, with numbers next to each.

Loud laughter from outside prompted him to switch off his flashlight. Having reconnoitered the hall, he knew campus police patrolled the perimeter twice a night. He listened to the voices. Students, definitely inebriated, singing, *"Young strump, old strump, every strumpet come, to the strumpet carnival, we'll have a lot of fun . . ."* They stopped outside the building, and Steve could hear the sound of running water—great time to take a piss. He saw a flashlight coming toward the boys as they were finishing their business in the bushes.

Shit, shit, he thought. *Get the fuck away from the building.*

As campus cops came closer to the building, Steve heard, "Come on, assholes. You're gonna get busted."

From the second-floor window, he watched one Brown cop break into a trot. There were shouts as the boys scattered into three different directions, the campus cop chasing one of the boys toward Waterman Street.

He sat on the floor, waiting, until the voices passed. He carefully opened the blind to see if the commotion had attracted any more campus police. He could hear his heart beating as he compressed each breath to regain control. Extracting his notebook and a brownie camera from his bag, he decided he didn't have time to edit here so he would copy everything. He was certain the files would point him somewhere. He set the folders under the desk to conceal the flash and methodically photographed each file. Changing film, he continued with other files from the east-side real estate files.

What was he looking at? He didn't have time to read it all. Just get it and get out. He looked at his watch: already twenty minutes had passed. How much longer would it take? He wanted it done in one trip.

When he finished with the drawer, he felt as if he had just finished wind sprints. Locking the cabinet, he looked around the room to see if there was anything else he had missed. He felt like pissing on the chair just to leave his mark, but he let the urge pass. At the door, he looked back across the room with the flashlight. Was anything out of place? He stopped and returned to push the desk chair back where it belonged.

As he inched his way down the steps, his hands were sweaty, but there was a giddy feeling of adrenaline racing through his body. He didn't want to fuck up now or trip an alarm. Did the place have an alarm? Fuck, he hadn't thought about that.

He paused by the door and examined the frame with the flashlight for any connectors. What was he thinking? It would have gone off when he came in. Too much overload; he had to get out. He turned the oval brass knob and slowly opened the door, pressing against the wall until he descended the steps. He began a steady walk, feeling the wetness in his armpits.

What was on the film? He would bring it to the photo shop in the morning—no, not in Providence. He would drive to Attleboro in Massachusetts, better to be sure of its security.

He wanted to break into a run, a sprint, as the excitement of what he had just done hit him. But he steadied his pace to that of a tired student. He exited the green, passed the grinder truck, and cut through the quad to Benefit Street. Better to take the long way around to the apartment.

After a night shift, Steve walked to grey granite City Hall, with the mansard roof. The Haven Brothers diner next to it was packed up and ready to leave. The tax assessor's office was located in the City Hall, and he thought that would be a good starting point. The files from Dean Toll's office gave him a list of names that didn't mean anything. There were lots of files about real estate and expansion plans.

But he didn't know how they fit together. He came prepared for a research project, ready to footnote every primary source. He had his note cards neatly organized in an envelope that was tied with a cord.

He asked for the real estate assessment records, and the woman clerk looked up from her coffee and pointed him to a room with large plat books measuring nearly two feet long. The clerk sat behind the large partition that separated her from the public. He was trying to be calm, natural, but was he trying too hard? He looked around the office; it was empty. No one had followed him. Why would they? They didn't know anything—did they? But what could they know, since he wasn't sure what he was looking for? But evidence didn't matter; it could be created, or it could disappear—that was one lesson he had learned early on the force. Was he taking all these risks for nothing? Still, he felt he had to try.

Because the books were arranged by plat numbers, Steve realized he had no clue which ones would be helpful. Asking the clerk for help was asking a blind person for directions. He began methodically narrowing his search by the part of the city. He finally located the Fox Point and East Side books. He was amazed at the prices for homes on Blackstone Avenue. Even the little colonial houses on Benefit Street were well beyond anything he could ever afford. He found 239 Williams Street and wrote the owner's name on an index card: Pawtucket Associates. He found 249 John Street—Pawtucket Associates. He wrote down the names and cataloged the cards by address.

He researched all properties on John and Williams Street. He expanded to Power, Arnold, Brook, Hope, Thayer, Benevolent, and Transit Streets. He would cross reference them with the files from the dean's office. What was the connection? They were just white pieces in a jigsaw puzzle—he needed some colored reference points.

"Where do I find out who these owners are?" Steve asked the bored clerk.

"The registered owner's name is in the book," she said without looking up.

He had the names. "And if it is a company?"

The woman shrugged, happy to get rid of him. "Well that's over in the State's files."

He looked at his watch. It was already after lunch. He needed to think through his next steps. For the last few days, he had dissected every file from the dean's office. He had them all cataloged on index cards, but they were just files. He knew the files led somewhere, or else why were they locked up? And who were these Pawtucket Associates? He would find out.

He called Sutton, the newspaper man, and suggested they meet. The reporter suggested Haven Brothers after his shift, but Steve knew that too many cops and city workers stopped at the diner. Being seen with Sutton would get people talking.

"How about up on the Brown campus—place called the Blue Room. It's on Waterman. Go through the arch and up the stairs to Faunce Hall. I'll meet you there on Tuesday around three p.m." Steve felt more secure on campus; if a Providence cop was following him, he would be easy to spot. He laughed at his own thought pattern—how fucking sad.

Sutton looked like a toad when he arrived at the buildings, intimidated by his surroundings. He was standing by the large brass grizzly bear in the foyer when Steve approached.

"I didn't know this place existed," he said and sat down with Steve at a small table overlooking Waterman Street. "I've never even been on this campus."

"Yeah, not too many outsiders come on campus. It's why it's such a bubble." Steve could see the doubt as Sutton raised his eyes.

"Ready to do a story about you? *Top Cop Gets Brown Pop—Ivy League Kid Joins Providence Police.* Now uniforms will have button-down collars." Sutton's mouth turned up on the side with amusement at his headline.

Steve smiled. "Thanks, but no thanks. I may have a better story for you. Anything seem strange to you about police calls in Fox Point over the last six months?" Steve asked, trying to figure how far to go with the reporter.

"No, not really. Some disturbances, drugs, gambling. Same old shit." Sutton was eying him with his narrow, sunken eyes. He was going bald but tried to hide it with a bad combover.

"You should take a look at the addresses. Not what you might think."

"And what might I think? You have something for me?"

"Not yet," Steve answered. "I'm playing a hunch, but I need more hard information. I also need to figure out what I do with the rest of the information, if it goes where I think it might."

"You're a cop; just go to your superiors. They'll do what's right."

Steve laughed with Sutton. "Never thought of it like that."

"So what do you have?"

"I think they're fabricating complaints—maybe a way to force the tenants out. I'm not certain of why, but I have a suspicion."

"Fox Point. Shitty neighborhood. Who'd want . . ." Sutton stopped.

"That's why I asked you to come up here. On your way home, drive by these addresses on Williams and John Streets. Then tell me if you're interested."

Sutton nodded and put on his grey fedora, looking like a reporter out of a black-and-white movie. Sutton had sources on the force and was old Providence. The *Providence Journal* wasn't the *New York Times*. The ownership was tied to Providence in ways he didn't pretend to understand. Maybe Sutton would start asking questions, raising suspicions, and fuck everything up.

"Let's keep this between us until I get you some hard evidence." Sutton nodded. "Sure. Mum's the word.'

Steve wasn't sure he could trust him but didn't have many options. The agent hadn't gotten back to him, and he was feeling very exposed.

Steve was pounding on the black typewriter with more than his usual vengeance, doing reports. It was his third cup, and he was so wired he forgot to put milk and sugar in the half-finished cup of bitter black coffee on the desk. The room was empty; Monday was a light crime day. Steve took the new reports, put them in a folder, and carried them to the Records Room. Joe Taylor, nicknamed Ole Joe, was the civilian records clerk who had been on the job forever. Asleep in a chair at the side of the room, the small, old man quietly snored, his head leaning back against the wall. Steve took a deep breath and held it to calm his stomach. He exhaled slowly and walked quietly. He was ready to cross another line.

His years of doing research in the stacks at the Rockefeller Library had prepared him to quickly sort through the index file. He looked up the incident reports on Fox Point. Several properties had a number of violations. He then picked a few files from Federal Hill on the mafia social clubs to see what the official records said. He was sure there would be a link to the city. He photographed some files with his Brownie and took carbon copies from others.

"What are you doing there?" Joe asked.

Steve was startled by the closeness of the voice, and his heart increased its pace. Quickly concealing his pad and camera in his shirt, he called back, "Just filing these reports, Joe."

He rattled some sheets of paper. He heard the file clerk push back his chair and start to walk to the aisle but stop. Steve rapidly closed the file drawer and walked quickly but under control to meet him.

Joe came into view at the far end of the file row. He was rumpled and small, a man who would disappear in a crowd. But in the records room, he was king.

"You know you're not supposed to be in here." He looked at Steve, the side of his mouth tilted.

Steve rubbed his chin. "Joe, I had these reports for the captain. You were sleeping so soundly, I didn't want to disturb you. I was putting them in the correct files when you called. Let me show you to make sure I did it right."

"Reports? Which reports? You don't file your reports; you give them to me, and I . . ." Joe's voice raised an octave.

Steve feigned disgust. "I wish they were my reports; they turned me into a fucking secretary. Wish I never learned how to type. Captain is giving me a month of *his* reports—cleaning up his fucking mess. I want to be out on the street."

A smile of recognition crossed Joe's face. He chuckled.

"Oh, you're that college boy. Heard the captain was pissed off at you. He's a sadistic old bastard. Does he make you shine his shoes and bring coffee, too? The brass, they run the joint for their own benefit. The things I could tell you. But thanks for letting me get some shut-eye."

"You got quite a filing system here. I think I put them in the right place."

"It's not that complicated. Let me show you how I put them in order. First you look at the date, then you look at the type of report . . ."

Steve listened and asked questions. Joe would stop in mid-sentence and run his right hand along his temple before answering. There were some tricks to the filing system, but it would make his research easier.

"You really are a pro. How do you remember all this stuff?" Steve asked as Joe beamed.

"Experience. You need years of experience."

Steve nodded in agreement. "If you need to get some coffee or take a smoke break, let me know. I can cover for you."

Joe nodded appreciatively. Over the next few weeks, Steve chatted up Ole Joe until he trusted Steve to spell him so he could go out for coffee and a butt. And the breaks stretched longer. One night, the door opened loudly, and Steve quickly closed the file folder in front of him as Johnson, the desk sergeant, came into the room. Johnson was a short-timer on restricted duty until his pension came through in a month.

"Logan, what are you doing here?"

"Covering for Joe, who went out for a smoke."

"This is a restricted area."

"Yeah." Steve grimaced for effect. "Rather be on the street. Fucking shit . . ."

Johnson shook his head. "You crossed the captain, you pay the price." He handed Steve a folder. "Tell Joe no more than ten minutes."

"Sure."

Johnson shook his head again as he closed the door. Steve took a deep breath—would he say anything? Possibly, but it would get involved. And there would be paperwork with the captain involved. Did Johnson care?

The Rhode Island state capitol building was modeled on the United States Capitol building in Washington, with a freestanding rotunda dividing the two houses of the legislature. Steve parked his car in a space behind the building with a sign on it that said *State of Rhode Island and Providence Plantations*. Office of Secretary of State. Dressed in a cotton knit shirt and jeans, he looked like a college kid.

The clerk was a short, middle-aged man with a highway bald. Rising from his desk, as if unaccustomed to walk-in public visitors, he asked brusquely, "Can I help you?"

"I'm looking for some incorporation papers." Steve smiled nicely.

"Are they for your corporation?" the clerk asked, looking Steve over from head to foot.

"No. I need to verify some information."

The clerk went into his practiced speech. "You need to write a letter to the Secretary of State designating what information you want, what the purpose of the request is for . . ."

Steve held up his badge, cutting the man off. "Let's not make a big deal of this. I'm doing some background checking for the boss. I need the incorporation papers of Pawtucket Associates, East Side Properties, Main Street Development—either you can find them or I can find them. Or . . ." he let the final alternative hang in the air until the clerk began to move.

Pausing for several seconds as if thinking about his options, the clerk asked again, "Pawtucket Associates? What were the other ones? What years were they incorporated?" He took a yellow legal pad from his desk.

"I don't know."

The clerk shook his head at having to do work. "Wait here."

Where was he going? Phoning headquarters to verify the investigation—the thought raced through Steve's mind. What was his answer? Not official business but working out a hunch? That didn't work. Maybe the complaints—that was it. Who needed to be held accountable for the complaints.

The clerk emerged from a side room with a large, black ledger book.

"Pawtucket Partners; Pawtucket Realty; Pawtucket Auto Body; Pawtucket Associates. Incorporated 1969."

He held it close. Steve put out his hand, and the man handed him the book. Steve thumbed through it, taking out his notebooks and copying the information on each corporation. He was careful to look at the incorporation dates, principals, legal address, as well as any attorneys who were involved. He spent most of the afternoon sitting in the corner of the room, much to the annoyance of the clerk. Steve was satisfied that he was an inconvenience rather than a threat to the clerk. Just another day on the job.

At the end of the day, the picture was still not clear. Many of the corporations were owned by other corporations, but a few familiar names began appearing. He would have to go to Boston to look into the Massachusetts companies. He also had to get the directory of city and state officials—probably legislators as well. He could find them at the library. There were some colored pieces in the jigsaw puzzle, so it was beginning to take shape.

Maybe Roxy could help. She was good at puzzles. They could do it together, lay all the files out on his floor, connect some dots, and figure out where the missing pieces were and how to get them. They would stay awake late into the night, drinking tea, and then they would make love, passionate love, releasing all the tension and stress building within him. He could still dream.

CHAPTER 14

REASON TO BELIEVE

Called in for the day shift, Steve entered the squad room. Fifty cops from different shifts mixed in a football team warm-up. Working a day off was not unusual, but the last-minute call for so many uniformed cops was; Steve knew it was more than construction site duty. A sergeant appeared with two carts filled with riot helmets and long batons.

"Listen up," Captain Lynch shouted. "You've been called in today because we've gotten word that there's some type of demonstration. It might stay peaceful, but we need to show sufficient force to make certain that happens. No valid parade permits have been issued. Men will go out four to a car and bring three wagons in case these assholes don't understand English. I expect all of you to stay in tight formation."

Dylan asked Steve as they left, "What the fuck?"

"Got me. I was told to report for day shift."

Steve and Dylan packed into a squad car with two other cops. Riding in back, behind the cage that separated the prisoner from the driver, Steve felt they were wild animals about to be set loose on an unsuspecting public. The cars formed a caravan from headquarters

243

over the bridge and pulled onto the streets of Fox Point. The squad cars parked in a double line, blocking off two intersecting streets. The captain ordered the men to line up in two straight lines.

With their longer riot clubs in front of them, Steve, in his riot helmet, was positioned at the far right of the first line. Captain Lynch marched in front with a bullhorn. On command, they slowly marched up the street, side by side in perfect unison, filling the entire distance from curb to curb. Steve saw windows in the wooden apartment buildings open, heads appearing to watch the scene below.

"This is an illegal assembly. This is an official warning to disperse," Lynch squawked through the megaphone as the police line stopped, facing the crowd.

The group of people had swelled to more than one hundred. The mixed crowd had many sightseers and well-wishers. On the front stoop of the house, elevated over the crowd, was Father Schmidt, in his grey Franciscan robes. Close to the priest were fifty to seventy-five people, including immigrant families and college students with signs that said *Stop the Greedy Landlords* and *Save our Homes*.

Steve looked at the people facing him, women with doughy faces older than their years, with clothes from secondhand stores, and men with hard hands from manual work, with resignation but resistance in their eyes. These were people fighting for their homes in this new country. College kids, kids he would see on campus in navy pea coats, stood up for the oppressed as acts of defiance to their privilege. Steve was standing erect, remembering the demonstration downtown, where the police phalanx had been impersonal and intimidating. He realized some of the cops next to him were nervously tapping their batons into their hands. Steve was tense; he didn't want to hurt these people in front of him. He should be on their side, but . . .

Without the aid of a microphone, Father Schmidt spoke in his accented voice. "You cannot seize these peoples' homes. They have nowhere to live. This is the greedy capitalists, grinding down the working man. This is wrong, an abomination against God and man."

Lynch replied through the grey bullhorn, "This is an illegal assembly. You must disperse. There is a legal order of eviction, and we will execute it. This gathering is illegal. I warn you: Disperse now." His voice had turned from patient to angry.

The crowd began to sing, "We shall overcome, we shall overcome, we shall overcome someday . . ."

"Father, please," Lynch said to the priest. "Tell these people to disperse or they will be arrested."

Father Schmidt replied, "We will not be moved." He signaled everyone to sit down and lock arms.

"Fuck," Lynch said under his breath, turning to his troops as two television news trucks arrived with cameramen and reporters scurrying to the scene.

"Let's clear this place quickly," the captain shouted to the officers closest to him. "Keep those news guys away, and get that fucking priest in the wagon first. Then this group will run. Clear the street," he ordered the men, waving his hand forward like a cavalry officer in an old Western. Steve saw the dark shadow of anger on the captain that he remembered from the march down the hill after Kent State.

The police line moved into the crowd. The cops began yelling at people, telling them to move and pushing them back toward the houses. The resistance was passive; each individual was a struggle to move as they flopped into dead weight. Steve saw a group of police officers advance toward Father Schmidt, who was still standing on the stoop, but now was surrounded by a human shield of his supporters. The police attempted to pry them apart, but the crowd pushed back, knocking over one cop, who fell heavily to the sidewalk.

Jumping up, the cop hit the man in front of him with his baton, drawing a scream of pain. The protesters screamed at the cops and pushed more aggressively at the line. The police surged forward, now using their clubs to part the crowd. Protestors were being pulled and driven to the wagons, some bleeding. Rocks and bottles sailed in a wide arc from the back of the crowd, hitting both cops and protesters.

The cops' surge became more frenzied, with a new urgency to get protesters into the wagons before they were overwhelmed by the crowd.

Steve could feel the adrenaline racing as he pleaded with a woman with dark, unwashed hair pulled tight under a striped green scarf.

"You don't want to go to jail. Please leave. *Por favor.*"

She sat, looking at him, arms crossed, although a bit of fear had crept in under her dark-hooded eyes.

"Come on then," Steve said, picking her up by the arms of her grey wool coat. She twisted away from him and sat back down. The battle in the center of the line was becoming more intense, but Steve told himself to remain calm. He wasn't going to allow the chaos to force him to react.

He picked the woman up more securely this time, and once she was on her feet, fast-walked her to the wagon, almost tossing her to the cop at the wagon door. He didn't want to be here arresting these people. From the corner of his eye, he saw that Roxy was among the protesters at the far left end. A surge of protective fear hit him. He had to get her out of there.

A bottle exploded on the street next to him, spattering a gooey liquid onto his pants. Several more followed in rapid succession, one glancing off his shoulder with a flat thud.

Steve worked his way behind the line of cops and toward Roxy, but the crowd was now belligerent, and the fighting was intensifying. He was being spit upon by the protesters. People standing behind the sitting protesters threw bags of feces at the cops.

A cop lunged over the prone crowd to get at his assailants, but they disappeared into the crowd. As men and women were pulled from the ground, Steve pushed them toward the wagon while fighting his way toward Roxy. Chants filled the space between the cursing cops and the screaming faces. There was blood on some batons and perspiration on the red faces of the officers.

Steve could see that Roxy was animated, chanting with the crowd. She was sitting when she was grabbed by a cop. He felt panic and pushed harder against the cops and protesters keeping him from her. *Don't do anything stupid,* he wanted to scream to her. She struggled and freed herself from the cop's grip, sitting back down and locking arms with the people next to her. The cop grabbed her again, and she twisted hard, throwing him off balance.

When the cop recovered, he raised his baton, and she collapsed to the ground with one stroke. Steve couldn't see who the cop was but wanted to hit the guy. The crowd's surge pushed him back, carrying him away from Roxy like a rip current. He fought more intensely, pushing cops out of his way as he tried to get to her before they put her in the wagon, but he was too late. The doors closed on the wagon as it pulled away.

Hit in the back with a bottle, he turned again to the demonstrators and continued to pull them into the empty wagons. He used his baton only to push the demonstrators and felt guilty every time he heard the dull thud and scream as a baton found a body part. His anger built at the protesters, the cops, Roxy, but most of all anger at himself for being on this side of the protest.

Hours later at police headquarters, there was chaos. Families and friends of the protesters were milling in front of the desk, shouting in multiple languages. Steve, still in riot helmet, approached the desk sergeant from the squad room.

"How's processing the demonstrators going?"

"Pain in the ass. Did you guys have to arrest all of them? The paperwork is killing us. Judge is downstairs in holding. The TV guys are out front, and the brass is hiding upstairs—are you here to help or watch?"

"What are we charging them with?"

"As few charges as we have to." The sergeant looked at the crowd of concerned relatives building in front of his desk. "This is not making us look good. The archbishop even called. He was pretty hot about us arresting a priest."

"Are we releasing without charge?"

"Yeah, if someone will sign for them. Otherwise, wait for the judge."

"Okay. I'll sign for Fisher. Roxanne?" Steve said.

Sergeant gave him a questioning look.

"Yeah, I know her from school. She's going to be a doctor. Gimme the paperwork, and it will be one less to deal with. I'll even type it up."

The desk sergeant looked skeptically at him but gave Steve a form as people yelled at him from the floor. Disappearing into the squad room, he quickly returned with it complete. The sergeant stamped it and returned it to Steve, who raced to the lockup door. The guard buzzed him through and he raced downstairs, two steps at a time, to the holding cells. Steve searched the two small cells crowded with women. He saw Roxy sitting on the floor; she was dirty and had obviously been crying. She looked up blankly at Steve, seeing only the uniform and the helmet, not the person. As she watched him take off his helmet, her expression slowly changed to recognition. A smile began to form, but she tried to suppress it. The security matron came over to Steve, and he handed her the form.

"Fisher. That one," he said in his official voice.

He pointed to Roxy, who was now standing. The matron looked at the form and at Steve's nametag.

"All right, Officer," the matron paused, "Logan."

She opened the cell with her roll of keys and brought Roxy out. She still looked slightly dazed. When Steve took her arm, she flinched in pain.

"Fucking pig hit me," she said, her fear changing back to anger.

"Language." Steve nudged her up the stairs.

"I don't care; he didn't need to fucking . . ."

Steve escorted her rapidly out the front door. There were three television news crews waiting outside. Steve and Roxy paused for a minute, hearing a commotion, when the newsmen all started shouting.

"Father! Father!" The newsmen surrounded Father Schmidt like schooling fish as he emerged from the police station. He stopped on the top step and turned to the journalists as the television lights went on.

"Father, can you tell us why you were arrested? What were you . . ." the newsmen shouted.

"For doing God's work. I am defending the rights of the poor against the landlords and other elites." The priest spoke slowly for the camera, elevating to his full height.

Another newsman yelled, the camera perched on his cameraman's shoulder like an electronic parrot.

"Police said the demonstrators started the fight and became aggressive."

Schmidt smiled a patient Franciscan smile at the crowd, continuing to turn his face from camera to camera. "We were assembled peacefully when the police attacked. The poor are the privileged channel of God's grace. The mission of Jesus Christ is to bring justice for the poor. I am just his humble vehicle."

"What will you do next?" another newsman shouted.

"We will continue to follow God's path, and we will resist the corrupt powers that oppress the poor. Thank you. I must return to my congregation, who so valiantly put their lives in danger for me today."

Roxy and Steve, still in uniform, were listening to the street interview when the cameraman who was panning the crowd fixed his lights and camera on them. Steve ducked his head to the side, but it was too late.

That evening in Roxy's apartment, Steve, Roxy, and other friends were watching the eleven p.m. television news.

In other developments, the Providence Police made several arrests . . .

The television showed footage of the police hitting people with batons and putting bloodied civilians in wagons.

. . .today for disorderly conduct during an eviction proceeding . . .

There was more footage of police clubbing unarmed civilians in Fox Point.

Father Bruno Schmidt, the leader of the protesters, had this to say:

The footage cut to Father Schmidt as he emerged from the police station.

"The order was unlawful, and it would have put poor people on the street. It is our duty to resist."

The camera scanned the crowd outside headquarters and slowed to a clear view of Steve in uniform, with Roxy holding his arm, listening to the priest.

"Oh, I look horrible. Did you see me?" Roxy scrunched her face and brushed her hair back.

"Shit." Steve was stunned, seeing himself as part of the crowd worshipping the priest. "I look so . . . visible."

They sat for a while in the living room, not paying attention to the sports report that followed. He knew the captain would be livid when he reported to work. He would have to play along, apologize, and be contrite. He needed more time. He didn't know what else they could do except bring him up on charges which they would fabricate. But he thought they would rather have him go quietly—he was counting on it.

Finally, Roxy and Steve went down the hall to her bedroom.

"Let me see that bruise," he said. She took off her shirt to show him the arm that was black and blue on the biceps. He touched it gently. "Sorry I couldn't get to you," he said, placing an ice-filled towel on her arm.

Roxy cuddled up with him, bringing his arm over her bare shoulder. "Did you hit anyone?"

"Hit anyone?" He was amused. "No, I was a target."

She looked up at him, smiling. "Thank you." She squeezed his arm tighter. "I was so scared in that cell. I was never in a jail; it smelled so horrible. But then I saw you when you came for me. You were my knight rescuing me. You're not like the rest of them. I can't believe you do that every day."

She put her head on his chest and quickly fell asleep. He sat, absorbing the rhythm of her breath, stroking her hair as he felt the warmth of her naked shoulder on his arm. Cyrano came over and lay down with them.

"Yes, I try to do the right thing." He wiped away some dirt on her cheek and rested his head against the pillow as the cat purred. He slept contently.

Bill and Steve were sitting in the IHOP, sipping coffee. Steve had a waffle with boysenberry syrup and Bill, his muttonchops gone, was eating his second silver dollar stack.

"Not the smartest thing I've ever done," Steve said. "I thought I was joining the good guys. You know: Roy Rogers, John Wayne."

Bill nodded agreement. "But you did it. You weren't just talk. I get so tired listening to these kids who lecture about what should be done—you at least are trying to do something. I wish I had your courage. You've making me reconsider my future; maybe I shouldn't go to business school."

"There's always time for school, but I've learned more in the last year than in all my time in school."

"I admire you and can't believe you're a fucking cop. You are actually doing something constructive."

"But it cost me Roxy."

"Just sooner than later, man. I'm your friend so I can say it—you were so blind in love, you couldn't tell if the sun was out. It was a pretty intense movie from the outside. Maybe the sex was that great, but . . ."

"I don't know if I'm Don Quixote or Sir Lancelot, but I could've made it work."

Bill shook his head. "Only in your dreams. You can't follow her around like a lost puppy for four more years. She's got bigger ideas than getting hooked up with a loser like you."

Steve smiled. "What a friend. Don't hold back. Maybe I got a little lost. Now, the next step is a big leap."

Bill raised his eyebrow. "What does that mean?"

Steve stared at the waffle before taking a forkful carefully coated with the syrup. "I have to decide: in or out. Ya know, once upon a time, I thought it was easy to tell right from wrong, but now, now . . . I can't tell which side is up. That's not true, either—I know but don't want to accept it."

"What the fuck are you talking about?"

"I'm talking about life. Decision time for me. I can't keep putting it off." He looked directly at Bill. "If you had a chance to really change things, but you knew that it would cause a shit storm and you would never be able to come back, that it could fuck up your life for good, would you do it?" He put the fork down without taking a bite, pensively looking at the square indentations in the waffle. He wanted to ask Roxy this question.

"I don't understand. Do what?"

There was no going back from it when he made the decision, no do overs. "Is it better to do the right thing, even if it might be the wrong thing for you personally?"

"You should do what you think is right. But what's this big decision?"

"Just thinking aloud. Got to make a decision. What time is lacrosse practice?" Bill was always there to listen, and he appreciated the friendship.

"Three, like usual."

"Maybe I'll talk to Coach. See if he needs an assistant."

"Great, a new incentive—if you're dogging on laps or sprints, Steve fires a couple of warning shots at you." They laughed.

"And yes, the sex was great."

Because the green VW was the butt of many jokes in the squad room, Steve knew it would be too conspicuous if a patrol car drove by the building he needed to access. He wanted to get in and out without being noticed, so he decided to walk. Wearing his camel blazer, shirt, and striped tie, he could pass for a young lawyer, except for the brown Star Market shopping bag. He had to carry it because he didn't have a briefcase, and his backpack would be out of place.

He turned onto George Street, the brick walls of Wriston Quad protecting the dorms and fraternity houses from the outside world. He was on the outside now, part of the world that was dirty, disorganized, unfair, and brutal. Not like inside the wall, where they wanted him to believe that fairness and truth existed. He was so young two years ago. He should just turn downtown, but he felt comfort in the brick buildings that evoked his innocent memories. He wasn't nostalgic, but he had warm memories of late-night hall discussions with preppies and townies. Kids with more worldly experience and money than he had ever dreamed were struggling to fit in. He realized he always knew who he was: simple, hardworking, and unwilling to give up. Keep your head down and your feet moving.

Keep your feet moving; he was doing it now. Not blindly, but with full knowledge of what he was about to do. *Treason*—that would be a word for it. *Courage to act* was another way to look at it. College logic: look at it from both sides. Let's debate it and let history decide the outcome. He passed the John Brown house; its nefarious history in the triangle trade with slavery was glossed over for years. But nothing stays hidden forever. Secrets—we all have secrets. He was carrying his secret now as he descended the steep hill toward the city.

It wasn't a dream. He had made the decision. He felt his stomach tighten. As he descended the hill as he had on the first day he entered the police department, he realized how little he knew. He was working from instinct—the right instinct. The one instilled in grammar school by the nuns. Do the right thing. That was his intention when the bayonet was at his throat. How far life had come. Now it was the next step—the crazy one—the right one, maybe. It could all blow up on him.

He avoided the major streets. He was fairly confident he'd successfully hidden his activities and no one knew where he was going or what he was carrying. Still, it was an effort to not keep looking behind him. Taking a deep breath, he looked at the grey building in front of him. He was on his own once again. He heard the Wishbone Ash song, *the fight is over and done, neither lost nor won.* Entering a side door to the Federal Court House, he went to the third floor as he had been instructed.

The FBI office was austere, with government-issued furniture and two-inch horizontal metal Venetian blinds with two-inch faded white tapes. On the wall were pictures of Richard Nixon and J. Patrick Grey, and a Georgetown Law School diploma. An American flag with a gold eagle on top stood by the door. Agent Adams, in his early thirties, sat behind the desk in a grey suit, white shirt, and striped tie. He was assigned directly to the United States Attorney. Steve had used the pay phone at the coffeehouse on Thayer Street when he spoke with the agent about the outline for their meeting.

"Have you consulted an attorney?"

"No," Steve replied. He had thought about it but wasn't concerned for himself since his information was just facts. He had scrupulously maintained his records of every call.

"You may be implicating yourself as an accessory." Adams' tone was even, and Steve couldn't tell if he was threatening or warning him. Either way, he had made up his mind to go forward after having thought about it every night.

"I could just go to the press if you are not interested," Steve said. "Do you already have enough evidence? Maybe you don't need any more?"

"You know I can't discuss any ongoing investigations or possible investigations. But I can tell you we have developed a very credible source within the department. If you can confirm facts, if you can give us additional specifics, it would be helpful to the case. Can you provide credible-enough information?"

"I'll give you what I have, and you decide," Steve said.

"I just need to warn you that your life could be in danger. These people can play rough."

Steve shifted in his seat, remembering the locker room. This was a bigger step. He nodded and handed the agent three large manila envelopes. He felt relieved that he had finally taken action. He already was in danger every day on the job.

He would have liked to see Roxy's face when he told her what he was doing. He wished things were different so he could have shared the decision. But now, he really wanted her to know—to know that he wasn't one of *them*.

As he watched Adams open the first folder, beads of sweat formed in his armpits. For Roxy to know that he had the courage to go through with it . . . This was his decision, his decision about his future—a final decision. And maybe it was his contribution to the future. In the first folder were numerous smaller envelopes containing cash and with dates, places, and names written on the front of them. In the other folders were papers, photos of documents, and carbon copies from the police record room, organized and cataloged. Also included were incorporation papers for Pawtucket Associates and many other corporations. Among the directors were W. McGuire, Chief of Police; G. Lynch, Captain of Patrol; and D. Toll, Vice Chancellor at Brown, as well as names from the city council, Democratic Party, and others of the city elite.

Agent Adams looked over the material carefully and nodded at Steve. "Very interesting and detailed. We didn't know all of these connections."

"What I promised?"

"Yes, and much more. How long have you been collecting this information?"

"Since the first hundred-dollar bill. Every envelope is dated."

"And these other documents?"

"From the police files—file numbers are on the envelopes, easy enough for you to subpoena." He didn't tell the agent how he had obtained the Brown files.

Adams looked down at the gift Steve had given him, and Steve could see he had opened some new doors for the investigation. "You seem to have done your homework well."

Steve looked back at him with satisfaction. "I always did my homework well."

"This is very useful. We'll be in touch." He stood, extending his hand. As he closed the door behind him, Steve felt a wave of relief sweep over him. *"Alea iacta est."* It now was the beginning of the end.

He arranged the meeting with Sutton for the next day. It would take some time for any criminal investigation, but a newspaper story would stop the Fox Point evictions. He had typed up his notes, including some of the information he had obtained from the Brown files as well as the police records. He laid out the lots and the ownership, and traced the ownership to interlocking companies, shell companies, and partnerships. But the names were the key: politicians, police, academic administrators, party bosses, as well as some legitimate landlords who might be willing to talk.

Toad read the material slowly. He kept looking up at Steve as he went through the thorough file. The university was expanding. A new medical school, more graduate programs, and increased student population. It all needed room, and the east side of Providence was already built out.

"I don't know if they will publish this," Toad said, setting down the third manila file. "I mean, this is the establishment of Providence."

"Is your publisher's name on the list?"

"No, but a lot of the Hope Club's membership is."

"And . . ." Steve had no illusions anymore. They would look to protect themselves. "There's enough for a story—maybe a Pulitzer. But it's yours for the running. You ask the questions; I just did the research." Steve said, setting down his coffee. The *Times* was willing to cooperate with Durk, so what about the *Providence Journal?* He didn't know because it was such a small town. They couldn't bury it now; the question was how far would they go?

"A Pulitzer?" Toad put down the package and looked out the window.

"Sure, why not you? You're a good-enough reporter." Now, Steve had to wait and see where Sutton would go with it—and stay alive.

CHAPTER 15

BOTH SIDES NOW

Four days after the demonstrations, Steve was at roll
call. When he entered the room, the normal chat-
ter dropped to a hush. The veteran officers gave him fleeting glances
and whispered to each other. Steve could tell the back-channel gossip
had already penetrated the room as hushed conversations started as
he walked into the room

"Logan, walking post 32," the sergeant announced as he read
off the assignments. A low whistle rose from the back of the room.

Steve followed Dylan out the door. "Guess everyone knew," he
said.

Dylan looked at him. "I don't know anything specific. Just that
it wasn't gonna be good. Why were you on TV?"

"Is that what this is about? I was standing there." Steve paused.
He'd been so focused on his activities at the Federal building and
the potential fall-out. He had done his best to check he wasn't followed, leaving by a side doorway. He'd forgotten he and Roxy had
been caught by the cameramen when he'd gotten her out of jail
after her arrest.

"Don't think that's how they see it. Media said Lynch used too much force, and then you show up with that fucking priest. They're out to finish you now."

"You suppose?"

"Post 32? It's in the projects. It's not a regular post. Be careful." Dylan nodded to Steve.

The rows of public housing apartment blocks in South Providence were littered with broken benches and shattered liquor bottles. Steve walked along the sidewalk on the street side. A car was parked by a fire hydrant. Stopping, he wrote out a ticket and left it on the windshield. A group of young black men, a bit in the shadows, were talking and trying to stay out of his view. Steve could see they were watching him, and he felt like an alien in their neighborhood.

Steve continued to walk through the project, making notes on lights that were out, benches that were broken, and sidewalks that were cracked. On the street, he saw a young man go over to the car, take the ticket from under the windshield wiper, rip it up, and drop it on the ground. Steve monitored the crackle of his radio, *Car 23, man down on Weymouth Street.* He continued to walk, aware of eyes on him from the shadows as well as from some apartments.

Hearing some shouting from around the corner, he walked faster, staying away from the few working streetlights while keeping the noise from his footsteps to a minimum. A group of young men gathered by a basketball court. The metal backboards had bent rims. The group was arguing loudly and waving their arms. There was only one streetlight at the far side of the court.

Steve took the radio out of its holster on his belt.

"Post 32. Post 32." He waited, but there was no response. "Post 32. Dispatcher, can you read?" Still no response. "Post 32, I have a group of men at Potters Avenue behind the buildings at the basketball court. Possible disturbance. Request backup." Still no response. "Fuck, fuck, fuck," he said into the radio. "So that's how it's going to be."

His voice attracted the attention of one of the young men, who had turned his back on the gang and now fixed an even stare on Steve instead. Should he even bother to investigate, knowing he was alone? He hesitated for a moment before he moved out into the pathway, taking his six-inch flashlight and holding it at his side.

"A lot of noise here. Any problem?" Steve announced in a strong voice.

One of the youths stared at him as he took a step backward. "Who the fuck? Where the fuck did you come . . ."

Another youth stepped to the side; the group quieted down and looked Steve over. He stopped and spoke into his radio loud enough for the group to hear him.

"Yes, Units 23 and 25. Basketball court on Potters Avenue. Seven men. Late teens, early twenties, blue sweatshirt, Celtics t-shirt, red striped shirt . . ."

Taking his finger off the radio, he looked at the men-boys and tried to interpret the nonverbal signals.

"I asked: Any problem here?" He looked up at the group and addressed the one who first challenged him, raising his flashlight to see his hands, then his face.

"I asked: any problem here?"

He had interrupted a tense stand-off. He shone the light on each individual. He stopped at the boy in the Celtics shirt who looked familiar.

"Norvell, Marvel?" He could see the boy's eyes were glassy from drugs—definitely more than pot. The boy had not looked at Steve. Rather, he was focused on a boy with a camouflage Army shirt with the name *Smith* on it. Norvell startled when his name was called. He looked more intently at Steve.

"Teach?" Disgust and annoyance filled his voice. He continued to look aggressively at the Army youth and made a gesture that things weren't finished. He and a few friends turned away and started down a pathway to one of the buildings. The other youth glared and then looked at Steve, who raised the flashlight again to his hands, then his face.

"Any problems?"

The youth looked to his friends.

"Naw. No problems."

The boy in the army shirt walked in the opposite direction from Norvell. Steve stood in place for a few minutes, watching the group part. He looked at his unanswered radio.

"Motherfuckers."

The bedroom was dark except for a row of lit votive candles around the room. Sweet incense wafted through the room from a brass Indian burner. Sitting on the floor, leaning against the bed, Steve was floating, allowing his mind to focus on the song. Music was playing, Joni Mitchell's *Both Sides Now*. On the floor was Carlos Castaneda's *Teachings of Don Juan, A Yaqui Way of Knowledge*. Heather, wearing a loose, flowing, thin print dress leaned down to pass him a joint, exposing her small white breasts.

"We change our reality many times during our lives. You had a child reality and with it, psychic and physical limitations. And then you get into your adolescent reality with your changed body and mind. Now you need to let go of your cruel world, this new aggressive reality you have entered . . ."

Steve puffed the joint and passed it back to her. She took a toke, tossed her long blond hair, and sat cross-legged next to him.

"It does suck out there. I . . . I don't know how I got myself . . ."

Heather stroked his arm.

"I didn't . . . don't know much. It . . . it would be . . . it would be a way . . . You know with the war, and I thought I would . . . could, would make a difference. I think I will but I can't tell anyone . . ."

"She's flying into her new sphere. You have to let that reality go. You are in the man-war reality. Fighting, combat . . . Prehistoric stuff before we evolved. The time now is to change . . ."

Joni Mitchell's music played.

"I try. I get up and go out there." He shook his head. "I want to be . . . what I want to . . ."

"The warrior mentality. You have to leave it. You should be working to create, not destroy. To build the new order."

She stood, reached across her shoulders, and let her dress drop to the floor.

"You are a good man. There is too much good in you, and you have to allow it to come out."

Steve rose, and she stripped off his t-shirt and unbuckled his shorts, letting them drop to the floor.

"I can try. Roxy said that I could . . ."

Heather put her finger to his mouth and then kissed him intensely as they fell onto the bed. He resisted for a moment before returning her kiss, releasing his pent-up passion.

The plaintive music about changing and acting strange continued as they floated through the night. Her strong hands massaged his neck as he nibbled her breasts, making his way to her stomach. She was an earth mother, warm and welcoming. She pushed him to his back, stretching his arms over his head as she explored his body with little kisses. She mounted him, her long blond hair falling over her breasts as she built to a climaxing rhythm. He turned her over, stroking the long blond hair on her legs. She had captured him so that he was with her totally, allowing him to escape all his other fears. And they spent the night making love.

Steve was up and dressed in the morning. Heather, still naked, walked slowly over to him. Putting her hands around his face, she stared deeply into his eyes.

"There is good, and you should be doing good."

He nodded. "I'm trying."

She kissed him, and he returned it, trying to pull himself away. He turned to leave. And turned back.

"And when you make love to a woman," she paused, "you shouldn't talk about your ex-girlfriend. It's not polite."

She smiled, and Steve sheepishly smiled back.

"Thank you." He quickly kissed her again.

As he skipped down the stairs, he felt liberated for the moment. But as he reached the front door, he stopped, quickly looking both ways. It wasn't done yet. He needed to be careful. He moved quickly, taking a short cut through campus to make certain he wasn't being followed.

In the projects that night, Steve stayed in shadows by the corner of the buildings, smelling the spring night air. After one in the morning, a quiet settled over the broken carcass of urban living. There were few sounds except the occasional car passing. He watched a car with its headlights off come into the parking lot at the far side of the open space. He couldn't see the driver or his passenger, but, as the car started to slow, Steve moved to a better vantage point. Two young black men came out from a cellar door in one of the buildings and approached the car. A man rolled down his window and spoke with the two youths. The boys exchanged something with the men in the car and then returned to the buildings. Steve figured it was a drug deal.

The two men got out of the car with guns in their hands and began moving toward the building. Steve inched along the wall, keeping them in sight as he quietly unsnapped the safety strap and took his gun out of his holster. He could feel perspiration on his forehead. He inhaled a long, deep breath and compressed it into his stomach to steady his nerves. He couldn't call for backup since no one was answering his radio. He was on his own. The two men stopped near the door the boys had disappeared through and appeared to be discussing their next step. Steve decided it was time to act.

"Halt! Police!"

"Fucking shit." The gunmen pointed their guns at Steve, who crouched into a shooter's position.

Shoot. The instinct was in his head. *Shoot before he does.* One gunman flipped open his jacket, showing a gold badge on a lanyard hanging from his neck. With greasy hair to his ears and the shaggy black beard of a street man, Steve had to look twice to recognize Detective Rizzo. He should end it here, kill the motherfucker. Justifiable homicide. *He pointed his gun at me.* No badge was visible; the situation was dark. He would be taking one bad guy out. He could feel the blood pumping at his temple—*do it, do it.* For the locker room, for setting him up, for the good of the community. His eyes met Rizzo's.

Pull the trigger, so simple. He could feel the drips of water rolling down from his armpits. There would be an inquiry but . . . but . . . He looked at the man and hated what he saw as he slowly lowered his gun.

"What the hell are you going here, asshole?" Rizzo hissed.

Steve could feel the adrenaline subsiding while his anger simmered just below the surface. "Doing my job." Steve's voice dripped with sarcasm.

"We might be able to use him," Bouley said.

Steve looked at them—*use him.* Like hell.

"We just made a buy: heroin from a kid in the building. We don't know how many there are, so we can go in as a team." Bouley motioned Steve to follow them into the building. They walked quietly down the hall, listening carefully, until they came to an apartment where music could be heard through the door.

Rizzo motioned Steve to the front of the door as he and Bouley stood on either side. Bouley motioned with his fingers—one, two, three—and they kicked the door open.

Steve waited for gunfire to greet him—he was the target out in front of the detectives, who slid to their knees as they entered the apartment. It would be over in a second. His eyes darted, looking for the danger.

"Freeze! Police!" the three cops shouted almost in unison. The room had a half a dozen youths of various ages sitting or sprawled on ash-stained furniture. Steve saw two faces peek from an adjacent room.

"They have a gun," Rizzo shouted, firing two shots as the bedroom door slammed and they heard the sound of a window opening.

The youths sat in stunned silence before a huge kid moved to get up.

"Be cool, Marvin," Steve said, recognizing the boy from school. "Nothing good is going to come of going outside." The boy nodded and sat back down.

"They're getting away," Rizzo said as he turned out the door. Steve followed. One youth was hiding behind some dumpsters. Steve worked his way in the opposite direction of the detective. The boy began to run. Steve started moving parallel to the running boy. Breaking into a sprint, diagonal to the boy, accelerating, he hit the boy with a solid open-field tackle, throwing the suspect to the ground.

Steve was quickly on top of him, pinning his arms as he put cuffs on. Rizzo followed the sounds and was breathing heavily. Steve lifted the boy to his feet and turned to Rizzo.

"Have a good run, Detective?" he smiled at Rizzo, who was still trying to get his breath. Rizzo slammed his fist into the boy's midsection, sending the boy in cuffs to the ground.

Bouley barked, "Where'd the second one go? Is he the one with the gun? Which way did he run?"

"This shit tried to kill a cop." Rizzo kicked the boy. Steve pushed him back. He moved aggressively at Steve, who stood his ground between them.

"Where's his gun?"

"He must have dropped it." Rizzo said.

"Fuck you. And if you drop one, I'll report it," Steve said.

Rizzo was nose to nose with Steve. "You're a dead man. You know it. We're gonna get you."

"I'm fucking scared," Steve hissed, smelling the stale tobacco on Rizzo's breath.

In the sliver of light coming from the exit sign by the door, there was sudden noise from the dumpster to their right. Steve could see a figure sneak through an opening in the low fence.

"Police! Don't move!" Rizzo yelled and ran toward the figure, who was running toward the parking lot. Rizzo and Steve gave chase. Suddenly the boy stopped, turned, and raised his gun. Rizzo, panting, was exposed in the streetlight, "Police! Drop the gun!" Steve yelled. The recognition was instantaneous, but Steve still had trouble processing it. "Norvell, no. It doesn't have to happen," Steve shouted as he crouched in a shooting stance. "Norvell, put down the gun."

The boy looked toward Steve and cocked his head as if he recognized Steve's voice. Steve hoped to see him lower his hand.

The explosions of the guns caused every pore to erupt with sweat. Rizzo screamed "Shit!" as he fell to the ground. The next explosion was from Steve's hand; the kick of the pistol was minimized by his stance. Steve could feel the blood pumping in his temples as he took deep breaths to try and calm himself.

The boy on the ground in front of him was screaming.

"Norvell," Steve yelled, realizing he had returned a round when the boy returned Rizzo's shot.

Bouley ran toward Rizzo, who was sitting.

"How bad?" Steve shouted to Bouley.

"Grazed him. He'll live," Bouley said as he applied compression to Rizzo's arm. Steve radioed as he ran to the boy, "Policeman down, Potters Avenue. Need ambulances now. Answer the goddamn radio. Policeman down."

"Roger that."

When Steve got to the boy, he saw the look of fear in his clouded eyes. "Why? why, Norvell?" The boy could only cry in pain. Steve frantically ripped the boy's shirt into pieces and tried to stop the abdominal bleeding.

"Attempted murder of a police officer," Bouley gloated as he walked up to the suffering kid.

"My collar," Steve yelled at the panting, angry detective.

"Bullshit. We've been working these drug dealers for months. He tried to kill me," Rizzo said, his face red and his eyes drawn tight. He was holding his arm, which had stopped bleeding. "And now we have attempted murder of a police officer."

"I had to shoot!" Steve screamed at him. "Why did you shoot?"

"He shot first. Our lives were in danger." Rizzo nearly spat it at Steve.

"Fuck you. You shot at him. I had it under control." His body was taut, nose to nose with the detective, ready to take him out, but the anger was self-directed. Did he kill the kid? He had fired without thinking. Instinct, but was it necessary? Norvell shot. Returned fire. But why? It was a drug bust. Now he would go up on attempted murder—twenty-five to life. He played the sequence back in his mind, trying to put it into slow motion. The stop, Norvell, the gun, the flash, Rizzo's cry of pain, the slow squeeze of the trigger, sighting over the barrel like at the range. One shot on the mark and another scream of pain. Did he have a choice? It happened so fast.

Bouley looked hard at Steve. "Why the fuck are you here?"

"I wouldn't know. Captain thought I liked the neighborhood. No one answers my radio." Steve spat the words at them as he heard the whine of multiple sirens approaching the block.

The ambulance arrived with many more police. Steve stood toe to toe with the two detectives while the area was turned into a blinking kaleidoscope of colors. Norvell was placed on a stretcher as the paramedics stopped the bleeding and tried to keep him from going into shock. Two cops were waiting to accompany him to Rhode Island General.

Bouley had retrieved the other boy while Rizzo was treated by the paramedics. The kids from the apartment were being led into a waiting wagon.

Steve was angry. Angry about being there, angry at Norvell for being there and being shot. He was angry at Rizzo and Bouley for their Dirty Harry police work. Steve was ready to fight; Bouley backed off a short distance.

"Bouley, recuff him. Your collar." Steve pushed the boy at him. "Want me to type your report?"

"Not necessary." Detective Bouley stared with hatred at Steve.

"I can't guess who the hero is . . ." Steve said.

Rizzo approached and threw Steve his handcuffs. "Fuck you, Logan."

Steve glared at him. "You're welcome. Maybe I should've shot you."

Rizzo entered the waiting ambulance as Bouley led the boy off. Steve saw him get hit again and watched two detectives roughly shove the boy into the backseat of the unmarked car.

One got in after him, and Steve heard another loud groan. He looked down at the ground, where his shoe had left a footprint in Norvell's blood. What had he done? He realized he had made a God decision while barely thinking about it. And he fucking hit the target. He felt weak, but the commotion of the scene, with brass arriving from everywhere, allowed him to move through the questions as the police tried to get their story straight. Could he ever tell anyone?

No one who knew him would think he would shoot someone, but he did. It was his job, but to save Rizzo, that lousy piece of shit. It was done, but would Norvell live?

Steve hoped so. How did it happen so fast? Should he have done something else? As the Lieutenant led him over to the car, he could feel the increased weight of the revolver on his hip. He was responsible for pulling the trigger, for good or bad. It wasn't what he signed up for, but it was done. Now the paperwork.

Several days later after his night shift, Steve drove the green VW aimlessly through the streets of downtown Providence, knowing he should go back up college hill. He was back on desk duty, typing reports until the investigation was finished, but he continued to turn the entire scene over in his mind. The *Providence Journal* reported that a drug dealer was wounded in a shootout with police, with a police officer slightly hurt.

The parking lot for Rhode Island General was in front of him. Hesitating for a split second, he shifted into second gear and guided the little car into the lot. On the third floor, he faced the ICU nurse's station.

"Norvell Thompson?" Steve asked the nurse behind the counter. Her bleary eyes showed she worked the night shift, too.

"Officer, the new guard is already here."

He realized the nurse only saw the uniform. The wing was beginning to come alive as doctors were arriving for their morning rounds and nurses were checking vital signs. "I know. How's he doing?" He smiled at her.

"Serious but stable. The bullet missed vital organs," she said, looking at the chart.

"What room?"

"Three twenty-six." She indicated the corridor behind him. Turning, he wondered what he was doing here. It was against regulations—he couldn't speak with the suspect. But he felt he had to. He had made his decision. To see Norvell, to see what he had done to him. To tell him . . .

The room was at the end of the hallway, secured with only one way in or out. Meatball was sitting in the chair outside the door with a cup of coffee, two donuts, and the morning paper. Steve smiled. This was the type of police work Meatball loved.

"Logan, you shouldn't be here," he said without getting up.

"I know, but I have to see him."

"Can't do that. He's a prisoner."

"Cut me some slack. I put the bullet in him."

"Scumbag deserved it. Ya should've killed him and saved the state some money."

Steve turned the doorknob and realized it was locked. "Key?"

"I'll have to report you."

"I'm scared. Key?"

Meatball shrugged and opened the door with the key on the lanyard around his neck.

"You're a fuckup."

"Yeah, I've heard," Steve said and closed the door behind him.

The room was dark. Norvell was connected to some machines, with several tubes in his right arm and mouth. His left arm was handcuffed to the bed. His eyes were shut, and his breathing was shallow. A green screen to the left silently charted his life.

"Why, Norvell? Why?" Steve asked, again reliving the split seconds of the noise, smell of gunpowder, and the screams. He started out to make a difference, which he thought would be better. Was it?

The boy opened his eyes, vacantly looking at the form in front of him. Steve took off his police cap and moved closer to the boy.

"You'll get through this. The doctor will fix you up."

Steve saw the recognition in the boy's eyes as he struggled to speak. "Teach, I really fucked up, didn't I?"

"Yeah, you did, Norvell. But you have time." The boy closed his eyes, turning his face away.

Putting a business card on the bed tray, Steve said, "He's supposed to be a good defense attorney. Listen to him; he'll get you the best deal." He didn't expect Norvell to respond.

Norvell had fucked up big time. There would be a plea of attempted murder. He was only seventeen, and the DA would want him to plead as an adult. Maybe the attorney could get a better deal as a juvenile. Twenty years with good behavior, maybe serve twelve. That would make him twenty nine when he got out—then what? Why? This wasn't supposed to . . .

He wasn't supposed to be the one to . . . Protecting Rizzo? It could have been done so differently, without the violence. Was he lying to himself?

Norvell died. The mood in the station was jovial. The case was open and shut, and with the death, there would be no long, drawn-out court trial with bad press. Captain Lynch branded the kid a cop killer, so there was no discussion with the media about who the kid really was.

The brass closed ranks quickly to protect Steve as if he was one of their own. But he wasn't. He was guilty of taking a life. He knew he was more respected in their eyes because he had acted as they expected. The fraternity slaps on the back from cops who would talk to him would fade as they remembered who he really was. And he knew he wasn't going to change. He had come too far to turn back; it was a fraternity he didn't want to join. The FBI had the files. It was up to them.

Steve climbed the familiar wooden stairs to his third floor sanctuary. He took the key from above her door, entering the room filled with her fragrance. Blue lace panties and a white bra were on the floor, not quite making the wicker hamper. Here was home, the secure feeling that he craved now. Her reaction would be anger, outrage. How could he have become such a monster? It was true: how did he become everything he wanted to fight against? It just happened. There hadn't been enough time to think, but the kid . . . He would always see his face in the front row, challenging for learning.

Sitting on his side of the bed, he leaned his head back against the pillow, closing his eyes, allowing his mind to relax. A soft purring against his hand brought him back to the moment.

"Hello, Cyrano. Have you been taking care of her? I should have been here to do that, but I know you've been watching over her." He petted the cat softly as it settled onto his stomach. How nice, he thought, being remembered and loved so easily. That is why people have pets; they make love so less complicated.

He remembered the first days after she moved in; he was awkward with a stunning female, naked in his room, casual with body, warm with her smile, sensuous with her touch. He was in heaven every moment, but he had thrown it away, chasing after what? Some idea that he would make a difference in the world. Now he had made a difference for one young boy, forever.

Hearing the key, he stiffened as the cat jumped to the end of the bed. She would not be happy he was there with no warning. He had to see her; there was nowhere else to go. She went to her desk, dropping her books as she turned on the light. Startled, she sat in the desk chair, looking at him.

"What's wrong?" she asked.

"Wrong?" he replied.

"You look like shit. Are you sick?" Her tone turned to concern.

"Yes, I think so. But not like you think. I need to talk to you. To tell you something." The waves of fear erupted inside, as he knew this would be the end. "Come over here," he said in a quiet voice, staying outwardly calm.

Roxy tossed her hair, grabbing it with one hand and pulling it into a ponytail. She sat at the foot of the bed, near enough for him to touch.

"Now what's so important? You look so serious." She ran her hand across his hair.

"I killed someone." He had to just say it. There was no other way. Just say it, admit it, be damned by it.

"What? What are you saying? You did what?"

"I killed someone. A young man, Norvell . . . One shot . . ." Then it began. He was trying to stay controlled, a man, but it just came out. "I didn't mean to . . . I did, he had a gun and fired . . . I just reacted . . . one shot. I'm so sorry. I'm so bad. I know you can't forgive me. I can't forgive myself . . ." He was crying full deep sobs with an expression he had never felt.

Her arms circled him, and he buried his head in her chest, his tears flowing as he sought forgiveness and comfort in her arms. She stroked his head until his sobs began to subside as he regained control of himself.

"Are you going to be arrested?" she asked.

"No way. They think I'm some kind of hero. High fives. Now I'm one of them." He leaned back against the pillow. "But I'm not. I'm done."

"But what does it mean? What's going to happen to you?" Her voice quavered slightly. Being clinical, she was diagnosing the problem, but he didn't care what happened. It was over. He couldn't take it back.

"Some cursory internal investigation, but he had the gun, fired . . . Oh shit, what does it matter? The boy didn't need to die. There is so much more to life than . . . I'm so sorry." He began to sob again, and Roxy stroked his cheek. He could feel her warmth, and her touch smothered his raw emotion. He was where he needed to be, and she was there for him. Maybe he didn't ask enough of her. Maybe she needed to take care of him, not he her. Now she was his strength. Maybe he had it wrong. Right now, it didn't matter; the stain would always be with him.

Sitting at the black Underwood typewriter, Steve inserted a blank piece of paper and rolled it to typing position. There was little noise or commotion in the room because the day shift was on. He typed, *Due to deep moral and philosophical differences with the Department, I hereby resign my position as patrolman.*

He looked at it. Short and sweet. He took it out of the typewriter, signed it, and went up to the second floor.

Colonel McGuire was behind his desk. Sitting to the side, in partial darkness, was Captain Lynch, who was smoking his cigar. Steve knew they had been waiting for this day, but he was surprised at how mixed his emotions had become. He didn't want to admit failure, but he knew there was no longer any chance for success. He had given the U.S. Attorney everything he had, but was it enough to change anything?

Steve walked up to the desk and handed the note to the colonel. He then took off his badge and gun belt and laid them on the desk. The colonel looked at the note, showing no emotion.

"Very well. Dismissed," the colonel said.

Steve turned and looked hard at the fat captain sitting in the chair before he went for the door. The captain gave the colonel a nod of satisfaction, but Steve smiled. It wasn't over yet.

Steve and Roxy walked down Bowen Street to Prospect Terrace Park, a small pocket park that overlooked downtown Providence. Set in a quiet enclave among the nineteenth-century luxury homes, it was neatly tended like an English garden. The state capitol building dominated the background, bathed in a necklace of light in the clear night.

The last month had disappeared in new love. They had talked more, laughed more, made love more to chase away his demons. He thought they were more deeply in love than when they first met. But the fantasy they created wouldn't last; they both knew it but kept chasing it away like fireflies in the night. Reality—they knew what it was and why they tried so hard to keep it at bay. He wasn't healed, but a scab had formed, and it was time to move on.

They sat on a wooden bench.

"I'll be gone for a while," he began. "It's time for me to go. I've done all I can do but didn't accomplish much. Maybe I can do something better this time."

"Are you afraid?"

"It's a new adventure." He smiled at her. "You know: Nothing better than another grand gesture."

Roxy was tearing a bit and nodding. They had been talking about it for weeks. "I'll miss you, you know."

"I hope a little, but you'll stay busy. Get into med school." He knew she was strong, maybe stronger than he was. He didn't want to put her in danger. He was being paranoid, but the system was cruel when defending itself. He wanted to be far away when the Federal Attorney came back with indictments.

"I'll write. Do you know where you'll be?"

"Far away." Steve paused, thinking that the distance might do him good. He couldn't help himself when he was around her. They fell in love too deeply and too fast. It consumed all the fuel. Now they would address their grown-up fears. "You'll be with me. We still have another chapter." He forced a weak smile because he didn't want to cry.

He handed her the keys to his green VW. "Think of me. I'll be back for your graduation. I'm not that easy to get rid of." He forced a laugh.

"This is another one of your crazy ideas."

Tears silently slipped down her cheeks as she tried to maintain some control. He began tearing as well and shook his head to clear his eyes. As they stood, Steve pulled her to him and hugged her very tightly. Burying her head in his chest, she clamped her arms around his back.

"I love you," he said softly in her ear.

"And I you." Absorbing the moment, they kissed. "Be careful."

Steve was in the open Jeep arranged by the Peace Corps with the windshield folded down on the hood. The driver, with ritual parallel scars on his face and forehead, sat stone-faced, unable to communicate with him in either English or his college French. The Jeep bounced on a deeply rutted African road in the arid landscape of the Mandara Mountains. The land was strewn with boulders from the worn-out hills they still called mountains. Only volcanic cores, giant phallus symbols, attested to the lost virility of the mountain range.

He felt the Jeep continue to slowly climb as it lurched around foot-deep ruts in the road. The Jeep approached a group of large women with straw baskets. They were filling the ruts from dirt piles dug with rusted shovels. The women left the road slowly as the vehicle neared, their leathered bare feet etching footprints in the soft dirt. Steve watched the women return to their work in the hot sun with little vigor or desire.

The Jeep stopped in the center of the village. It was Wednesday, market day. The market consisted of two rows of stalls made of spindly poles and dry thatch for shade. There were dried fish, peanuts—raw and roasted—canned goods smuggled across the border, cotton, kola nuts, and live chickens. A barber had an old aluminum chair in the shade of a tree. Several horses were tied to a pole, and men in full boubas were squatting on the ground, exchanging money. Brightly colored cotton cloth waved seductively in the soft breeze by the corner stall.

Steve tried to absorb the assault on his senses. A cow's head stared at him from a tree stump. It had open eyes, as if surprised by his arrival. An old man with facial tattoos in purple ink, his long sleeves dotted with remains of cow blood, swished a carpet of flies from the freshly killed meat as he cut a piece with a long, thick blade for a waiting woman.

The women in the market, young and old, noticed the Jeep and the newcomer and rushed to surround it. Steve scanned the faces in the crowd—new and unfamiliar—looking at him with curiosity and without fear. As he stepped out of the Jeep, his tan desert boots sinking into the sand, the women, from grandmothers to young girls, came closer to stare at him before a woman with red kola-juice-stained teeth whispered to the assembly, who broke into a cacophony of laughter, some turning their faces away from him. He smiled at them, knowing he was the butt of their joke.

Settling into a routine as weeks turned into months, he walked two miles every morning to the concrete secondary school. Teaching math and science in French, his classes were ninety-five percent boys. It was very different from Providence. Here, the students passed a test to get into school. And when they graduated, they were assured of good-paying jobs—real motivation.

He was feeling good about himself, though the monthly pay was less than what Bouley would stick in his pocket for not seeing anything. But there was nothing to buy but food, and not much choice there, either.

Kutok, the boy with the bright eyes, was his star student. He came from a small tribe near Mora. The other students looked to him because he was unafraid to ask the questions they were thinking: Did Americans really walk on the moon? How big of a television do you need to see the moon? Is everyone in America rich?

He engaged Steve in conversation after class in the shade of the porch as the other boys gathered to listen and occasionally participate. Steve's basketball skills delighted the boys when he played with them, teaching the step-back jump shot. He knew he was doing good this time.

Several months later, Steve walked to the small concrete block colonial post office that also served as the government hub of the little village. The mail came to the village less than once a week, and letters from the United States sometimes took a month. The building had a telegraph line to the outside world, but no telephone.

He recognized Roxy's handwriting on the thick brown envelope covered with postage. Sitting on a rock on the shady side of the building, he took out a clipping from the *Providence Journal*. The headline read:

> *Feds Crack Providence Corruption*
>
> *Federal indictments were handed down in a massive investigation into corruption in Providence by Federal Authorities. Bribery, corruption, collusion with organized crime, extortion, and a wide range of other charges has shaken the Providence Police Department. In addition, several high-ranking officers have been forced to resign based upon what they knew or should have known.*

There was a picture of several men in cuffs being led into the Federal Building. Detectives Bouley and Rizzo were among the men in handcuffs.

A second story read:

> *Acting Police Chief Appointed as Inquiry Spreads*
>
> *Mayor Joseph Assensen has appointed Captain William Krieger acting chief of police as the continuing investigation of corruption by the FBI continues to spread.*

In the picture, Krieger was in full dress uniform, with the mayor standing next to him, looking drawn and uncomfortable. Captain Krieger was shaking hands with the United States Attorney. Agent Adams was standing behind them, looking pleased.

Krieger was quoted.

> *"The Providence Police department is cooperating fully with the FBI to root out any corruption in the department and to get rid of any bad apples that are tainting the good name of the brave men in this proud department. We intend to professionalize the department with higher educational requirements and more training."*

A third article with a picture of Colonel McGuire in full dress uniform read:

> *Providence Police Chief Suicide.*
>
> *Today at police headquarters, Colonel McGuire apparently committed suicide in his office, among continuing revelations about corruption in the department. Unnamed sources confirm that the chief was to be arrested on Federal racketeering and corruption charges.*

Steve looked at Toad's byline above the fold of the newspapers. He returned the clips to the envelope. Maybe Sutton would get that Pulitzer. Steve opened the blue envelope, written in Roxy's hand.

> *Dear Steve: I hope you are taking care of yourself. I knew but never realized everything you were up against in Providence. I guess it was me being selfish about what I wanted to do and wanted to see. Got into Yale, Georgetown, and NYU. Graduation is in three months. I miss you so much and can't wait till you come home. With all my love, Roxy.*

He checked the postmark: only two months now. The words to a song jumped into his mind.

Then he smiled, thinking about seeing her again.

I've got sunshine on a cloudy day . . .

The End